Silently John Saxon looked down at the young beauty before him, trying desperately to forget his impending departure. But the chill of the night pierced his senses, and he suddenly felt overcome with grief at the thought of losing her. He longed to shout out his love for her, but could he? Dare he try something so bold? After all, they had just met a few hours ago.

It was Mary Elizabeth, with her wonderful perception, who broke the silence.

"Aren't you even going to kiss me good-bye?"

THE STRANGE PROPOSAL

Living Books®
Tyndale House Publishers, Inc.
Wheaton, Illinois

This Tyndale House book
by Grace Livingston Hill
contains the complete text
of the original hardcover edition.
NOT ONE WORD
HAS BEEN OMITTED.

Living Books is a registered trademark of Tyndale House
Publishers, Inc.

Printing History
J.B. Lippincott edition published in 1935
Tyndale House edition/1994

Library of Congress Catalog Card Number 94-60395
ISBN 0-8423-5944-3

Printed in the United States of America

99   98   97   96   95   94
6   5   4   3   2

JOHN Saxon saw Mary Elizabeth for the first time as she walked up the church aisle with stately tread at Jeffrey Wainwright's wedding. John was best man and stood at the head of the aisle with the bridegroom where he could see everything.

First came the ushers stealing on the picture with earnest intent to get the business over, then the four bridesmaids in pale green crisp organdies,—and then Mary Elizabeth! She was wearing something soft and delicately rosy like the first flush of dawn in the sky, and bearing her armful of maidenhair fern and delicate blossoms like a sheaf of some lovely spring harvest. She preceded the bride, Camilla (on the arm of her father's old friend Judge Barron) as if she delighted to introduce her to a waiting world.

But John Saxon had no eyes for the lovely bride, for they had halted at Mary Elizabeth and held there all the way up the aisle.

Mary Elizabeth had eyes that were wide and starry, fringed with long dark lashes under fine level brows. There was a hint of a smile on her lovely unpainted mouth, a little high-born lifting of her chin, a keen interest and delight apparent in her whole attitude that distinguished her from the rest of the bridal party. To her it was all a beautiful game they were playing and she was enjoying every minute of it. There was none of that intent determination to get each step measured just right, each move made with the practised precision that characterized the procession of the bridesmaids. Mary Elizabeth moved along in absolute rhythm, as naturally as clouds move, or butterflies hover.

The wide brim of the transparent hat she wore seemed to John Saxon almost like the dim shadow of a halo, as she lifted her head and gave him a friendly impersonal glance before she moved to her place at the left of the aisle head.

The bridesmaids wore thin white hats also, but they were not halos, they were only hats.

John Saxon suddenly remembered the bride whom he had not sighted as yet except as background, and lest he seem to stare at Mary Elizabeth, he turned and looked back down the aisle to Camilla. Camilla in her mother's lovely old embroidered organdy wedding dress of long ago; Camilla, wearing the ancestral Wainwright wedding veil of costly hand-wrought lace, and John Saxon's orange blossoms from his own Florida grove; Camilla, carrying Jeff's white orchids and looking heavenly happy as she smiled up to answer her bridegroom's welcoming smile.

Yes, she was a very lovely bride, with her gold hair shining beneath the frostwork of lace and waxen blossoms! How splendid they were going to look together, Jeff and Camilla! How glad he was for Jeff that he had found a girl like that!

Then he stepped one pace to the right and front and took his place in the semi-circle as had been planned, with the old minister standing before them against the background of palms and flowers that the old home town people had arranged for Camilla's wedding.

He raised his eyes again to find Mary Elizabeth, wondering if she might not have vanished, if she could possibly be there in the flesh and not a figment of his imagination. He met her eyes again and found her broadcasting that keen delight in what they were doing, found himself responding to that glint in her eyes, that bit of a smile in the corner of her lovely mouth. It was as if they had known one another for a long time. It couldn't be true that he had only just now seen her and for the first time felt that start of his heart at the vision of her! It couldn't be true that he had never been introduced to her!

John Saxon had arrived but the day before the wedding and spent the most of his time since in acquiring the necessary details of raiment in which to appear as best man.

Quite casually he had asked when he first met Jeff at the train, and as he pocketed the directions Jeff had given him to find the right tailor and haberdashery shops:

"And who is this person, this maid of honor I'm supposed to take on as we go back up the aisle after the ceremony? Some flat tire I suppose, since you've picked the one and only out of all the women of the earth," and he gave Jeff a loving slap on the shoulder.

"Why, she's quite all right, I guess. I haven't seen her yet, but she's an old schoolmate of Camilla's. She's on her way back from California just to attend the wedding. Camilla says she's a great Christian worker, and interested in Bible study, so I guess you'll hit it off. Anyway I hope she won't be too much of a bore. She's expected to arrive to-morrow afternoon sometime. Somebody takes her place to-night at the rehearsal I believe, so she won't be around long enough to matter anyway. Her name is—Foster—I think that's it. Yes, Helen Foster."

Nobody had told John Saxon about a washout on the road half-way across the continent, a wreck ahead of Helen Foster's train and a delay of twenty-four hours. He had not heard that in spite of frantic attempts to reach an airport from the isolated place of the wreck, in time to arrive for the ceremony, the maid of honor had telegraphed only two hours before the wedding that she could not possibly get there. John Saxon had spent most of the day in shops perplexing his mind over the respective values of this and that article of evening wear, and arrived at the hotel only in time to get into his new garments in a leisurely manner and repair to the church at the hour appointed. In fact he was there even a few minutes before Jeff. And so he had escaped the excitement and anxiety consequent on the news of the missing maid of honor. He did not know how hurriedly and anxiously the troublesome question of whether or how to supply her place at this last minute had been discussed and rediscussed, nor how impossible at this last minute it had seemed to get even a close friend to come in and act in a formal wedding without the necessary maid of honor outfit.

Excitement had run high and Camilla had just escaped tears as she thought of the Warren Wainwrights, and the Seawells of Boston, and the Blackburns and Starrs of Chicago and New York, all new unknown to-be-relations. She went down the list of all the girls she knew who would be at all eligible for the position of maid of honor and shook her head in despair. There wouldn't be one who could take the place at a moment's notice that way and fit right in, and if there were one what would she do for a dress?

Dresses could be bought of course, even as late as that,

but no ordinary dress would be able to enter the simple yet lovely scheme of the wedding without seeming to introduce a wrong note in an otherwise perfect harmony. Oh, of course it might be bought in New York if one had the time to shop around, but the home town wasn't New York, and no one had the time. Camilla stood in the sitting room of the hotel suite she and her mother were occupying together, and drew her brows together in perplexity, trying to think of some dress she had herself that would do, that she could lend to someone, no matter who, so that the wedding procession should not be lacking a maid of honor, trying to decide to do without a maid of honor, when Jeffrey Wainwright walked in and wanted to know why Camilla's eyes didn't light at his coming as they had lighted all day whenever he had appeared on the scene.

Camilla told him anxiously what was the matter, but he met it with a smile.

"That's all right," he said gaily when he had listened to the tale, and stood looking at the telegram over Camilla's shoulder, "get Mary Beth! That is if you don't mind having one of my cousins instead of one of your own friends. Mary Beth always has oodles of clothes along of every kind. She'll find something that will do. She's just arrived, and she'll just love to do it. You haven't met Mary Beth yet, have you? She's my very best cousin just got back from abroad. Shall I go get her? She's only down the hall a little way. Just show her what you want and she'll manage it somehow, she always can."

And so Mary Elizabeth had come smiling at Jeff's summons, had kissed Camilla and her mother, had looked over the bridal array, including the bridesmaids' crisp pale organdies, and then had departed with a confident smile and a lift of her happy chin as she said:

"Leave it to me! I'll love to do it. I've got just the right thing, a pale rose chiffon I picked up in Paris—a little confection and just as simple as a baby!"

And when Camilla saw her an hour later as she slipped in for inspection, she forgot her worries, knowing that the simple little dress from the exclusive Paris shop knew how to keep its distinguished lines in their place and would never stand out as being too fine for its associates.

And so quite unexpectedly, Camilla came to know and love Mary Elizabeth. But of this John Saxon knew nothing at all.

And now though John Saxon was sorely tempted to study the face across from him to the exclusion of everything else, he was a dependable person, and he knew his responsibility as a best man. He had a ring to deliver at just the right moment, and he was not a man to forget his duty. So he held his eyes and his thoughts in leash until the ring was safely given to Jeff and Jeff had placed it on Camilla's finger, and then his glance lifted and met the glance of Mary Elizabeth full, and both of them smiled with their eyes, though their lips were perfectly decorous, but each of them knew that they had been enjoying that little ceremony of the ring together. Mary Elizabeth was now holding the great bouquet of orchids, along with her own green and white and blush-rose sheaf. Sweet, fine Mary Elizabeth! John Saxon thought how sweet and unspoiled she looked, and stood there watching her with his eyes alight, thinking quick eager thoughts, his mind leaping ahead. In a few minutes now, or it might be even seconds, it would be his duty to turn and march down that aisle by her side, and he could actually speak to her. They had not been introduced, but that was a mere formality. They were set in this wedding picture to march together and they could not go like dummies because they had not been introduced. He thrilled at the thought of speaking to her.

The prayer was over, the solemn final sentences said that made Camilla Chrystie and Jeffrey Wainwright man and wife, the tender consummating kiss given, Mary Elizabeth handed Camilla her lovely white orchids, adjusted the veil and the quaint old-fashioned train and Jeffrey and Camilla started down the way of life together. Then Mary Elizabeth adjusted her own flowers and turned smiling to greet the best man who stood there breathless above her.

John Saxon laid her hand on his arm as if it had been something breakable. The thrill of it gave his face a radiance even through the Florida bronze. He looked down at her eagerly, just as though they were long-lost friends who had by some miracle come together again.

"I've been looking for you for a long time!" said John Saxon, as they wheeled into step and Mary Elizabeth looked up and saw something arresting and almost disturbing in his glance.

"Yes?" she said brightly. "I have been running around a good deal to-day. I guess I was hard to find."

"Oh, not just to-day!" said John Saxon, conscious that the next measure was the one they should start on to follow the bride and groom. "A long time! Years! In fact I guess I always knew there would be you sometime! But will you mind if I'm abrupt? We've only got from here to the door to talk and then the mob will snatch us apart and I've got to leave on the midnight train!"

"Oh!" breathed Mary Elizabeth looking up wonderingly into his eyes, a sparkle in her own.

They were off in perfect time with the stately old march now, quite unconscious of the eager audience watching them with keen eyes, not realizing that they were the next most interesting pair in the whole show, after the bride and groom who had now passed out of sight of all except a few who deliberately turned around and stared at their backs.

"Who is she?" whispered Sallie Lane to Mrs. Sampson.

"Some relative of the groom I heard."

"But I thought it was to be Helen Foster!"

"Oh, hadn't you heard? There was an accident and Helen's train was late. They had to get somebody at the last minute. Don't you see her dress is different? It isn't the same stuff, doesn't stand out so stiff and crisp, and it's terribly plain. Too bad! I heard the bridal party all had their dresses made off the same pattern."

"I like it. It kind of fits her. Say, don't they look wonderful together? I shouldn't wonder if they're engaged or something. Look at the way he looks at her! They certainly know each other well."

"I love you," John Saxon was saying in a low thrilling voice, a voice that was almost like a prayer.

And Mary Elizabeth, quite conscious now of the many eyes upon her, kept that radiant smile upon her lips and the sparkle in her eyes as she looked up to catch the low words from his lips.

"But you couldn't, of course, all at once like that!" she said smiling as if it were a good joke. "Is this supposed to be the newest thing in proposals of marriage? I've never had one going down a wedding aisle, though I've been maid of honor several times before."

She looked up at him archly with her sparkling smile to cover the trembling of her lips, the strange thrilling of her heart over this stranger's words.

"Is there any reason why it shouldn't be that?" he breathed as they neared the door and the wedding party began to mull about them in the vestibule. It seemed to him they had fairly galloped down that aisle.

"If my gloves had been off I suppose you might have thought there was," said Mary Elizabeth with a sudden memory in her eyes.

"Your gloves?" said John Saxon, looking down at the little white scrap of a hand that lay there like a white leaf on his arm.

Then suddenly he laid his other hand upon hers with a quick investigating pressure, and looked at her aghast.

"Then,—you mean—that I am too late?" he asked, caring not that they were now in the midst of the giggling bridesmaids, whispering what mistakes they had made, and how this one and that one had looked.

"Oh,—not necessarily!" said Mary Elizabeth now with a wicked twinkle in her eyes. "It was only an experiment, wearing it to-night. It came in the mail a few days ago with an importunate letter and I thought I might try it out. But there's nothing final about it!"

And Mary Elizabeth gave him a ravishing childlike smile that left him bewildered and utterly routed. He didn't know whether she was trying to be flippant, or merely making talk to cover any possible embarrassment, for they were right in the thick of the crowd now, with someone outside directing traffic loudly, and suddenly John Saxon realized that he was still best man and had duties about putting the bride and groom in the right car. He fled into the street precipitately.

He was a fool of course, he told himself. He had gone off on a tangent and no girl in her senses would take sudden words spoken like that seriously. Oh, he had probably messed the whole thing now. She wouldn't even recognize him when she got to the hotel, or would call a lot of her friends to protect her. What a fool! What a fool he had been! He hadn't thought that he could ever be impulsive like that!

But when he had slammed the door on Jeff and his

bride and turned about with his miserable eyes to see what he could see, and whether she was still in sight, someone caught him and whirled him into a car.

"Here, Saxon," the unknown voice said, "get in quick! Jeff wants you there as soon as he is!" and the car whirled away before he was fairly seated. In fact he almost sat down on someone who was already there in the dark, sitting in the far corner.

He turned to apologize and she laughed, a soft little silvery laugh.

"I bribed the traffic man to give us a whole car to ourselves," she said gaily, "so that you could finish what you had to say."

He caught his breath and his heart leaped up.

"Do you mean that you are going to forgive me for being so—so—so presumptuous?" he asked.

"Do you mean you didn't mean what you said?" rippled out Mary Elizabeth's laughing voice, the kind of a laugh that sometimes covers tears.

"Mean what I said?" said John Saxon, in the tone he often used to rebuke a boy whom he was coaching when he was scout master in Florida. "I certainly did mean what I said!" he repeated doggedly, "and I'll always mean it. But I know I ought not to have flung it out at you that way in public, only I didn't see that I would ever get another chance if I didn't do something about it right away."

"Why, I didn't mind that," said Mary Elizabeth gravely, "it was quite original and interesting. It made the walk down the aisle unique. Something to remember!" There was a lilt in her voice that might be suppressed mirth. John eyed her suspiciously through the dark, but she sat there demurely in her corner, and he felt awed before her. Perhaps he had been mistaken and she was one of those modern girls after all.

But no! He remembered the haloed face, the lovely unpainted smile. He would never think that! She might not be for him, but she was what she seemed. She could not be otherwise.

"Yes," he said with a tinge of bitterness in his nice voice, "something for you to laugh about afterward! A country hick come to town to make a fool of himself, putting a girl in an embarrassing position in public!"

"No!" she said sharply. "Don't say that! You didn't! I wasn't embarrassed! I liked it! I really did! I—felt—honored!"

And suddenly one of the little white hands stole out of the darkness and crept into his hand with a gentle reassurance, and—it was ungloved!

Awesomely he folded his hand about it marveling at its delicacy, its softness, the way it lay relaxed within his own strong hand. It was then he remembered the ring under the glove.

"But—you are already engaged!" he reminded himself aloud sternly. And then he felt for the ring again. This was the same left hand that had lain upon his arm as they went down the aisle together,—galloped down!

Then he sat up sharply, felt the little hand all over, and then reached over to the other hand that lay in her lap. It still wore a glove!

He sat back again and drew a breath of relief.

"Where is that ring?" he said.

"Here, in my handbag," she said, sweetly offering him a tiny scrap made of white beads and gilt, "did you want it?"

"Was it a joke you were playing?" he accused sternly.

"Oh, no," she answered lightly, "I told you it wasn't at all final. I've had that ring several days, and I just thought I'd try it out to-night and see if I cared to keep it."

He hesitated a moment still holding the little ungloved hand that lay so yielded in his own.

"Then—there—is no reason—why—I may not—tell you of my love!"

"Well, I would have to consider that," said Mary Elizabeth gravely. "It was rather unexpected, you know. But here we are at the hotel, don't you think perhaps we'd better get out now?"

John Saxon helped her out, thrilling with the thought of touching even the hem of her garment, guarding her flowers, picking up her glove from the cushion, touching her belovedly, his heart pounding away with an embarrassment and trepidation that was quite new to him. John was usually at his ease anywhere, and he had been in the world enough not to feel strange. But he felt a perfect gawk when he thought what he had been saying, and recalled the keen, gay retaliations.

They hurried through the hall and up in the elevator to the big room set aside for the wedding reception, and John blessed the fate that gave him even this silent bit of time more before they had to face the others. He looked down upon her, in her lovely halo hat, and she looked up and smiled, and there was no scorn in her smile as he had feared. Yet she had in no way put herself in his debt. She had held her own. His eyes drank in her delicate beauty hungrily against a time of famine he feared might be swiftly coming. He would never forget her nearness, the soft fragrance that came from her garments, the natural loveliness of her. He tried to summon her name from his memory, where it hovered on the edge of things and evaded him. Was it Helen? But that was not the type of name for such a girl as this.

Then the elevator door clanged back and they stepped into the big room smothered in ferns and palms and flowers, and there in a distant bower that seemed almost like an orchid-hung hammock in one of his own Florida forests, the bride and groom were taking their places, Camilla smiling up at Jeff so joyously that John Saxon's heart gave another leap. Would such joy ever come to him?

He looked down at the girl by his side and their eyes met and something flashed from one to the other, a gleam that thrilled them both.

2

"COME," said the girl with a certain possessiveness in her voice, "we must go over and stand by them, you know," and she put her still ungloved hand on his and led him across the room. Behind them the elevator clanged again and opened its doors to let the green bridesmaids surge in with the ushers, and the reception was upon them in full blast. But somehow John Saxon didn't mind. His heart was leaping in new rhythm, and a song was in his heart.

"Hold this for me, please, while I put on my glove," said Mary Elizabeth handing over her little pearl purse as if she had been used to having him all her life for an escort.

He took the purse shyly in his bronzed hands. He had not been accustomed to hold such trinkets for ladies. Not that he didn't know plenty of ladies, but he had always shied out of paying them much attention. But he liked the feel of it when it was in his hand, and while he watched her putting on the glove so expertly, he grew bold enough to gently prod the purse till he had located the ring, a great ox of a stone, he told himself as he carefully appraised its value. He could never get her a ring like that, he thought to himself dismally in one of the intervals of the passing throng of guests. Even if he succeeded beyond his hopes he couldn't. That ring had been bestowed by some millionaire of course, and she had been weighing its worth, and perhaps its owner. He frowned so hard that Uncle Warren Wainwright asked his wife afterward if that best man wasn't a rather stern-looking fellow. But his wife said, no, she thought he was splendid-looking, so nice and tanned and well built, so he said he guessed he must have been mistaken. Uncle Warren was like that, always ready to concede to his wife's opinion. He had made his money in spite of doing that.

The long procession of gushing or shy friends had surged by at last and the bridal party were seated around the bride's table in the "throne end" as Jeffrey called it, of the banquet hall.

"There," said Mary Elizabeth as John Saxon seated her, "isn't this nice and cozy? You didn't know we were going to sit together, did you?" John sat down beside her feeling like a prisoner on parole.

There was comparative privacy where they were, amid the gay laughter and talk of the rest of the wedding party. The wedding roses, the tall candles, all made it a fairyland and they carried on their little private conversation there between themselves, the girl continually ready with her sparkle and smiles. And nobody wondered that the attractive best man was absorbed in the lovely maid of honor.

Quite suddenly, it seemed, the wedding supper was over. He found his heart sinking. Soon the beautiful links would be broken and when would he ever see her again? He tried to make some plans, say something to her about it, but the glamour of her presence somehow dazed him. He ought to tell her that he was a poor man. That it would be some time before he could claim her. He ought to let her know about his one year more of graduate work in the medical college. She ought to know that his wedding could never be the grand affair that this was. He was not a Wainwright. There were things he ought to say to arrange what they should do in the future, but to save his life he could not say them, could not put them into the words that ought to frame them. Not with all these gay kindly people around them, shouting pleasant nothings across the table, mixing together for that one night, strangers, but with a common interest in the bride and groom. His tongue was tied! And perhaps there would be no other time!

"And I don't even know your address," he wailed, as suddenly the bride arose and everybody got up with her.

"I'll write it for you and give it to you before you leave," she assured him with a smile. "Where is my little bag? I have a pencil and card in it."

He handed it forth reluctantly. It seemed he was giving up one of the slender links that bound them.

"I'll have it ready for you when you come down." Her smile was bright. "You have to go upstairs with Jeff, don't you? Well, I'll be waiting over there by the alcove, and—you know *I'm* driving you to the station afterwards, so don't go and order a taxi or anything. That's the business of the maid of honor after her duties for the bride are done. She has to look after the best man, you know. That is—when he needs looking after."

She slipped away up the stairs with one of her sparkling glances, and looking after her he had to own to himself that he actually wasn't sure yet, whether she was only playing a game with him, or had taken his words seriously. Nevertheless he went to Jeff's room with something singing down in his heart.

So while the guests waited below to play the usual bridal tricks on the departing couple, with a sentinel stationed at every hotel exit, Camilla with the help of her mother and Miss York, their friend, got out of her bridal array and into the lovely simple going-away outfit and calmly kissed them good bye, including Mary Elizabeth who had slipped in a minute before and now stood holding the precious orchids.

"But what are you going to do with your bouquet, Camilla?" she asked. "You can't go away without the time-honored ceremony of throwing your flowers for the bridesmaids to catch."

"You'll have to do it for me, new cousin," said Camilla smiling. "Or perhaps you'll prefer to keep them yourself. If they bring any potent virtue I'd rather you'd have them, Mary Elizabeth, dear! I'm going to love you a lot."

Then Camilla put on a stiff white starched nurse's uniform and a tricky little cap, tucking her own soft hat under the big blue nurse's cape. She stepped to a door connecting with another suite of rooms, unlocked it, and stood a moment looking at them all with happy eyes.

"Good night!" she said sweeping them a courtsey.

"But, Camilla, where are your bags?" said Mary Elizabeth.

"Safe in our car and waiting for us in a little village three miles from town. Jeff saw to all that. Goodbye, and it's up to you, Mary Elizabeth, to go down and announce that I've fled and you've found nothing but my bouquet, and therefore it's yours because you found it first."

And with another smile and a kiss blown at them all, she turned and went into the other room closing the door. Nurse York swiftly locked it after her, and the three conspirators hurried downstairs by devious ways looking most innocent.

No one noticed a nurse with a tray of dishes slip out of the end room and hurry down the servants' stairs.

Down at the back of the building the caterer's car was drawn up for hampers of silver and dishes to be stowed away, and two young men in chefs' linen coats and aprons stole through the basement kitchens with the nurse behind them. They slipped into the back of the caterer's car, that is, one young chef and the nurse slipped in, and one chef stayed behind. And not even the careful watchers in the yard had a suspicion. The back door of the car was slammed, and a driver got into the front seat and put his foot on the starter.

"Oh, by the way," said John Saxon slipping up again to the little window at the back of the car. "I liked your Miss Foster a lot. Thanks for helping me to meet her!"

"But you didn't meet her," giggled the young woman in nurse's uniform.

"Oh, but I did," said John Saxon heartily, "we didn't mind a little thing like that. We introduced ourselves!"

"Oh, but you didn't," cried the soft voice again. "She wasn't there at all!"

But the driver had put his foot on the starter and the car clattered away and John Saxon was none the wiser for that last sentence.

He stole back through the servants' corridors, rid himself of his disguise, and mingled again with the guests unobtrusively.

"Oh, hello!" said someone presently. "Here's the best man! Where are they, Mr. Saxon? Which way are they coming down?"

"Why, there isn't any way but the elevator, is there?" said John Saxon innocently. "Jeff was all ready when I left him."

There was excited gathering of guests in little groups, then the appearance of the bride's mother, smiling and a bit teary about the lashes, brought about a state of eager intensity. The elevators came and went, and there was a dead silence every time one opened its noisy doors to let out some guest of the house. They all stood in the big entrance hall clutching their handfuls of paper rose leaves and rice and confetti. Outside the door stood a big car belonging to Mr. Warren Wainwright, understood to be the going-away car, well decorated in white satin ribbons and old shoes and appropriate sentiments, but time went on and nothing happened!

"I'm going up to see what has happened!" announced Mary Elizabeth when excitement grew to white heat and suspicion began to grow into a low rumble of anxiety.

Mary Elizabeth stepped into the elevator and disappeared, and a breath of relief went up from the guests.

Then Mary Elizabeth descended again with the great bouquet of white orchids in her hand! The bouquet that every one of those four bridesmaids had so longed to be able to catch for herself!

And when they saw the orchids it did not need Mary Elizabeth's dramatic announcement: "She's gone! And I've got the orchids!" to tell what had happened.

A howl went up from the disappointed tricksters and if it had been anybody else but Mary Elizabeth with her gay friendly smile, she might have been mobbed.

But Mary Elizabeth had disappeared in the excitement, slipped up to her room, and by the time the guests had begun to drift away, she appeared with a long dark wrap over her arm, jingling her key ring placidly, with no offending orchids in sight, and when John Saxon came back after seeing Camilla's mother to her room as he had promised Jeff he would do, there she was sitting demurely in the alcove, the long satin cloak covering her delicate dress, and her eyes like two stars, waiting for him.

It thrilled him anew to see her there, and meet her welcoming smile, just as if they had been belonging to one another for a long time. Even in the brief interval of his absence he had been doubting that it could be true that he had found a girl like that. Surely the glamour would have faded when he got back to her.

But there she was, a real flesh and blood girl, as lovely in the simple lines of the soft black satin cloak as she had been in the radiant rosy chiffons.

She had taken off her gloves, and he thrilled again to draw her hand within his arm as they went out to the car.

The doorman put his bags in the back of the car and Mary Elizabeth drove away from the blaze of light that enveloped the whole front of the hotel. They were alone. Really alone for the first time since he had seen her! And suddenly he was tongue-tied!

He wanted to take her in his arms, but a great shyness had come upon him. He wanted to tell her what was in his heart for her, but there were no words adequate. Each one as he selected it and cast it aside as unfit, seemed presumption.

John Saxon had a deep reverence for womanhood. He had acquired that from the teaching of his little plain, quiet mother. He had a deep scorn for modern progressive girls with bloody-looking lips, plucked eyebrows and applied eyelashes. Girls who acquired men as so many scalps to hang at their belts, who smoked insolently and strutted around in trousers long or short. He turned away from such in disgust. He hated their cocksure ways, their arrogance, their assumption of rights, their insolence against all things sacred. He had had a great doubt in his mind about even Camilla until he had seen her, watched her, talked with her, proved her to be utterly unspoiled in spite of her wonderful golden head and her smartly plain attire.

And now to find another girl with beauty, and brightness, and culture, who assumed none of the manners he hated, almost brought back his faith in true womanhood. Certainly he reverenced this girl beside him as if God had just handed her to him fresh out of heaven.

"Well," said Mary Elizabeth presently as she whirled the car around a corner and glided down a wide street overarched with elm trees, "aren't you wasting a great deal of time? Where are all those things you were going to say and didn't have time for while we walked down that aisle?"

"Forgive me," he said, "it seemed enough just to be sitting by your side. I was trying to make it seem real. I wasn't quite sure but I might be in a dream. Because you see I was never sure whether my dream of you through the years would be like this when I found you—*if* I found you!"

"That's one of the nicest things anybody ever said to me," said Mary Elizabeth softly, guiding her car slowly under the shadow of the elms.

"I suppose scores of men have said nice things to you," John Saxon remarked dismally.

"Yes," said the girl thoughtfully, "a great many. But I'm not sure they were always sincere. They didn't always please me. Yours do. You know it's rather wonderful to find someone that doesn't have to be chattered to in order to feel the pleasant comfort of companionship. Even if I never see you again we've had a lovely evening, haven't we? I would never forget you."

John Saxon started forward and closer to her, looking in her face.

"Is that *all* it means to you?" he asked searchingly.

"I didn't say it was," said Mary Elizabeth with a dancing in her eyes that gleamed naughtily even in the dark as she turned toward him. "I shouldn't prevent your seeing me again, of course, if you want to. I only said, even if I never saw you again, I wouldn't forget that we've had a most unique and wonderful evening. You must remember that I have no data by which to judge you, except that presumably you are one of Jeff's friends. Remember I've just arrived on the scene this morning and not a blessed soul had time enough to gossip about you!"

"They wouldn't," said John Saxon ruefully. "There wasn't enough to say. But I was presumptuous of course to dare say what I did right out of the blue. I'm only a plain man, and you may be bound irrevocably to someone else."

"I told you it was not final!" said Mary Elizabeth driving smoothly up to the station and stopping her car.

"Yes," said the man giving a quick startled look out at the station. "Yes, you said it was not final, but you gave me no hope that you would listen to me."

"But I listened to you!"

"But you didn't give me an answer."

"Did you expect an answer?"

"I don't know," said John in a low tone, "I wanted one."

"Just what did you say that needed answering?" Mary Elizabeth's tone was sweet and courteous, and also the tiniest bit reserved.

"Why, I told you that I love you, and—I asked you to marry me!"

"Did you?" said Mary Elizabeth, still sweetly and innocently. "I wasn't sure. I thought I sort of dragged that out of you!"

He looked up quickly at her and caught that starry look in her eyes, and yet was there a twinkle of mischief too? Could it be that she was still making fun of him, able to hold her own until the end?

"You surely didn't expect me to tell you that I loved you, going down a church aisle at another girl's wedding, did you?"

There was still the twinkle in her eyes, but there was something dear and tender in her voice, as if she were talking to the little boy he used to be long years ago when he dreamed her into his life some day in the far, far future.

"You couldn't, of course. I wouldn't expect you to feel the way I did," said John Saxon humbly.

"I'm not saying how I felt," said Mary Elizabeth with her head held high, "but even if I felt it you surely wouldn't expect me to blurt it out that way right before the assembled multitude, would you?"

"No, I suppose not!" said John Saxon in a very dejected tone.

"And as for marrying, people always have to have time to think that over, don't they?"

"I suppose—some people—do. I didn't!"

"But you should have, you know," said Mary Elizabeth still in that sweet tone in which one imparts knowledge to a small boy, very gently.

"I'm glad I didn't!" said John Saxon quite suddenly, with a firm set of his jaw in the dark, that Mary Elizabeth could see because his profile was perfectly outlined against the bright light of the station platform.

"Yes,—and so—am I!" said Mary Elizabeth with an upward fling of her chin, ending in a little trill of a laugh with a lilting sound in it. "John Saxon, there comes your train, and you have to get your bags out! Do you really *have* to go to-night?"

"Yes, I really have to go!" said John Saxon through set teeth, giving Mary Elizabeth one wild look and springing out of the car.

He dashed to the back of the car, opened it, slung his bags down, gave a furtive glance down the track at the great yellow eye of light that was rushing toward them, so speedily to part them, and before he could look into the car for a hasty farewell he found Mary Elizabeth beside him.

"You haven't given me your address," he said breathlessly, measuring the distance of the track with another glance. "Tell me quick!"

"Here it is," she said, slipping a small white envelope into his hand. "When am I—? When—are—you? I mean—you'll let me hear from you—sometime?"

Her voice had a little shake in it, but she was looking steadily up with that brave smile on her lips—no, it wasn't a mocking smile, he decided. His eyes lighted.

"I'll write you to-night, at once!" he said. "Oh, I'd give anything if I only had another hour. How I have wasted my time!" He looked down at her tenderly.

"Yes," she said sweetly, "you have, perhaps, but it was nice anyway, wasn't it?"

He caught his breath at the sweetness of her voice and longed to catch her and hold her close, but dared he, now, without knowing how she would take it? His own reverence held him from it. And the train was slowing down a few steps away.

"Oh!" he breathed, "I love you!"

"But—" said Mary Elizabeth with a wistful little lifting of her lashes, and that twinkle of a glance, "aren't you even going to kiss me good bye? Just friends often do that you know!"

But the words were scarcely out of her mouth before

his arms went eagerly round her and he laid his lips on hers.

"My darling!" he said. "Oh, my darling!"

Into the tenderness of his whispered words stabbed the sharpness of the conductor's call:

"All aboard!"

John Saxon released her suddenly as if he were coming awake, seized his bags and took three strides to the step of the nearest car which was already beginning to move slowly. But when he turned about, there was Mary Elizabeth beside him walking composedly along the platform, her cheeks very rosy, and she did not look angry. In fact her eyes were still starry and there was a twinkle of a smile about her lips. Her chin was tip-tilted a bit as if she were proud of it.

Then did John Saxon's heart leap with joy.

"That was final, dear!" he shouted down to her through the noise of the train.

"Yes?" said Mary Elizabeth. "You certainly did it thoroughly."

And then the train got alive to its duty and swept them apart like a breath that is gone, and Mary Elizabeth stood alone on the long empty platform gazing after a fast disappearing red light at the end of the train.

Gone!

She put up the back of her hand to her hot cheeks, she touched her lips softly, sacredly, and smiled.

Had it been real?

Finally she turned, got into her car, and drove away.

When she reached her hotel the doorman summoned a man to take her car to the garage, and Mary Elizabeth went up to her room, turned on all her lights, and went and faced her mirror to look straight into her own eyes and find out what she thought of herself.

3

MEANTIME out in the silence of a smooth dark road in their own luxurious car, the bride and groom drove happily through the night to a destination that Jeffrey Wainwright had picked out, and not even Camilla knew.

They had completed their exciting trip in the caterer's car, had made a quiet transfer to their own in the haven of the back yard of an old farm house where a friend of Camilla's mother lived. Not even the farmer and his wife were there to interfere though they did stand a-tiptoe behind a sheltering curtain and watch the car move smoothly out of their drive and down the road, and they felt the thrill of their own first journey as man and wife.

There had not been opportunity to talk in the caterer's car, nor safety, lest they be followed, and by the time they were launched on their own way there were so many other thrilling things to say that they forgot that last encounter with John Saxon. But an hour later as they swept over a hill and looked down across a valley to where the lights of another small city blazed, the memory of John Saxon recurred to them.

"What did he mean, Jeff, about Helen Foster? Did no one tell him she wasn't there?"

"Evidently not from what he said. You see we didn't really have much time to talk. He probably confused Mary Beth with her. But what's the difference?"

"A great deal, I should say," said the bride in a wise tone. "If you'd noticed his eyes when he looked at her!"

"Now, Camilla, don't go to being a matchmaker!" laughed Jeff. "Because if you do you'll be disappointed. Those two will never get together. They're as wide apart as the poles."

"Any wider apart than we were, Jeff?"

She laid a caressing hand on her new husband's arm and he looked down on her tenderly, and then leaned over and gave her another kiss.

"I insist," he said and kissed her again, "that we were never far apart. If we were I never could have made the grade."

Then they floated off to reminiscing again, but eventually got back to John Saxon.

"What did he mean by saying they had introduced themselves? Can it be that nobody looked after that little matter?"

"It must have been. But it strikes me that John Saxon is able to get around and look after himself pretty well. It looked that way to me. They seemed to be having an awfully good time together."

"Well, they would," said Jeff thoughtfully. "They're both unusual. But I'd hate like sixty to have John get interested in Mary Beth. She's always been my favorite cousin, but I'll have to own she's a bit of a flirt. I don't know how many men she's kept on the string for a number of years now, and they're all deeply devoted, but Mary Beth goes smiling on her way and takes none of them. I wouldn't like John to get himself a heart and have it broken. He's a constant old fellow, and he doesn't care much for women, doesn't have much opinion of the modern ones, and wouldn't understand it. It might go hard with him."

"But she seemed so sweet and genuine," protested Camilla, perplexed.

"Yes, she is," said Jeff, "but she's always had her own way. Her father spoiled her, and her mother spoiled her, and then when her mother died and she inherited all that money besides what her father will leave her some day, she did more and more what she wanted to. Oh, I'll admit she usually wanted to do nice things. She wasn't bold and arrogant like the modern girl. She had ideals of her own and she stuck to them. And that's remarkable too, since she's traveled the world over a lot, and had plenty of chances to go modern. She's kept her smile and her natural face and hasn't taken on rowdy airs and habits. She's a great sport and I admire her a lot. But she does let a lot of men trail after her, and just smiles and plays with them a while and then lets them go. They are just a lot of toys to her it seems. And I'd hate to have John Saxon treated that way. He's too genuine to be played with. And I'm not sure whether she could understand a man like John. I guess it's a good thing that they're not likely ever to meet again. I wouldn't have John hurt for the world."

"He looks to me as if he could take care of himself," said Camilla.

And then they turned to the right and swept down into the heart of the little city, and drove to their hotel, forgetting all about John Saxon and his affairs.

Back in the hotel where Camilla's mother and Miss York were preparing for rest Miss York was saying:

"What kind of girl is that Miss Wainwright who took the place of maid of honor to-night?"

"Why, I think she's very sweet," said Camilla's mother. "It was so nice of her at the last minute that way to be willing to fill in, not having the regular dress or anything."

"She had a stunning dress!" said Miss York, "and she certainly was agreeable. Of course most girls love a thing like that, and she certainly did the part well."

"A great deal better than Helen Foster would have done," said Camilla's mother. "Poor Helen isn't very pretty and never has known how to dress, but she's a lovely girl and Camilla was very fond of her. But Miss Wainwright was sweet. I liked her very much. She seemed a good deal like Jeffrey, didn't you think? The same blue eyes and clear complexion with dark hair. He's always been very fond of her. She seems almost as if she might have been a sister."

"Yes," said Miss York reluctantly, "if she's like him in spirit she couldn't be improved upon. I was just wondering whether a girl *could* be as beautiful, and as rich as they say she is, and not be spoiled."

"Jeffrey wasn't spoiled," said Jeffrey's new mother-in-law.

"Jeffrey is unusual," owned Miss York. "You know he's unusual. You said so yourself!"

"Well, couldn't his cousin be unusual too?"

"She *could*," said the nurse. "I was wondering whether she *is*. I've been watching her all the evening. That friend of Jeffrey's is a very fine young man."

"Yes, he is," agreed the mother. "He is very wonderful! Camilla has been telling me about him."

"That's it," said Miss York, brushing out her long old-fashioned hair that still had a pleasant natural wave in spite of the threads of silver here and there. "That's just what I mean. He's fine. He's rare! And is that girl good enough for him? I watched them all the evening, and sometimes I thought she was and sometimes I wasn't sure."

"Well," said Camilla's mother smiling, "isn't it good that we don't have to settle that? I suppose our heavenly Father can look out for those two as well as He has looked out for my child. My, how strange it is to think that Camilla is married! And how glad I am it is Jeffrey she married instead of that other man I was so afraid she would take. Oh, God is good!"

And so the discussion ended, and presently the light was out and the two women lay quiet with their own thoughts.

Down the hall a few doors Warren Wainwright was struggling with the collar button of his dress shirt.

"Who's that chap Mary Liz was running round with to-night, Fannie? What do you know about him?" he said as he conquered the button at last and flung his collar down upon the bureau, drawing a relieved breath as his constricted flesh relaxed in his puffy pink neck.

"Why," said Mrs. Warren Wainwright placidly as she unwound the heavy ropes of pearls from her own ample neck and took a satisfied look at the set of the frock she had been wearing all the evening, noting that it was exceedingly becoming, "why, he's one of Jeff's friends. Jeff speaks very highly of him. He told me he's very scholarly and very keen. He's going to be some special kind of doctor I think, though I believe he hasn't much money at present."

"Mary Liz has enough money of her own of course," growled the uncle, "but I'd like to see her happy. I wouldn't like to see Mary Liz get some puppy she'd have to divorce in a few months, or years. I'm very fond of Mary Liz. She's a fine girl!"

"Yes, of course," said Mary Elizabeth's aunt yawning

delicately and placidly, "but you know Mary Elizabeth can look out for herself, and she always would."

"Yes, and that's the very reason we ought to find out about that chap and manage somehow to get her away from his vicinity if necessary till he lays off her, if he isn't all right. Where is he staying anyway? I saw how he looked at her when they came down the aisle. I'm not so old I don't know what a look like that in a man's eyes means."

"Why, he's left already," said Aunt Fannie beginning to take down her hair, and wishing she hadn't sent her maid to bed.

"What?" said Uncle Warren Wainwright sharply. "He's left already? I don't think much of him for that!"

"Why, you were just worrying about him staying around," laughed Aunt Fannie. "And very likely Mary Elizabeth turned him down anyway. You know her! Besides, I saw her wearing a perfectly gorgeous diamond on her left hand just before she went down to the church. I think it came from Boothby Farwell, I really do. I saw the white case it came in lying on her bureau and it came from Tiffany's. There's been a rumor around about them for months and I suppose it's settled at last."

"H'm!" said Uncle Warren relieving himself of his dress shirt. "He's too old for her! And by the way, he wasn't here, was he?"

"Jeff doesn't like him!" said Aunt Fannie in her placid tone.

"H'm!" said Uncle Warren. "The little jade! Well, she's bound to have a good time wherever she goes, isn't she?" and he laughed grimly. "Even if she is engaged she'll have her little fling!"

"Now, Warren," said Aunt Fannie, "I don't think you're fair to Mary Elizabeth. She isn't a flirt. She really isn't. She's just friends with them all."

"Yes, I know," said Uncle Warren. "I'm not blaming her. But I hope she keeps 'em all just friends till one comes along fine enough for her. She's a sweet girl."

"Yes, she is!" agreed the aunt.

"That's what I'm saying about this chap, Saxon, is that the name? Queer name. We must look him up. Get Jeff to give us his credentials when he gets back. That is if she hasn't forgotten him by that time! But somehow I don't think she'll forget him so soon. I shouldn't if I were a girl."

"You don't know what you'd do if you were a girl, Warren. Now do get to bed. You know we've got to take a journey in the morning," soothed Aunt Fannie.

And very soon in that room also all was quiet.

But Mary Elizabeth lay in her bed with her eyes wide, her cheeks burning and a thrill upon her lips, thinking over every instant from the moment she entered the church door and caught that look of John Saxon as he stood there beside her cousin Jeff, down through the unprecedented events of the evening until she saw him swept away from her by the train in the darkness, with only a little red light winking back at her.

Would she ever see him again? Would she ever hear his voice again thrilling into her soul? Was that little red winking light at the end of the train that took him away by any possibility a warning, a danger signal to her, to stop right here and not carry it any farther?

Well, in the morning she would wire to Jeff to tell her all about him. No, she couldn't do that. She didn't know where Jeff was going. And there was Camilla. She didn't want Camilla to know that she was interested. That was the trouble when your favorite cousin got married, there was always his wife, no matter how nice she was.

And she didn't want Jeff to know either that she was interested. Any question would have to be oh so casual, and that couldn't be accomplished as things were now. No telling when she would see Jeff alone again.

And besides, of course she must wait to see if John Saxon ever came again or wrote. Oh, strange sweet perilous situation!

Then she thought of his voice whispering, "my darling!" and fell asleep with her cheek against his.

To-morrow she would have to see about sending back that ring, but to-night was hers and John Saxon's.

4

JOHN Saxon made his way to the club car and sat down at the desk to write his letter. It seemed the most momentous thing of his life. In his hand he still clutched the tiny envelope Mary Elizabeth had given him at parting. He hadn't as yet looked at it. But he glared around on the other inhabitants of the car sternly. They were not his kind. Three men at a table were playing cards and drinking, had been drinking for some time if one might judge from their loud, excited voices. A highly illuminated girl was smoking in the far corner and watching the men sleepily. An old man with cigar ashes sprinkled over his ample vest front was audibly sleeping in the chair next to the desk, his rank cigar smoldering in his limp hand.

Saxon turned away in disgust. It seemed a desecration to write to her in such surroundings. Such thoughts as he wished to pen to her were not fitting here.

He arose and went back to his section. It would not be comfortable to write there, but at least he would not be annoyed by others talking. John Saxon had not spent a large part of his life roughing it for nothing. He could make the best of circumstances. So he disposed of his baggage as best he could, got out his writing materials, folded his length up in as comfortable a position as he could beside the tiny light of his berth, and started to pour out his heart to the girl he had just left. He had promised her a letter at once and she should have it.

"My dear—" he began. He did not want any names interfering in this first letter. He wanted to tell her all that was in his heart before his thoughts would be entangled with the things of this world, including even a name. As he remembered it she didn't have a very pretty name anyway, but what was in a name? So, "My dear—" he wrote and lingered over the writing of it pleasantly.

> I want to tell you what you seemed like to me when I first saw you, to tell you all the things I wanted to say going down that aisle and couldn't because there wasn't time, to let you know what you seemed to me all the blessed evening while we were together. They are things of course that I should have said on the way to the station when I was tongue-tied with the thought of your nearness and my privilege. Yet the time was not wasted for I learned that just to be quietly near you was enough to bring great joy and peace and preciousness.
>
> And now, I find there are no words that will express the depth of my thoughts about you—as if I were a painter and, getting out my pigments, I find none of sufficient clearness and depth of color to paint you as you are. I should have to mix the colors from my heart. That's how I feel about you.—As if I were a poet and could find no new phrases not worn dull and shabby by other men's

thoughts about other girls down the ages. You are too lovely to be described by worn out words.

If I could summon all the lovely descriptions by poets of all ages, all the wonderful portraits ever painted, and select the best and put them together, they could never equal you. There hover in my mind phrases I have read and admired, loved indeed sometimes, one that likens hair to a glossy raven's wing, but it seems stale when I think of the beautiful crowning of your dark hair, and the way it waves away from your white forehead.

There are lines that stand out in literature likening a beloved one's eyes to stars, and there is a starriness in your eyes, but there is something more. None of the words I find cluttering about in my mind quite satisfy. It must be because my love for you goes deeper than the mere outer look of you. It recognizes a spiritual glow from within, a radiance that does not come just from feature or form or color, though you have those to perfection.

But words, mere words fail to help me tell you what you are to me. I would have to lay my lips again upon yours, to hold your face close to mine once more, and to fold you close in my arms to make you understand what I mean. And you will readily understand that I could not have done that coming down the church aisle.

When I looked down toward the church door and saw you coming with your lifted face and that inner glow lightening your eyes I cannot express to you what it meant to me. The years will have to tell you that, if in the kindness of God He gives us years together. I only know your face is like a flower, lovely and full of sacredness, and I thought your eyes spoke to my eyes, an understanding look, and told me I might dare.

These things seem hard and cold when written down upon paper, and the thought that you may laugh at them makes me quiver, for although your laugh is very lovely, these feelings I here hand over to you are delicately sensitive, for I love you, love you, love you. And that after all is the most satisfactory thing I can write, for it is true and deep and will reach out to eternity.

And now there are things I must tell you, though I can tell them better and more in detail when I get to a quiet room and a desk. But they are things you should know at once.

I am just a plain, poor, young man with a lot of hard work behind me, and probably a lot still ahead. I finished my course in medicine a year ago and have been working since to get together enough for a special graduate course which I need for what I want to do. This has been arranged for, and it was to meet by appointment the great man with whom I am to study that I had to tear myself away from you to-night. If I had missed the meeting it might not have come my way again. As I look back on the possibilities of the evening I find that in case I had had no opportunity to talk with you I would certainly have missed my appointment, much as it meant to me, and difficult as it was to arrange, rather than run the risk of losing you. As it was I found it by far the hardest thing I ever had to do to leave you. And after I was under motion and it was too late to go back it came to me what I had done, and I was appalled that I had let you bring me to the station, much as I delighted in having you to myself, and that I had left you at that hour of the night to go back alone! Oh, I realize that it was but a short distance in a well-traveled district and that you are probably quite used to being out that way alone. But it is not my idea of the way to take care of a girl, and it is not the way I shall want to take care of you if the precious privilege is ever mine.

I want you to understand that my people, though educated and cultured to a wide degree, are very plain, and not well off. I go from my appointment in New York back to our Florida orange grove where I have duties to that grove that mean hard work and plenty of it if the grove is to bear our fortune's worth this next season.

Be sure I would be planning to return straight to you, wherever that might be, before going south, but that the simple fact is, I cannot afford to be away from my work another day just now. The wind and the sun and the weather are doing things every day to my grove and my garden that will hopelessly tie my hands for the immediate future if I do not get right back to my work there. Even a day more makes a difference.

But know this, beloved, the moment I am free I shall come to you if you will let me, even if I have to walk to get there.

Now there is just one more thing, and perhaps it should come first instead of last, for after all it is paramount to everything else in my life. I want you to know that the first, foremost, and highest thought in my life, is of my Lord and Master, Jesus Christ, the Saviour of my soul. What He says I must do, where He leads I must follow. To study His Word is my greatest delight, and to witness of Him my highest joy.

Your place in my life, if you grant me your love, will be second only to my Lord.

I have been trusting that these standards are yours also, and surely, if that is so, we should have great joy in living our life together in Him.

Earnestly wishing that I might give you good night face to face instead of on paper, and eagerly awaiting some word from you, at the above address,

Your lover,
John Saxon.

John folded the letter carefully, and put it in an envelope. Then he drew the little missive she had given him from his pocket and read it.

"Miss Mary Elizabeth Wainwright."

He stared at it in dismay! Wainwright! Was she a Wainwright? What could it mean? Had some one played a joke on him? Had she put some one else's card in the envelope? Hadn't Jeff said that the maid of honor was named Helen Foster? Surely his memory had not played him false.

Carefully he went back over the time since he had arrived from the south. He recalled distinctly that Jeff had said he would like the maid of honor, that she was his kind, or something of the sort, a great church-worker. He had said that positively. He had certainly conveyed the idea that the girl was a Christian, in sympathy with his own beliefs and standards.

And now he recalled the bride's words from the back of the caterer's car, "But you haven't met her!" It hadn't meant a thing then but that nobody had introduced him, and he had to perform that function for himself. But now he began to see that something must have happened to the original maid of honor, and this girl had been substituted.

Wainwright! Now what would that mean? Wealth, honor, sophistication, all that made up a different world from his, and no guarantee whatever about her being a Christian! His heart began to sink.

And he, what had he done? Rushed ahead and committed himself without so much as an upward glance to see what had been his Lord's will in the matter! He had been so sure that she was all right. Her face had been so wonderful, her whole manner so lovely, so in keeping with what a servant of the Lord should rightly be, that it had never entered his mind to question, to hesitate. And now here she was a *Wainwright,* and he knew what the Wainwright tradition would be. He had come close enough to Jeffrey Wainwright before he had been born again, and closer still afterwards, to know that the family were utterly worldly. Jeff had mentioned no exception in his family, and he most certainly would have done so if there were one. They had had many a heart to heart talk about what Jeff's new life was to be after he took the Lord for his Saviour and Master. Jeff had known that he would meet with opposition on every hand. He had said that his family, though tacitly connected with church life, had no understanding whatever of the truth of the Gospel, nor of true Christian life. They had only a feeling that it was the respectable thing to do to belong to a church and might perhaps pave the steps to heaven by and by. Oh, God! Could she be like that? And he, pledged to give his life to the service of Christ! There was no turning back for him. There was no possibility of compromise.

Into his mind surged verse after verse of scripture. "Be not unequally yoked together with unbelievers!" "Can two walk together except they be agreed?" If his earthly love and his heavenly service did not agree his love would have to go. There was no question about that. His

Lord came first. And he was glad that before he knew who she was he had made that plain in his letter. But oh, what pain this might bring!—Certain pain to himself. Would it also perhaps bring pain to her, to whom his soul clave already?

John Saxon buried his face in the pillow beside him and began to talk to God, letting God search his heart, owning his own impetuous fault, asking for guidance and strength.

Gradually a number of things became plain as he prayed. For one thing he realized that a Wainwright was a very different proposition from a quiet, plain, village girl who had been a friend of Camilla's. He knew that Camilla had worked for her living. Likely her friends were of her status socially. A Wainwright would expect larger things in the way of wealth and position. A Wainwright would laugh at his presumption. He writhed as he thought of these things, as he remembered the mocking light in her eyes sometimes, the twinkle of fun at the corner of her mouth. Could it be that she was not what she seemed to be?

He remembered her lips on his, remembered her hand nestling in his. Was she only playing with him? Did she practise this sort of thing? No! His soul recoiled from the thought. He had given her his love, whether right or wrong, impetuous or wise, it was done, and he must trust her until she had been proved false. That was the first exaction of such love as his. And yet it must be in obedience to his Lord, or it could never be blest.

"Lord, Thou canst make her a child of God. Thou canst send Thy Holy Spirit to draw her to Thee if she is not already Thine. I do not deserve that Thou shouldst do this for me, but I ask it in the name of the Lord Jesus, for Thy glory, if it be Thy will. Nevertheless, not my will but Thine!"

Somewhat refreshed from contact with his God John Saxon sat up and read over his letter. After due deliberation he decided to send it. It was all true. It was no more than he had told her before he left her, and it was her due after what had passed. But there was a little more that he should say. So after some thought he wrote again.

The foregoing letter was finished and signed before I opened the envelope you gave me. I find now to my consternation that you are not the girl I was told I was to partner with. She was an utter stranger to me as much as you were. I knew nothing of her family or station in life. Her name, they told me, was Helen Foster, and I was not greatly curious about her, till I saw you coming up the aisle and knew that you must be the maid of honor, and my heart went out to you. I felt I must not run the risk of losing you.

Now, when I see your name, and know you are a Wainwright, my heart is turned to water and my hope sinks low. You come from a family of fabulous wealth and station, and I am a plain man with my way to make. I had no right to presume without knowing all about you. You must have laughed quietly to yourself over my presumption, for doubtless you knew more of me than I did of you. Also, I see another cause for blame in me. What right had I to assume that that other girl, whoever she was, would not be wealthy and socially prominent and resent an impetuous courtship as well as yourself? Oh, the whole thing has made me despise myself. I never knew I was impetuous before. Yet like any school boy I have confessed my love for you before you had a chance to judge me. It wasn't fair to you.

And yet, I love you, O I love you, Mary Elizabeth! I write your beautiful name reverently. Mary Elizabeth. How wonderful if I might some day say, *my* Mary Elizabeth!

I shall love you and pray for you. John Saxon.

Having addressed and sealed this letter John Saxon lay down to sleep. He was more weary than he remembered to have felt ever in his life, and as he sank off to sleep he had the feeling that something so fine and lovely that he was almost willing to give his life for it, had touched him and glanced away.

It wasn't a long night. The porter awakened him before they reached New York. He had time to get himself garbed for the day and pack away his evening clothes smoothly for the journey south. He would not be needing them again. At least not till he came back in the fall,—*if* he was accepted, and *if* he came back.

The morning light had not taken away his submission, but it had brought sober second thoughts. It had made him grave and almost sad. It had made him see his own act of proposing to a stranger, and such a stranger, as almost unforgivable. It had made him judge himself most severely. It would seem that he had entered this race with several handicaps that he was not even aware of until it was too late. His judgment had been on a debauch, and had landed him in a situation out of which there seemed no possible escape.

Now and then there would return to him a swift vision of the girl, and his heart would thrill to it instantly. Whatever she was she was not false, not mocking. He was sure of that. That clinging form, those yielded lips were not merely playing a part. The fact that they were not painted lips bespoke in part an inner cleanness of mind that would not yield to falseness of this sort. He found that most of all he wanted to find her true. Even if it meant a parting from her forever, he kept praying that she might be clean, might be true, as she had seemed to him.

Ordinarily the errand upon which he was bound that morning, the meeting of a world-renowned scientist who chose his associates from among the greatest scholars, and refused students at the slightest whim, would have kept him on the *qui vive*. He had so longed, so prayed for this opportunity, yet now that it had arrived it seemed small in comparison with what was occupying his mind.

He ate a meager breakfast sitting on a stool in a cheap restaurant, and thought in humiliation as he lifted the thick coffee cup and put it to his lips, that the girl whom he had dared to kiss last night might even now be driving in a great limousine up Fifth Avenue, or Riverside Drive or wherever the Wainwrights of the world took their morning airings.

Fool that he was, he might have known when he saw the make of her luxurious little car, and heard its costly purring, that she was not of his class at all. The very size of the stone she had worn under her glove, which he had touched there on his arm, might have taught him that a girl who could command gifts like that was not the girl for him to dare aspire to. Fool, fool, fool!

And presently, after she had gently and kindly told him where he belonged, she would tell her cousin Jeff, and he would have to go through all his life knowing that Jeff, whom he loved like a brother, despised his good sense, and regarded him less because of his impulsive act.

Lower in spirit John Saxon could not possibly have been, as he started out that morning to meet his appointment with the great man. He had borne poverty, toil, sickness, even sorrow like a man, sometimes almost like an angel, but this new form of trial, that was thrillingly sweet, and bitterly tender, and gallingly humiliating, really got him down and out. For a few hours a little demon sat on his throat and laughed to his fellows about how John Saxon, Christian, had surrendered to the common passion of love, and compromised with his good sense as well as his trust in God.

"I told you so!" the little demon cried to the others gathered round to gloat. "I told you his trust wasn't so great! I told you he'd forget his Guide and go the way his feelings led him when it came to something he really wanted!"

But John Saxon had not his trust in God for naught. The habit of prayer was too firmly fixed upon him to be long intermitted, and in his despair he turned to God. He prayed on the street as he went, threading his way among traffic and pedestrians. His heart was in touch with heaven, and his soul was crying out for help, for confidence, not in himself, but in the God Whose he was.

By the time he reached the place of his appointment he was steady and calm. His natural gravity sat well upon him, and there was none of the trepidation he might have felt at another time.

It was good to get in touch with every day affairs again, to be planning his life's work, to look into the face of the great man and read the genius that made him eminent among his peers. Saxon felt again the enthusiasm for his profession, the zest to do his best, and although he did not realize it, he made a fine impression upon the man who was accounted to be hard to interest.

The interview was not long. Dr. Hughes asked him a few crisp questions about his work so far, about his interests, and where he had pursued his studies, about his financial state, and how he had earned his way. He seemed pleased with the answers, and then, just as if it had been a foregone conclusion that he would be accepted, John Saxon found himself accepted and approved, was told briefly when and where and how to present himself in the fall, and with a brief handshake was dismissed.

He carried with him a glow from the last smile the great man had given him. Now, at least, he had something to say for his own prospects that needn't make him feel ashamed. It was not everybody who could claim to be this great man's special student. If all went well his professional future was assured.

And then his heart sprang back to last night. Sharp as a sword thrust through his heart went the thought that he ought not to think about Mary Elizabeth any more. And yet his human heart went throbbing on and loving her in spite of all.

How he longed to jump on a train and go back to the place where he had left her. Of course she wouldn't still be there. She didn't live there and she would have started home by this time. Finally he could stand it no longer and he got Long Distance and called the hotel, asking for Miss Wainwright. He had decided that he would tell her he had been anxious lest she had not reached the hotel safely alone last night. That was a poor excuse of course, she would laugh at it, but it would be so good just to hear her voice, even in a bit of laughter.

But he was promptly told that Miss Wainwright had checked out early that morning, and he hung up with a dreary, desolate feeling that his dream had turned into practical every day living and wouldn't ever come back. He had mailed his letter early that morning, against his better judgment. His judgment said it ought to be revised and less revelation of his own foolish heart and its deep feeling made known. But judgment had been set aside and he had sternly mailed the letter. He told himself that he had promised to write that letter and now that was done and it was up to her.

He wandered up to the shopping district which he knew well from his college days, and bought his mother a lovely little soft gray dress. It wasn't the kind of dress she usually wore, and she wouldn't likely have much place to wear it, but something in him yearned to bring into the life of his sweet little patient mother a bit of the beauty he had seen in other women last night. He got his father some shirts and ties, things he knew he needed, and his heart went out to them in a deeper love than he often took time to realize. They might be plain and unsophisticated, and many people might despise them, yet so all the more he would love and be loyal to them.

When he had finished his purchases, spending more than he really could afford, he idled past Tiffany's, lingered, went back, and finally went in. He wanted to find out just what really nice diamonds cost. Not as large and wonderful perhaps as that diamond must have been that she wore last night. He knew that there were rings of comparatively small dimensions that cost fabulous sums, but he wanted to see for himself just what one ought to spend for a reasonable ring, if ever he should see his way clear to get one—and if he should have anyone to get it for.

He came away from Tiffany's a sadder and wiser man, and went thoughtfully to the Museum to use the remaining hours before his train left in something more profitable than dreams.

5

DESPITE the fact that Mary Elizabeth had slept very little the night before, she was up and around quite early the morning after the wedding. She had several fish to catch and fry before she left the town, and she didn't intend to miss one of them.

She had her door a tiny crack ajar and kept watch as the different members of the wedding party came from their rooms, and it wasn't an easy thing to do either, because she wasn't sure how early they were going to start.

The bride's mother was the first to come out, with Miss York in trim traveling suit of sheer brown and a becoming brown hat.

Mary Elizabeth was on hand, fresh as a rose, as the elevator clanged its doors open to take them down. She had a letter in her hand to mail and she greeted Mrs. Chrystie enthusiastically. Mary Elizabeth liked the bride's shy sweet little mother, and looked her over approvingly. Her dress of soft black and white silk was most becoming, and there was a faintly haunting memory of Camilla in her eyes. Mary Elizabeth had fallen very much in love with her cousin's new bride, although she had had such a brief fleeting acquaintance on the wedding day.

"My dear!" said Mrs. Chrystie, "I'm glad you are here yet. I was so troubled last night when I couldn't find you. I wanted to thank you personally for coming in at the last minute and taking that important place in the wedding party. So many girls wouldn't have been willing. It was most gracious and lovely of you. And you did your part so perfectly without having to be told a thing. Of course you've been in so many such functions before it wouldn't seem the bugbear to you that it would be to a lot of girls."

"Oh, I just enjoyed it, Mrs. Chrystie. Jeff has always been like a brother to me and it was lovely to have an intimate part like that in his wedding," said Mary Elizabeth.

"Well, Camilla appreciated it more than she had time to tell you. The last word she said to me was to ask me to please hunt you up and tell you that you were just wonderful. She'll write you of course but she wanted me to tell you especially."

"Oh, I'm so glad she was pleased. She's lovely, Mrs. Chrystie. I was afraid I was going to be horribly jealous of anybody who married Jeff, we've always been so close. He couldn't have been dearer to me if I had been his own sister, though of course we haven't seen so much of each other the last five years while I've been abroad. But he's a dear! And I'm just crazy about Camilla. She just suits him. She's perfect. I couldn't have dreamed a girl for him any better. I'm so pleased. I do hope we're going to be so situated that we can see a good deal of each other. I never had a sister, and I've always wanted one. She looks like the sister I've always imagined."

"Why, how sweet of you, dear. I know Camilla will enjoy you. And by the way, she wanted me to tell you that Jeff was so pleased that you made his friend Mr. Saxon have such a pleasant evening. He said Mr. Saxon was usually rather quiet and reticent, especially with ladies, and he had been afraid he wouldn't have a good time. He had asked Camilla to be sure to introduce her old friends to him, but really, Camilla's old friends all seemed to have so many of their own friends around them that there wasn't any chance. And you took the whole responsibility and made Mr. Saxon feel at home. Camilla said she watched him and she was sure he had a good time."

Mary Elizabeth was not pale, even after her night's vigil, but the quick eyes of Miss York saw the color rise a little warmer in her smooth cheeks and a softened light come into her eyes.

"Yes?" said Mary Elizabeth quickly, her voice in perfect control. "Why, anybody would be honored to have the privilege of entertaining Mr. Saxon. He is—a most interesting—person, don't you think, Mrs. Chrystie? I certainly enjoyed every minute of the evening. I thought Jeff ought to be proud that he came so far to be best man. And I understand he is a very busy person indeed. Science of some sort, isn't that his line? He was—very—versatile. I—didn't find him reticent at all!"

Mary Elizabeth's eyes were dancing now with subdued lights and Miss York didn't miss a glint, but there was a little upward curve to her lips that had not been there last night when she had discussed Miss Wainwright with Mrs. Chrystie. She was beginning to feel that there was more to Mary Elizabeth than she had at first thought.

"Well, then, you must have interested him," laughed

Mrs. Chrystie. "And now, I do hope we shall see more of you. Are you leaving for—where?—this morning?"

"Yes, I suppose so," said Mary Elizabeth. "It all depends on Aunt Clarice. They're driving home and I promised to drive in their wake, and there's no telling what time they will appear on the scene. Aunt Clarice likes her morning rest. You know I drove Dad down yesterday afternoon, but he took the midnight train back home. He had some business this morning that he couldn't be away from, so I'll just take in some other member of the family I suppose. Are you leaving?"

"Yes, Miss York and I are driving up in Camilla's old car. She's willed it to me though Miss York is the driver. You met Miss York last night didn't you? She's our good angel, you know."

"I didn't meet her," said Mary Elizabeth with a warm little smile, "but I wondered who she was last night, and I'm glad to know her. I often need angels myself, guardian ones, and I might want to borrow her."

She put out her soft shapely hand and gave Miss York a warm grip, and that woman was heartily won over. She noticed too, as Mary Elizabeth turned away that the big glowing diamond she had glimpsed on her hand last night wasn't there this morning. Perhaps she had been mistaken in her judgment.

Mary Elizabeth went over to the desk and mailed a letter she had written about some trivial matter, and buying a morning paper sat herself down to watch the elevators for the next one of her victims. While she pretended to read the news in which she wasn't in the least interested, she reflected that she hadn't got much information so far concerning John Saxon. And yet, as she held the paper before her eyes her lips were smiling. John Saxon was reticent, was he? He hadn't sounded especially so as they came down the aisle together last night!

It was Uncle Warren and Aunt Fan who came down next to breakfast, and paused in the lobby to greet her.

"What, up so early, Mary Liz?" greeted Uncle Warren playfully. "I thought you'd have to take your beauty sleep this morning after being up so late last night."

"I wasn't up so very late last night, Uncle War," protested Mary Elizabeth quickly. "I wasn't up much later than you, I'll dare to say. I'm sure I saw your evening coat disappearing into the elevator just as I was about to go up myself."

"You don't say!" said Uncle Warren. "And what did you do with the big bronze giant? Or are you waiting now for him to come down and play golf or something? I saw you took quite a shine to each other last night. But look out, Mary Liz! He's a poor man. Jeff told me that yesterday. A poor man and a genius! You should never break the heart of a genius, Mary Liz. It unfits him to be a public benefactor. And besides, Mary Liz, I understand Jeff picked him up in a Florida swamp somewhere, and he wouldn't be your style nor able to go your gait, so I suppose you're wise to take up with that nice, settled, staid Grandpa Farwell. He can give you quarts of diamonds, and take you to all the horse shows in the world, and keep a general eye on your behavior. For you must own, Mary Liz, that you're an awful flirt, and I don't want any of Jeff's protégés trifled with!"

"Oh, Uncle Warren, aren't you complimentary!" said Mary Elizabeth with a gay little ripple of a laugh. "As if you didn't know that it was part of my duties last night to entertain the best man and make sure he had a good time! But you needn't worry about him, you gorgeous old fraud you, I understand he's left for parts unknown and he probably won't appear on the scene again."

"You understand! H'm! You understand!" grinned Uncle Warren.

"And as for Boothby Farwell," said Mary Elizabeth coolly, "I'm not looking for an overseer just now, thank you, though I suppose from your point of view I need one badly."

"Well, forget it, Mary Liz!" said her old uncle patting her cheek. "Had your breakfast? Why don't you come on in with us? Or are you waiting for some younger man to stroll by and ask you, my dear?"

"I'm waiting for Aunt Clarice to come down. I promised I'd take some of their party in my car, and I've got to find out just what she wants of me."

Aunt Fan patted her hand lovingly, and passed on to the dining room with her jocular old husband, and Mary Elizabeth settled down to her paper again.

But she had time to read the paper several times through before the other Uncle and Aunt appeared for they were having a discussion while they dressed.

"I liked that best man Jeff selected," the bridegroom's father was saying as he stretched his chin to give the last jerk to his tie.

"He was all right," said Jeffrey's mother, "only I did think it was such a pity he couldn't have chosen one of his own classmates, or some one in our set. It really isn't worth while to go out of your way to hurt people's feelings. There is Gerry Appleton, Jeff knows his mother is one of my very dearest friends."

"I don't see what that has to do with it. Jeff only gets married once—I hope—and why in Sam Hill can't he choose whoever he wants to be his best man? I can't think of Jeff ever choosing that little sissy of a Gerry, anyway."

"Really, Robert!" said his wife with dignity, "I don't understand your speaking that way of a son of an old family. It's bad enough for Jeff to have chosen a wife from an obscure family, a wife who had to work to earn her living, without having him go to the ends of the earth to haul up a nobody for his chief attendant at the wedding."

"Now look here, Clarice, it's time you got this thing straight," said her husband, facing her firmly with a glance of intensity from under his shaggy white eyebrows. "I told you very clearly that Camilla's family is just as fine and old as our own, and there have been several men of note in both her father's and mother's lines. I think you ought to put that idea out of your head once and for all. She is good and beautiful, and she loves Jeff and he loves her, and that is enough anyway. It was noble of her to go to work to support her mother when her father's fortune was destroyed through the wrong doing of their bankers. Would you have admired her any more if she had settled down on some of her distant relatives to be supported, or let her mother go to a Home? Now for Jeff's sake and for her sake and for all our sakes, you've got to put that snobbery away forever. Camilla is just as good as we are. And I'm saying that I liked that best man very much, and I thought you did too. You said so last night when you told me how much Jeff admired him."

"Oh, yes," said Mrs. Robert Wainwright. "He was all right. He is very good-looking of course, and appeared quite impressive standing up there by Jeffrey. But I am annoyed at Betty Wainwright that she should have made herself so prominent in his company all the evening. It wasn't required of her at all. She could have been polite without fairly falling in his arms. We certainly don't want two of our family going into obscurity for life, do we? Really I am worried about Betty. Her father lets her have her own way too much. Your brother Samuel always was too easy! You know I said that long ago."

"I wish you wouldn't call Mary Elizabeth 'Betty'!" said Uncle Robert in an irritated tone. "'Betty!'" he snorted. "It undignifies her good old-fashioned name. And as for the way she treated Saxon, I thought it was modesty itself!"

"Oh, yes, you always think everything that girl does is all right. You're just like Samuel. You haven't an idea how careful a girl has to be in these days. It's a good thing we didn't have any daughters, for you would have spoiled them terribly. I shall have to speak to my niece I'm afraid. She needs a woman's advice."

"You let Mary Elizabeth alone!" said her husband. "She's nice and sweet and good, and she doesn't need any advice. She's doing well enough bringing herself up. Now, are you ready at last? Where is Sam? Talk about spoiling, I don't see why you can't understand you are spoiling Sam, letting him sleep every morning as late as he pleases. He'll never amount to shucks if he doesn't learn to get up early in the morning. I've threatened him with cutting his allowance, but you always manage to excuse him somehow."

So they went down to meet their niece, who arose with a smile to welcome them and did seem to justify all that her doting uncle had said of her.

Aunt Clarice gave her an indulgent kiss and surveyed her critically.

"You're looking a little pale, Betty dear," she said as they walked together to the dining room. "I do hope your duties last evening as maid of honor were not too strenuous. It was hardly fair of Camilla to ask you that way at the last minute, you having no chance to prepare a special dress or anything. You did very well of course, but it must have been trying, dear."

"Oh, not at all, Aunt Clarice," twinkled Mary Elizabeth slipping on the armor that she always used in conversation with this aunt. "I had the time of my life. I enjoyed every minute of the evening."

"Well, that was good of you, but I think, if you ask me, that they might have raked up somebody from their own friends, if they had to have a maid of honor at all, since they didn't ask you at first. They really should have asked you in the first place you know, Betty Wainwright! It was quite the proper thing, since Camilla hadn't seen her own friends in a long time. It is certainly a wonder it all went off as well as it did."

"Oh, I thought it was beautiful!" said Mary Elizabeth. "And Camilla made such a precious bride. I'm just going to love her, Aunt Clarice!"

"Yes, she did very well," admitted the bride's new mother-in-law with a sigh. "It wasn't what I'd planned for my son, but I think she'll be all right. Of course it's a satisfaction that he's settled down at last and didn't do any worse. Jeff always was erratic you know. But—I'm very well satisfied."

"I thought it was a perfect wedding, Aunt Clarice, with not a thing to be criticized. Those bridesmaids were sweet, and the ushers were all Jeff's friends, and the best man was a peach! I'd never met him before, you know. How long has Jeff known him?"

"Only just this winter!" said Aunt Clarice with a resigned sigh. "And that was another regrettable thing of course, though it went off quite smoothly thanks to your kind offices. He's only a passing acquaintance that Jeff took an interest in. He's really nothing but a sort of teacher, or coach, scout master I believe they called him. He took Sam out with a crowd of boys for a camping trip. Jeff went along to see that all was right, and this is the result! But then Jeff always was so democratic! And

Sam just simply lost his head over him. I can't quite make it out, though I suppose it's all right, now it's over anyway, and we'll likely never see him again. Are you going to have grapefruit or melon, Betty dear? They do have such a limited menu in this rural hotel, though it's very good what they have, of course, and it did turn out to be quite convenient."

Mary Elizabeth's eyes danced. She had found out something more about John Saxon. So Sam was crazy over him! Then perhaps Sam could be made the key to her situation.

"Melon, please!" said Mary Elizabeth, and then turned a glowing face to her aunt.

"Aunt Clarice, you said your car was rather full. Why can't I take Sam with me? I haven't seen him much since he is growing up and I'd like to renew my acquaintance with him."

"Oh, would you want to bother?" asked her aunt thoughtfully. "I don't know but that might be as good a solution of the problem as any. Sam is always so restless in a car that he makes me nervous. He is always teasing to drive, and of course he can't. I certainly shall be glad when Sam grows up."

So Mary Elizabeth finished her breakfast hastily and went in search of her young cousin Sam.

6

JOHN Saxon in his upper berth—because it was cheaper and he felt that he should save every penny—tossed about uncomfortably, trying to keep his thoughts on something he had read in a medical journal during his long evening in the railroad station. Finally he threw discretion to the winds and let his thoughts drift back as they would to last evening. Was that perfume, borne to his mind above the stuffiness of sleeper curtains and the rank tobacco fumes from the smoking room? Perfume! Yes, the perfume of her hair as he held her in his arms when they said good bye. It didn't assert itself as perfume, just the fragrance of flowers. She seemed a lovely flower herself.

And there he was off thinking about her again! Fool that he was. A rich worldly Wainwright. Well, at least a Wainwright, and likely worldly too in spite of her delicacy and sweetness. And who was he to have presumed? He ought never to have mailed that letter of course. Very likely she didn't expect him to write any of the time. Very likely it was just a game with her for the evening, and she would think him an innocent that he kept it up.

Well, the letter was gone, he told his persistent soul that would keep defending her, and hurling the lovely thrills of memory at him to prove it. The letter could not be recalled, and he would have had to send one eventually. It was gone and if she never answered it, it would serve him right of course, and would probably be the best dose of medicine to cure his madness that he could take.

And then he went to calculating how long it would be at the shortest that he could possibly expect an answer. Inconsistency was in the ascendancy. Well, probably when he got home and got down to good hard work again he would settle down to sanity as well, and he would take good care never to let himself get caught in social life again. Here he had been always sneering at the follies of the social set, and then had fallen as far and as hard as anybody he knew. Fallen in love at first sight, committed himself without knowing a thing about her except her lovely face and manner!

He would get so far and then falter. The memory of that face and manner, even if there had been no words, even if she had not yielded those exquisite lips to his, disarmed every one of his efforts to put her away from his thoughts. She hovered quietly about him, like a lovely precious atmosphere that breathed balm and healing. And here was he who had always controlled himself, body, soul and spirit, utterly unable to keep his thoughts away from the dear memory of her!

Well, perhaps in the future years the time would come when he could think of her calmly, remember the sweetness of her, without that hungry longing for her, without that fierce desire to possess her for his own. It might be that in the ages to come he would even be glad that he had her safe in his memory, a lovely picture to look back upon, a picture that could never be sullied by human faults and frailties because he had known her only one brief evening. Even that was more than some men had, an eternal ideal never shattered by everyday living. At least, that much was his if nothing else ever came. Almost he felt like praying that nothing would, that she would somehow be prevented from destroying his beautiful vision of her, that she might never answer his letter rather than answer it with mockery, or worse still with gentle pity and kind refusal.

He groaned aloud and rejoiced that the train made so much noise that he might groan again and again and nobody hear but God.

And then suddenly he remembered that he was God's child in God's care, and this affair belonged to God—he had put it in the will of God to do with as was best and right. He must not meddle further.

Then softly there came a peace upon him, and he sank to sleep with that breath of fragrance drifting about him, soft arms clinging about his neck, soft lips, sweet lips on his. The memory of her smile! God, how lovely she had been! How wonderful that it had fallen to his lot to know her even for one brief evening!

Young Sam Wainwright when approached by his cousin Mary Elizabeth scowled. He did not take kindly at all to the idea of being shunted off from the general party. He had hoped to ride with his father and bully him into letting him drive perhaps, or into giving him money for a motor cycle in case the driving was beyond a possibility.

"You're riding with me, did you know it, Mr. Wainwright!" said Mary Elizabeth.

Sam's experience with older cousins, any older relatives, especially of the weaker sex, was that if they noticed him at all they wanted something of him.

"Aw, heck!" he answered ungraciously. "What's that for?"

"Well, you see," confided Mary Elizabeth in a low tone, with a furtive glance about, as if the family *en masse* were spying about to hear what she was saying, "I was just thinking there might be a bit of a crowd, and I was afraid they'd expect me to take Cousin Eliza Froud, so I thought I'd forestall that. I'd so much rather have you to buddy with. You know I haven't seen you for so long I'd just like to get acquainted with you over again, and have you tell me all about your school and your sports. They tell me you're a great sportsman."

"Aw, they're kidding you," said Sam, still with his unbending frown. "You can't get anywhere in sports with the family I've got. Mother thinks I'm a kid, and she puts her foot down on every blessed thing I want to do."

"Say, that's a shame!" said Mary Elizabeth sympathetically. "I wonder if she couldn't be made to understand? Suppose you tell me all about it and I'll use my influence."

Sam eyed her doubtfully.

"Nothing can influence my mother," he said sadly, shaking his head, "she thinks for herself."

"Yes," said Mary Elizabeth crisply, "but there are ways. We'll see what can be done. In the meantime you're going to help me."

"Oh, yeah?" said the incredulous youth. He thought the crux of the matter had arrived, and he didn't intend to be tricked into anything by a smooth-tongued cousin if she had been round the world.

"Yes," said Mary Elizabeth, "I need a man to-day to travel with me. A girl doesn't like to travel alone. Beside my car has been behaving badly. I might need you. Can you help change a tire?"

"I can change a tire all by myself!" said Sam with contempt. "I've done it in our garage when the chauffeur was out for the day, and he never knew it."

"Did you really?" chanted Mary Elizabeth like a fellow-conspirator. "How perfectly spiffy! Didn't he ever find it out?"

"Not yet. It was last week and he was too busy going on errands before the wedding to notice. He will though. He has eyes like ferrets."

"Well, he certainly won't know who did it, will he? You were careful to wipe off the finger prints I suppose?"

Sam laughed. He exploded first as if it came unexpectedly, and then he looked at her a minute and bent double laughing.

"Okay!" he said when he'd recovered, "I'll go with you. I wasn't going to, but you've got a sense of humor. So many relatives haven't. Jeff's the only other one that has and now he's gone."

"Oh, no, he's not gone. He'll be back sound as a nut pretty soon, and you'll like your new sister Camilla, too. She's a peach!"

"Oh, she's awright I guess," said Sam with a grimace. "But I don't see Jeff's getting married. Why couldn't he have stayed at home?"

"Well, it is strange, isn't it?" said Mary Elizabeth. "However I guess we can't do anything about that now. Now, partner, how much baggage have you got? Is it all packed? When do we get started? Or do we have to wait for the rest of the crowd? Because you know we might have some of our plans upset if we did."

"That's right," said Sam with another frown.

"Had your breakfast?" asked Mary Elizabeth.

"Sure thing!" said Sam contemptuously. "Had my breakfast an hour ago and been down to the wharf watching the boats. You didn't think I was going ta stick around till the family got up and then go in the dining room and have 'em all telling me what I was to eat, did you? It makes me sick the way they treat me, just like a baby."

"Well, that is hard lines, isn't it? Then suppose you hustle up and get your bags and bring them down to that side door over there, and I'll go and tell your mother we're starting ahead because I have a place I want to stop a few minutes on the way. There's a place I saw on the way down where they have the darlingest wire-haired terriers for sale, puppies, the cutest ever. Like wire-haired terriers?"

"Betcher life I do," said Sam, now wholly won over, his eyes shining with a great relief. "Gee, we're gonta have fun, aren't we?"

"Sure thing!" said Mary Elizabeth boyishly, giving him a real boy grin that endeared him to her, even as many an older youth had been endeared in the past.

So Mary Elizabeth ordered the porter to bring down her luggage, and went on her way to the dining room to let the uncles and aunts, principally the aunts, know that she was starting.

"But we wanted you to go along with us," said Aunt Fannie buttering and syruping her waffles.

"Sorry, Aunt Fan," said Mary Elizabeth sweetly, "I've promised to get home as soon as possible. I'm expecting some mail that is very important. And we couldn't see each other very much anyway on the road. You know it's terribly hard to follow a car and try to keep together in traffic."

"You'll drive carefully, won't you, Betty dear?" said Aunt Clarice.

"Oh, I'm the world's best, Aunt Clarrie, don't you know that?" smiled the girl.

"Well, be sure to see that Sam washes his hands and combs his hair before he leaves. I declare that child can acquire more dirt in a given time than any other of the human species I believe. Where he's been this morning I can't think! I went in to wake him up and found him gone. I don't know what he's going to grow up to! A tramp, I'm afraid. Well, I hope you won't regret your bargain taking him along, but it's a real charity, he makes us all so nervous. He gets restless you know, wants to get out and chase butterflies and dig up plants. Since he went on that camping trip in the winter he's simply impossible! You don't know what you're letting yourself in for, Betty dear!"

"Oh, I don't mind," said the girl with a happy smile. "We'll have a good time. Good bye. See you tonight sometime."

"Well, if you get tired of Sam just stop at that place where we took lunch on the way here and wait for us. We'll take him over and let you have Miss Petty, or Cousin Eliza Froud, you know."

"All right," said Mary Elizabeth, "I'll remember, but I won't get tired of my bargain so don't look for us." And Mary Elizabeth hurried out of the dining room.

She found young Sam with a suitcase, standing uncertainly by the door, an anxious eye on the dining room entrance.

"Didn't they can it?" he asked eagerly. "There must be some reason then. They likely wantta talk over the wedding and say how they hate somebody or they would."

"You uncanny child!" laughed Mary Elizabeth. "What made you think of that?"

"Oh, I've heard 'em when they didn't know I was

listening. They've made me like a lot of folks different times, talking against 'em."

"You're a scream!" said Mary Elizabeth. "I foresee we're going to have the time of our lives. Now, put your baggage in behind and hop in. Let's get started or somebody will try to go along with us."

"You said it!" said Sam, jamming his suitcase into the back of the car and letting down the cover carefully. "This is a peach of a car, isn't it?"

"It is rather nice," said his cousin settling down to her wheel as Sam sprang in slamming the door proudly as if he were the owner.

They rolled away from the hotel and around the little circle park in front and two blocks further on came to a halt before a candy shop.

"Like chocolates?" asked Mary Elizabeth fishing around in her hand bag for her purse.

"Sure thing!" said Sam with shining eyes.

She handed him a five dollar bill.

"Well, slide in there and buy as much as you want of anything that appeals to you. Get several kinds."

Sam took the money and crammed it into his side pocket with the studied indifference toward money he had noticed in all male persons when they were attending a young lady.

He came out so eager that he had almost lost his grown-up manner.

"I got several kinds because I wasn't sure which you'd like best," he explained as he climbed in and shut the door importantly again. He felt it was great, her using him this way, as any lady would send a young man on her errands. And she hadn't limited him as to how much to buy. He almost forgot that he wasn't driving the car.

"That's fine," said the lady curving smoothly into

traffic again. "I like them all. We're going to have a good time!"

"I'll say!" said the young cavalier. "Here's yer change!"

He almost felt that she was another boy and dropped easily into the boy vernacular.

"Oh, you'd better keep the change for any expenses we have. There is at least one ferry to cross if I remember rightly, and there'll be gas. You'll need more than that. Just put it into your pocket and look after things for me, won't you? It's such a relief not to have to bother. It's so nice to have a man along."

He gave her an appreciative grin, and after a minute said:

"Say, d'ya know, you remind me an awful lot of my scout master, Mary Beth?"

"Your scout master?" said Mary Beth with keen interest in her eyes. "Who is he? I hope he's nice."

"He is! He's a peach of a man. Why, he's Mr. Saxon, the one that was the best man last night at the wedding. You know him. You were talking to him a lot last night. Only he didn't look a bit like himself in those glad rags."

"Glad rags?" said Mary Elizabeth. "Doesn't he usually wear glad rags?"

"Naw, he wears khaki mostly, and flannel shirts and leggings. He's a crackerjack in the woods."

"He was rather nice, wasn't he?" said Mary Elizabeth with dreamy eyes as she guided her car out of traffic into a lovely country road. "I should think he would be good company in the woods. Tell me about it."

The boy's eyes grew dreamy too, and he stared off into a maple grove and saw live oak trees and palms instead. His thoughts were back in Florida with his idol.

"I don't know as it'll tell," he murmured. "You'd have to be there."

"I'll try," said Mary Elizabeth. "How does it look, the morning we start, or do we start at all? Do we just be there?"

Sam grinned.

"We start!" he said, entering into the game that his cousin was making. "We get up very early before it's light."

"I see," said the girl, her eyes half closed, "it gets light all of a sudden in Florida just as it gets dark all of a sudden at night. I know. I've been there. I only wish I could have been along with you. We wear old clothes, don't we, and don't take along a trunk, nor even a suitcase?"

The boy chuckled again.

"That's right. Just a pack. And we meet on the beach when the sky and the sea are altogether and look like mother's big opal."

"But that's very pretty," said Mary Elizabeth looking at him appreciatively. "Did anybody else notice it?"

"Aw, no, I don't even know as I did, but it was there if you wanted ta notice it. Mr. Saxon looked off at it a good deal. But he didn't say anything much. He doesn't. He only talks when it's necessary, except sometimes."

"What times?"

"Well, at night when we're sitting round the fire."

Mary Elizabeth thought that over while they were passing a series of trucks carrying a lot of new automobiles fresh from the factory.

"Well," she said, "what comes next? We don't just walk by the sea all the time."

Sam grinned.

"Next we have lunch. We boys rustle a fire. We were divided into squads you know, and each man had his duty. Jeff cut the bread and handed out butter. Mr. Saxon did most of the cooking at first, but afterwards we boys learned how."

Mary Elizabeth took in the picture.

"I certainly would have liked to be there. So Jeff was along too. That must have been grand."

"He was all right," boasted the proud brother. "He took care of the little kids. You know Mother had him go along because she didn't know Mr. Saxon, and I don't think Mr. Saxon liked it much at first, but afterwards they got to be buddies. And Jeff was fine, especially when the kids got scared of the snakes and things. There was one little kid hadn't any father and mother, or at least they didn't have any home together, and he was scared of snakes something awful. He just froze on to Jeff for a while till he got more brave."

"Snakes?" said Mary Elizabeth. "I don't know that I should care for them myself. *You* weren't afraid of them of course?"

"Naw, I don't mind snakes. There's nothing in snakes! Mr. Saxon told us a lot about their habits and things. He knows a lot about them. He isn't afraid of them. When he was a boy he used to have them for pets sometimes. His mother let him. He's got a swell mother! Mine would never stand for that! And once on the way we found a big red moccasin as big around as his arm and more than two yards long, and Mr. Saxon just picked him up by the tail quick and swung him around his head several times and flung him off, just like that!"—Sam demonstrated the manner vividly with his arms—"and Mister Snake he just lay still for a second and then he wabbled off all crooked, as if he was drunk. Mr. Saxon said it made him dizzy."

Mary Elizabeth considered this phase of her new friend several minutes. At last she said:

"He's not afraid of *anything,* is he?"

"I'll say he isn't!" said Sam.

"And what was it like when you got there?" she asked. "You finally got somewhere, didn't you?"

"Sure thing!" said the boy his eyes gleaming at the memory. *"And were we tired?* And *hungry!* We could have eaten nails. Sure, we got there. Why, it was all water, not the sea, just smooth water. First a little stream, and there were two Indians there with canoes, and we paddled till we came to a big lake with palms and tall pines around it, and across the lake was the camp. We got supper and sat around the fire on the sand to eat it. The sun went down before we were done, and the lake got all black like velvet, and then pretty soon the moon came up and made bright splashes like silver, and the rest of the lake was all like it had been lacquered. And then Mr. Saxon read—"

"How could he read if it was dark? You didn't have electric light in the camp did you?"

Sam threw back his head and laughed.

"I'll say we didn't. We had pine knots lighted and stuck in trays of sand, big wooden trays up on a post, and they flared like torches. They burned all night."

"And he could read by that light?"

"Sure, he read to us every night before we went to bed. Just read, and sometimes told us what it meant, just a word."

"What did he read?"

"Oh, the Bible," said Sam as if he was surprised that she didn't know. "He reads that all the while anyway, when he isn't doing anything else. You come on him lying in the hammock with his little Bible. He carries it in his pocket everywhere and gets it out any time when he's resting or anything. And he sure does make it plain when he reads it, just the way he says the words, without any talk at all, just reading. We fellas all liked it a lot. We wished he'd read longer, but he never did. It was always short. And then he'd sing."

"Oh, he sings, does he?"

"I'll say he sings! He's got a peach of a voice. And when he sings out in the open like that it's great! It just rolls out and echoes all across the lake. And then he made us sing too."

"What did you sing?" Mary Elizabeth's voice was filled with a kind of wonder. This Bible-slant on the man was something unexpected. Was it a part of his duty as a scout master? Was he under some kind of religious organization and had to read to the boys? She was considering this as she asked about the singing.

"Why, that first night we sang a chorus. He sang it first and then he taught it to us. Even Jeff sang. You know Jeff can *sing!*"

"Yes, he's got a wonderful voice," assented the audience.

"Well, when the two sang it was great. They took different parts, and say, it was silky!"

"What was the chorus?"

"Why, it was just a chorus. We learned a lot of them. Want me to sing it for you?"

"Oh yes, that would be great!"

Sam's clear treble piped out sweetly, every word distinct:

> *"I know a fount where sins are washed away!*
> *I know a place where night is turned to day!*
> > *Burdens are lifted, blind eyes made to see,*
> *There's a wonder-working power*
> *In the Blood of Calvary."*

"That's good!" said Mary Elizabeth hiding her astonishment. "Sing it again!"

Sam sang it again.

"It's very catchy. Try it once more and I'll hum it with you."

They sang it together several times and Mary Elizabeth saw it gave the boy pleasure.

"Gee, we had a good time down there!" he said, his face kindling with memory. "We useta sing till the old palm trees would rattle. We learned a lot of those choruses. I got a book home full of 'em. I'll show it to you sometime when you come around."

"I'd like to see it."

"Here's another. We useta sing this for a sort of grace sometimes before we ate.

> *"Everything's all right in my Father's house,*
> *In my Father's house, in my Father's house,*
> *Everything's all right in my Father's house,*
> *There'll be joy, joy, joy all the while!"*

"That's rather rousing, but wasn't it a bit hard on the little kid who hadn't any house because his father and mother were separated?"

"No, he just loved it. He useta go around singing it. It doesn't mean this earthly house down here, you know. It means heaven, and God's your Father."

"Oh!" said Mary Elizabeth in a small rebuked voice, marveling at the freedom of childhood. There was no embarrassment in Sam's voice. And yet she was positive most boys wouldn't speak like this of religious matters. Probably it was just this camp experience that had given him a different slant on such things. And that, of course, would be due to John Saxon! Amazing John Saxon!

She gave a little nervous shiver, warm though the day was. Serpents and gods! Her new friend and lover was as familiar with one as with the other. No wonder he had

dared propose to a stranger going down a wedding aisle!
Was she sure she wanted a lover like that, even though
he could make love in a deeper strain than any who had
ever come courting her before? Even though every new
thing she heard about him but thrilled her the more?
Gods and serpents!

Sam was singing over again that everything was all
right in his Father's house and presently Mary Elizabeth
was singing it too, taking the alto and delighting the boy
with the blending of harmony.

"Say, that's great! I wish you had been down there,
Mary Beth, you'd have just fitted!"

"H'm!" said Mary Elizabeth. "I don't know what
your Mr. Saxon might have thought about it. By the
way, Sam, why did you say I was like him? I'm curious
about that."

Sam grinned.

"It was you sending me for those chocolates. And,
gee! Isn't it about time we ate some?"

Mary Elizabeth handed over the chocolates with a
smile and Sam crammed in a big chocolate peppermint
and went on.

"Gee, you were nice, just handing over a lotta money
and not saying how much to spend. If my family had sent
me they'd have counted out the money and told me just
what kind I hadta buy because it was 'wholesome.'
Gosh! I hate that word wholesome! But you just let me
have the fun of choosing. And that's the way Mr. Saxon
does. He makes even work, fun, and he's always doing
something for somebody, no matter whether he can
afford it or not. Why he hocked his watch and some of
his best medical books to send a little kid up north to a
special hospital where he needed to go."

"He did?" said Mary Elizabeth, soft color stealing into

her face. "How kind of him! But—hasn't he got any watch now?"

"Oh, yes, Jeff found it out and bought his things in and managed to get 'em back to him so he didn't know who did it."

"That was nice of Jeff!" said Mary Elizabeth drawing a long breath and wondering why she was so glad that John Saxon did not have to go without his watch and valued medical books. "Sing that first song again, Sam, it kind of haunts me. There's something catchy in the tune."

So they sang it again and again, till Mary Elizabeth knew the words by heart.

"I'll sing ya another!" volunteered Sam. "Here's one we useta sing for morning prayers. It's to the tune of 'The Bells of Saint Mary's.' You know that one, don't ya?"

Mary Elizabeth hummed a little experimental bar or two.

"That's it. Only ya don't know the right words. You just haveta remember four kinds of songs and you have it. This is it:

"We'll sing in the morning the songs of salvation,
We'll sing in the noontime the songs of His love,
We'll sing in the evening the songs of His glory,
We'll sing the songs of Jesus in our Home above!"

They sang that several times together and Sam settled back replete with chocolates and happy as a boy of thirteen could be.

"Gee! Aren't we having a good time?" he said with a sigh of joy. "Gosh! I'm glad I came with you instead of the family."

"Well, that's nice," said Mary Elizabeth feeling a new

kind of joy in the boy's pleasure. She wondered if she hadn't been missing something in life by not cultivating children before. Then she remembered Aunt Clarice's words.

"By the way," she said quite casually, "how would you like to get out and stretch your legs a few minutes? See those three butterflies out there over that patch of buttercups? How about seeing if you can catch one of them."

Sam looked at her awesomely.

"You don't mean you'd stop on the way and let me chase butterflies?"

"Why not, if you'd like to?"

"But I thought you were in an awful hurry to get home?"

"Well, I thought I was," said Mary Elizabeth slowly, "but I don't know as it makes so much difference as that. I'd like to see you chase butterflies. If I didn't have my good shoes on I'd come and try my own hand at it."

Sam gave her a glowing look and started out of the car with a bound, but when he reached the fence rail and was about to spring over he suddenly turned back and hurried to where the car was parked.

"Say, I don't know as we'd better stop," he said cautiously casting a furtive eye back on the road. "The folks might catch up with us and Mother'd give me the dickens for holding you up when you are in such a hurry."

"Oh, that's all right," said Mary Elizabeth with a grin, "we're not on the regular highroad that they will take. I thought it would be more fun to be by ourselves."

The boy's eyes were filled with comprehension of her complicity, and with the deepest admiration that the eyes of a boy can hold.

"Say, you're swell!" he said eagerly. "You're just like

Mr. Saxon! I didn't know there were two folks in the whole world like that! You and he oughtta—oughtta—"

"Oh, that's all right, Sam," laughed the girl hastily, "don't worry about that. Run off and catch your butterflies before they are gone. I'll just sit here and think of something else nice to do."

Then Mary Elizabeth lay back on the cushions, with her cheek against the fine leather of the upholstery, and her eyes upon the dreamy, lazy, little June clouds that floated across a faultless blue, and thought of the new things she had been hearing about John Saxon. And then she closed her eyes and felt again his lips upon hers, thrilled again at the memory of his arms about her, at the words he had whispered in her ear. John Saxon! Oh, John Saxon! Why did you come marching down the aisle disturbing all Mary Elizabeth's well-ordered conventional life, and stirring up all sorts of longings that had never wakened before in her heart? Why did you make yourself the answer to every yearning of her heart, and yet be a new kind of person who would not fit at all into life as she knew it?

7

SAM came back eagerly with two butterflies, one pinioned in his cap, the other in his handkerchief. His face was dirty, and wet with perspiration, his hands were grimy, and his hair stood on end, but he was happy and his eyes were dancing.

"Gosh! That was fun!" he said as he climbed into the car.

Mary Elizabeth made him mop up to a certain extent at a brookside before they stopped for lunch, gave him an extra handkerchief for a towel, loaned him a little gold-mounted comb she carried in her hand bag to comb his recalcitrant hair. By this time he was as wax in her hands, and she felt another thrill of having captured his heart.

They had a wonderful lunch at a wayside dairy with milk in tall foaming goblets and ice cream made from rich cream, a few cakes and crackers for foundation, and they both decided it was the best lunch they had tasted in a long time.

Resting back on the cushions after lunch, Mary Elizabeth driving along through a bit of woodland, and Sam with the map on his lap, pointing out the turns to take in the road, the boy fell to singing again.

"I know a fount where sins are washed away!"

"Sam, why do you like that song so much?" she asked. "What have you to do with sins? You never did any very great sinning yet. You're only a kid."

"Oh, that doesn't make any difference," said Sam soberly. "Mr. Saxon said there was only one sin God judges people for anyway. All the others come outa that."

"What's that?" asked Mary Elizabeth sharply, wondering what new revelation was to come.

"Unbelieving," said Sam.

"Unbelieving?" said the girl in surprise.

"Yep! That's the big sin. That's sin. The others are only sins, and they're the result of it."

"What on earth do you mean, child?"

"Well, it's right!" said Sam with conviction. "It's all in the Bible. Mr. Saxon read it to us, and made us say it over and over and over. There isn't one of us will ever forget it."

"Well, explain, Sam. I don't understand."

"Why, you see, sin began in heaven," said Sam.

"In heaven? How could it? I thought heaven was perfect and everybody there was supposed to be sinless!"

"It was till Lucifer got stuck on himself," said Sam earnestly. "He thought he was It and wanted to be like God. He really wanted to be God and have everybody worship him and so he had to be thrown out of heaven."

Mary Elizabeth looked down at him in amazement.

"Go on," she said.

"Well, then Lucifer—he was called Satan by that time—came down to the Garden of Eden after God made Adam and Eve, and got in a snake and told 'em it wasn't so what God had said. You see God said they'd die if they ate any fruit off that forbidden tree, and they believed him instead of God, and did what God told them not to, and that's how sin got on earth. And death. That's why death hadta come. 'Cause God hadta keep His word."

Mary Elizabeth stared at the boy astounded. This was extraordinary talk for a boy. Also it was a story Mary Elizabeth had never heard before. She wasn't very familiar with the Bible, and Satan to her had always been something to joke about. It had never occurred to her that he was a literal person. Could it be that Sam had this right?

"Where did you get all this?" she asked after a moment's thought.

"Oh, it's in the Bible! Mr. Saxon read it to us. We studied Genesis an hour every morning while we were off on that trip. It was great. We liked it. Everybody liked it. Jeff did too. We had an examination on it the last day, and I had ninety-eight. I passed all right. And Mr. Saxon is sending us lessons this summer to do by correspondence."

"He is?" said his astounded audience. Then after an instant's hesitation, "Do you—*pay* him for that?"

"Pay him? Not on yer life. He does that just because he's interested. He wants us to get on. He wants everybody ta be saved. That's the most he cares about."

"Saved?" said Mary Elizabeth with puzzled expression. "Just what do you mean by that?"

"Why, saved! Eternal life and all that! 'God so loved the world that He gave His only begotten Son that whosoever believeth in Him should not perish, but have everlasting life.' Doncha know that? Everybody knows that. That's John 3:16 ya know."

"Why—it seems to me I've heard it somewhere," said

Mary Elizabeth uncertainly, perceiving that she was losing caste fast with her young companion.

"Well, that's about the most important verse there is, I guess. People can be saved just knowing that and nothing else."

Mary Elizabeth looked at him as if he had suddenly begun to speak in an unknown tongue.

"Just what do you mean by being saved?" she asked at length.

"Why, saved from punishment from yer sin. That's eternal separation from God ya know. I'm saved!"

He said it with an air of quiet conviction that was startling.

"How do you know?" asked Mary Elizabeth.

"Because Christ said so," said the boy. "He said: 'He that heareth my words, and believeth on Him that sent me, *hath* everlasting life, and *shall not* come into con-demnation, but *is passed* from death unto life.' Mr. Saxon drilled us a lot on that. He said we might havta tell someone someday that was dying and afraid."

"And aren't you afraid to die?" There was awe in her voice now as she studied her young cousin's face.

"Not any more. Not since I was saved."

"How do you get 'saved' as you call it?"

"You just believe Christ died in place of you. Not just believe it with yer head ya know, but with yer heart. You just accept Him as yer personal Saviour. Then He sends His Holy Spirit to live in ya, and tell ya what's right and wrong, and help ya ta be pleasing ta Him. That's all there is to it. He does the rest."

Mary Elizabeth was quiet a long time and then she asked:

"Did all the boys in the camp get saved?"

"No," said Sam thoughtfully, "not all. There was Flinty Robison. He just listened. He seemed interested

GRACE LIVINGSTON HILL

enough but he wouldn't ever give in and say he'd take Christ fer his Saviour. And he wouldn't pray. He said it was nobody's business what he did. And there was Stew Fuller and Corky Mansfield. They really didn't pay much attention. They snickered a lot. They haven't got much head, those guys, anyway. But we all are praying for 'em. I somehow think Flinty'll come sometime."

"Oh, you pray?"

"Sure thing! We got a prayer league. We write and tell each other who ta pray for. And Mr. Saxon writes ta us about it!"

They drew up just then at a filling station and no more was said about it. After they started on Mary Elizabeth seemed very quiet, and Sam was occupied in counting the different makes of cars they passed. He got out a pencil and paper and jotted them down. It seemed quite important to him. Mary Elizabeth was in deep thought adjusting this new light on her amazing lover.

She was realizing that the impetuous stranger had taken a deep hold on her inner life, and that everything she heard about him but filled her with more wonder, but this religious slant frightened her. Here was something in which she could not follow him. She wasn't sure she wanted to follow him even if she could. It would be almost like living with God to live with a man who thought about Him that way and was interested in the things of the Spirit. Mary Elizabeth realized that it would be wonderful to be loved by a man like that but wouldn't it be more than one like herself could ever live up to?

She thought of her other lovers in contrast. Rathbone Royce, steeped in art and literature, sophisticated to the last degree, adoring her languidly, critically, half sarcastically, bringing her gifts of rare editions of musty old volumes in which she had no interest, discoursing on

80

modern philosophy. Herbert MacLain, gay, irresponsible, handsome, a bit given to drinking which he had promised to give up entirely if she would marry him. He was a dear and she was fond of him, but did she want to devote her life to keeping him straight? She wasn't fool enough to think that merely marrying the woman he wanted was going to change his habits. There was Raymon Vincente, a musician of real worth, successful, devoted, urging her at intervals to link her life with his. Last year she had almost thought at one time she would. But time had gone on, and the lure of his music, while still enchanting, had ceased to cover the multitude of his sins, till at last she saw the real man, a weak selfish character. There was Harry Kincaid. They had been going together more or less since their kindergarten days. There was nothing wrong with him. He was part of her everyday life, and often she had thought that fate had set them apart for one another, yet she continued to laugh him off. There was nothing thrilling in the thought of marrying Harry.

And lastly there was Boothby Farwell, he of the great square diamond, which last night she had been fully persuaded she was going to return as soon as she reached home. Was she?

Boothby represented perhaps the cream of all her lovers, not excepting a couple of men in Europe who had been quite attentive. Boothby was handsome, cultured, successful, prominent, popular, so rich that one didn't stop to think of a limit to his wealth, perfect in his manners, interested in science, art, music and literature, owning several city residences of royal dimensions and charm, and as many country estates, in addition to a castle in Scotland. She might live in a palace if she chose, if she were his wife. Horses and chariots and yachts, even airplanes would be at her command at any hour of the day. He could give her diamonds galore, and pearls; he was wanting now to buy her a rope of pearls and an emerald bracelet. His flowers were the costliest that came to her. He had intimate friends among royalty, an *entre* everywhere. His entertainments were always in good taste. Private views of pictures and plays, paintings and statuary, private hearings of great music performed by greater musicians, these were among the attentions he lavished. If she married him there would be practically nothing that money could buy that she could not have for the wishing. And he was only ten years older than herself, splendidly set up, with just a distinguished gleam of silver on the edges of his hair. He was not tied down by business, for his business had reached the pinnacle where it could take care of itself, and he would be free to take her where she would!

All this and yet she had let a poor young doctor make violent love to her going down a church aisle in the presence of an assembled multitude. All these other desirable lovers and yet she was still thrilling to the clasp of his arms at the station, the touch of his reverent lips at parting, the vibrant voice that told her he loved her!

And he was poor, and a stranger, a man who had to work for his living, and religious! Could any more incongruous set of descriptions be imagined for a possible aspirant to the hand of a Wainwright heiress?

It was late in the afternoon that they stopped again to let Sam forage in a great open space toward which he had turned wistful eyes. He came back this time with a big bunch of swamp lilies, like lovely flames, and Mary Elizabeth helped him to bank them up back of the seat where they would get the air and be out of the way. She noticed as she turned back to smile at Sam that his whole face was aglow with joy, and a certain interesting beauty had begun to dawn in it. For the first time she saw a slight likeness to her cousin Jeff in its happy lines.

"This is a great day!" he said reminiscently. "Gosh! I wish it could last! When I get home there's no one cares a rap if I have what I want or not. They don't pay the slightest attention to me except to tell me to stop whatever I wantta do!"

"Well, why don't we do this again?" asked Mary Elizabeth. "I'm thinking of going down to look over our shore cottage and see if I want to open it a while this season. How would you like to go with me?"

"Gosh, I'd like it!" he said earnestly. "I'd like it a lot. When ya going?"

"Why, I'm not sure," said the girl thoughtfully, "soon, perhaps."

"Gee! I wish I could go!" he said plaintively. "But I suppose they'll begin ta talk camp again as soon as I get in the house."

"And don't you like camp?"

"I'll say I don't!" said the boy with bitter emphasis. "Not the camp I'm supposed ta go to summers. I don't like the man that runs it, but his mother belongs to my mother's bridge club so she thinks I havta go. He's the biggest fake I ever saw. He isn't fair to anybody. And he's a coward too. He was afraid of a snake last summer. I hadta kill it myself!"

"Really?"

"Yep! And then he had the nerve to say 'we' killed it when we got back ta camp and he was telling about it. Just because there wasn't any other fella along who saw what happened, and he knew I wouldn't dare tell 'cause he could mark me down for insolence if I did!"

"Well," said Mary Elizabeth, "he can't be much like your Mr. Saxon then?"

"I'll say he isn't!"

"But don't you have a lot of fun at camp?"

"Naw! They're a lotta Miss Nancys! They aren't my crowd! They all live up on Bleecker Hill and go to the Prep School. I suppose I'd be there too if it weren't fer Dad and Jeff. They don't like that school a little bit. Mother's tried to work it several times, but they just told her I'd gotta have a real he-man school."

"Of course!" said his cousin. "You go to the same one where Jeff went?"

"Yep! And Mother thinks it's old–fashioned, but Dad says it has the best English department in the whole city. So at least my school's safe. I got on the right side of Dad about that. And Jeff was with me. I'm gonta miss Jeff a lot!"

He sighed a deep boy-sigh.

"But he's not going so far away!"

"No, but it won't ever be the same of course!"

"Don't you like Camilla?"

"I sure do! She's a peach! I've always wanted a sister. Course I'd rather have you, if you just lived at our house."

"Thank you!" Mary Elizabeth smiled. "I'll be a sister to you, Buddie, and I'll see what can be done about that camp, too. It's a shame when you know what a good camp is to have to stand a poor one."

"Oh, gee! I wish you would!" said the boy. "I just wish Mr. Saxon would start a camp up north!"

Then he suddenly put his head back on the cushion and began to sing:

> *"Calvary covers it all!*
> *My past with its sin and shame,*
> *My guilt and despair*
> *Jesus took on Him there,*
> *And Calvary covers it all!"*

Again and again he sang it, till Mary Elizabeth joined in. Then they went back over some of the songs of the morning, but came again to the "Calvary" one.

"I don't understand, Sam," said his cousin looking at her young companion through the dusky shadows that were beginning to settle down over the world as evening drew on, "a lot of your songs talk about how bad you feel that you're a sinner. That doesn't seem real. You haven't got any 'past with its sin and shame,' have you? You never felt you were much of a sinner, did you?"

"Sure!" said the boy in a diffident tone. "Sure thing, I'm a sinner! You see it's this way, you don't feel it so much till you're saved. You think you're pretty good till you know Christ, and get ta talking to Him, and reading about Him, and thinking about Him. Then ya begin ta see yerself. That's how 'tis. I can't tell you how 'tis, but it's so!"

"Oh!" said Mary Elizabeth in a small voice as if she were once more filled with awe over the knowledge of this scarcely more than a child.

Very soon after that the lights of the home city began to appear through the evening and the boy watched them grow nearer with gloom deepening in his face and voice, gloom that settled into silence.

"Oh, gosh!" he breathed as they turned into his own street.

"Don't despair, Buddie," smiled Mary Elizabeth. "This isn't the end, I promise you. You and I have found each other and I at least don't intend to lose you again."

"You're some peach!" murmured young Sam shyly, and then sprang out of the car and gathered up his things. "Can't-cha come in?" he asked wistfully. "Just a min-ute?"

"Sure!" said Mary Elizabeth, "I'm coming in!"

The family had arrived only a few minutes before and

there was a bustle of getting settled at home, but they pressed Mary Elizabeth to stay. Answering the wistful gaze of the boy she assented.

"I'll just telephone Dad that I'm back safe," she said, "and unless he's waited dinner for me I'll stay."

Sam waited anxiously outside the telephone booth, and was radiant when she told him that her father had a directors' meeting and hadn't been able to wait for her.

"You must be all worn out, Betty dear!" said Aunt Clarice as they sat down to the table. "I declare you certainly were a godsend to-day, taking Sam. I just couldn't have stood his restlessness."

"Why, we had a beautiful time!" said the girl with a quick look of sympathy for Sam. Poor kid! Was this the thing he had to stand continually?

"Well, you certainly are a wonder, Betty!" said Sam's mother. "He's the most restless creature! Now Jeff was different. Jeff never wriggled."

"You weren't quite so old then, Mamma," said Robert Wainwright bluntly, "your nerves can't stand as much as they could when you were young. As I remember Jeff he had a lot of spirit in him too."

"Now Robert, I'm not talking about spirit, I'm talking about wriggling and sighing and wanting to get out and run, and things like that!"

"Mary Beth doesn't mind that, Muth!" growled Sam protestingly.

"Your cousin Betty is very kind, Samuel!" said his mother firmly. "She probably minds it as much as I do but she doesn't let you know it!"

Sam cast a quick suspicious look at Mary Elizabeth and met the disarming steady look in her eyes, and the wide understanding smile.

"No, Aunt Clarice, I don't mind restlessness, I get restless myself. I like to stop and do things too, and Sam and I had a wonderful time. Butterflies, and lilies,—by the way, Buddie, did you put the lilies in water?"

"I sure did!"

"Yes," said his mother ruefully. "He took one of my priceless jardinieres and filled it full of weeds!"

"Oh, but they were wonderful in the swamp, Aunt Clarice," said Mary Elizabeth enthusiastically. "But say, Aunt Clarice, why can't you lend Sam to me this summer? I'm thinking of opening the shore cottage, and if I do I'd love to have him there. We could practise tennis together, and go swimming and sailing. Of course if we open the cottage at all Dad would come down every night, or week ends anyway, and I'd take Roger and his wife, and some other servants. It wouldn't be lonely for him even if I were away a day now and then. You know Roger just adores boys, and he would look after him."

"That's awfully kind of you, Betty dear, and I must say you are brave after having him all day long, but we couldn't think of taxing you that way, especially this summer. You'll be having a lot of guests, and you couldn't depend on Sam. He'd come down to meals with his face dirty and his hair sticking every which way. And that nice particular Boothby Farwell there so much! Sam would disgrace you."

"I'll take the risk on Sam," laughed Mary Elizabeth. "Besides Boothby Farwell won't probably be there very much. If I remember rightly he said he was going abroad this summer."

Mary Elizabeth's voice was very blithe. She didn't say that he had asked her to go along with him, but she was jubilantly remembering that she had decided not to go.

"Oh, but Betty! Europe?" said Aunt Clarice in dismay. "Surely you don't mean he's going this summer!

Why, I thought he—I was sure you—that is—why, I supposed you were engaged!"

"Nothing of the sort!" said Mary Elizabeth in a ringing tone. "He's just one of my friends, and as such if he were to object to my cousin Sam he wouldn't be any friend of mine any more. Really, Aunt Clarice, I mean it seriously. I'd love to have Sam stay with us this summer, and I know Dad would just be delighted."

"Let him go," said Sam's father suddenly. "That is, if he wants to. Do you want to go with your cousin, Sam?"

"I sure do!" growled Sam dropping his long lashes over his big eager eyes to hide their eagerness.

"Then let him go, Clarice. It'll be a change for him, and you know you don't want to bother with him up in the mountains!"

"Of course not!" said his wife firmly. "But Robert, I've already written and registered him at the camp where he was last summer. It's quite too late to make a change. You know they have a long line on their waiting list and it's a great honor to get in."

"That's all right! Let somebody else take the honor then. I'd like Sam to go where he wants to this summer. And it will do him good to be with Mary Elizabeth. She's a good girl to want him, Mother!"

"Oh, certainly," said Aunt Clarice severely. "Betty is very good. But it's really too late, Robert, I've already paid the registration fee!"

"Well, lose it then, if they aren't honest enough to refund it. I don't see making Sam a martyr for the summer if he doesn't enjoy the camp. You know he didn't like it last summer."

"But Robert, it's so good for him. They are such a refined set of boys that go there."

"Refined *nothing!*" murmured Sam under his breath.

"And the young man who has charge is such a marvelous person!" said his mother waxing earnest. "His mother is one of my dearest friends! I really couldn't go back on it now, the matter has gone too far."

"Nonsense!" said her husband. "Sam is old enough to choose where he wants to spend his summer, at least within limits. We always allowed Jeff to do that and it seemed to work well. Look how he turned out!"

"Now, Papa," protested his wife, "you know I always felt that that one summer he spent with those quite common friends of his in Canada did more harm—! He got notions about being democratic. He seemed to think that all people were alike and one was as good as another."

"Well, aren't they?" snorted Papa, who always grew exasperated right at the start. "I'm sure Jeff turned out all right anyway."

"Well, of course," said his wife elevating her eyebrows, "but look at all the worry I had about him while he was going with that impertinent presuming movie star, expecting him every day to announce that he was going to marry her."

"Well, he didn't, did he?"

"Well—Papa,—you certainly don't think he looked very high when he did marry, do you?"

"I certainly do!" snorted Papa. "Camilla is a good girl. What more could you want?"

"Oh, yes, she's *good!* Of course she's a good girl. I have nothing to say against her."

"Well, you'd better not have since she's your son's wife. And she's beautiful! You couldn't find a more beautiful girl than Camilla if you searched the earth over."

"Oh, yes, she's beautiful; I admit that! She's good and beautiful!"

"And she loves him, doesn't she?"

"Obviously."

"And he loves her?"

"Quite obviously, of course. Still, you must own she hasn't anything to boast of in money or family."

Aunt Clarice was in her most disagreeable form, with cold steady gaze down into her plate, and impenetrable front.

"No, she is only the daughter of a highly respected man who lost a good fortune through the fault of others, just as nine out of ten business men have been doing to-day. And honorably, too, which isn't the case with many of them. And as for money, hasn't Jeff got enough for both of them?"

"Oh, yes, you Wainwrights are so open-handed about money," sneered his wife.

"And if I mistake not," roared the head of the house, now thoroughly aroused, "the girl that you most highly favored as eligible for Jeff was the daughter of a scoundrel who was convicted of graft and crime of the most flagrant sort, and is outside of jail only because he was able to pay three hundred and fifty thousand dollars to get free. Yet you shut your eyes to all that! You wanted our son to marry her and partake in the money gained through crime. I'm thoroughly ashamed of you, Mamma, and I don't want another word ever said reflecting on Camilla. She is our daughter now, and as such her name and antecedents are irreproachable, in my presence at least. And I'm surprised that you will cast such insinuations on her before Sam."

"That's all right, Dad," said Sam, "I think Camilla is a peach!"

"Certainly, Son," said Robert Wainwright, "of course she is. And that's what your mother really means, only she has got herself all wrought up over this camp business. But I'm putting my foot down, now, Clarice. Sam goes to no camp this summer, unless he wants to, and he will never go to that special camp again, no matter how much money has been paid. If Mary Beth wants him, he can go with her."

Sam drew a breath of relief and grinned across at his cousin.

"I think you are very unwise to discuss such matters before Sam," said his mother offendedly. "And as for aspersions, I certainly didn't cast any aspersions on Camilla. I'm exactly as fond of her as you are, and I don't know what Betty dear will think of you."

"That's all right, Aunt Clarice," smiled Mary Elizabeth with a sly twinkly-wink at Sam, "I'm so glad you're going to let me have Sam. I'll try to look after him and make him have a good time, and we're going to get really acquainted this summer, aren't we, Buddie."

"Sure thing!" said Sam, and arose gallantly to help her pull back her chair as they were leaving the table. Mary Elizabeth soon went home, wondering if it would be possible for that promised letter to have arrived yet?

8

MEANTIME, down in Florida, a little light twinkled in the inner recesses of a small neat house deep in an orange grove, and two people sat outside on the porch watching the great June moon come slowly up.

"Well, Mother," said the man, "I suppose the festivities must be about over now. John's probably marching down that church aisle with some high and mighty flibberty-jib of a bridesmaid, now."

"The maid of honor," corrected the sweet old wife. "Yes, I've thought about her, too. Oh, I do hope John won't fall in love with somebody utterly unsuitable. He's such a wonderful boy."

"And being a wonderful boy of course he won't!" said the father decidedly. "I'm sure I don't see what you find to worry about, Mother. He's steered himself safely through all kinds of groups of girls, and isn't scathed yet. You don't suppose he's going to lose his head just because he's best man at a wealthy wedding, do you?"

"No," said the mother with a slow little trembly sort of sigh. "I suppose not. But—life is so full of pitfalls."

"Meaning girls," said Father.

"Yes, meaning girls. You know that yellow-haired girl that came out here one day last winter hunting for Jeffrey Wainwright after he had gone home to his Camilla. She was—unspeakable!"

"Yes," said the father, "she was, but don't you know John would have thought her unspeakable too? And besides, Margaret, have you forgotten that John is under guidance. Our Father isn't going to let our John go through anything that He doesn't want him to meet and pass safely through!"

"I know." The voice was very sweet and low. There was strength and sweetness in the dim outline of her cameo face, a hint of John Saxon's seriousness and depth of character in the soft brown eyes she lifted to gaze at the moon. Her hair was soft and white. She reminded one of a delicate flower, fragile and sweet.

They were silent for a long time watching the moon march up the heavens. At last the old man spoke. He was fine and strong himself, though a bit bent with hard work, but there was still the ring of the conqueror left in his voice.

"Isn't it time you went in, Margaret?" he asked at last. "You know these nights are really chilly even in June, after the terrible heat of the day."

"Oh, Elam, it's such a relief after the heat of the day. I can't bear to leave it, this sweet coolness. I love to watch the dark shadows among the orange trees, and I love the perfume in the air. I sort of dread to-morrow again. That intermittent rain, and steamy sunshine are almost unbearable sometimes."

"You poor child!" said the man regarding her anxiously. "I'm almost afraid this is going to be too much for you. It will likely be only another year or two before we can afford to go north for the summers. The grove is coming into bearing so nicely now, and if we just don't have another freeze we'll be on our feet. But Margaret, we could have borrowed money on the grove and sent you north this summer. You ought to have gone with John. Even a few days in another climate would have done you good. You've been down here too long."

"And what about you, Elam?" said the sweet old voice.

"Oh, I—I am all right! You know I like this hot weather! I just thrive under it. It's you I'm thinking about. You've been down here too long. You ought to have gone with John. He would have found a nice quiet place for you to board cheaply—"

"I? All alone? Oh, father! I couldn't stand it alone. I'd just mourn for you. Nonsense! Don't talk like that! I can't even bear to think about it!"

"Well, I'm not so sure John won't say something more about it when he gets back. If he gets the chance to study with that wonderful doctor he's talked so much about, there's no reason why he couldn't take you with him and let you mend his socks and cook his breakfast at least."

"No, Elam! I'd never consent to go and leave you! Never! And as for John he needs every cent he has saved. He's got to have these advantages he's worked so hard for, and we ought to save everything we have to help him out."

"Oh, John'll do all right. Don't you worry about him, Mother. He's young and strong. Mother, do you realize how late it is getting? That wedding must be about over. They've eaten the ice cream and cut the wedding cake, and maybe thrown rice, or is it old shoes they throw at the bride? And it's time you and I went to bed."

"We don't go to a wedding every night, Elam," said the old wife wistfully. "I've been looking down that aisle in the orange grove watching the bride walk away from the altar and thinking about our wedding, Elam. We had a nice wedding too."

"We certainly did, Margaret, and you were the most beautiful bride a man ever had. And you're beautiful to-day, Margaret. Your hair was brown then and it's silver now, but it's just as lovely. In fact I don't know but you look even more beautiful to me to-night than you looked then. You were almost a child then, a bonny child, but untried. But now I can see the dear lines that time and care and pain and sickness and trouble and poverty have graven on your face, and they have only made you more lovely. I think it'll be like that in heaven, Margaret, we'll see the graving that life has put upon us; in some it will have cut away all the faults and mistakes and follies and there will be little left, but with those who have been faithful in the testings it will show up a wonderful beauty!"

"You're a foolish old flatterer, Elam Saxon, and you always were, but I like it of course, and I could say a great deal more about the way you've been true as steel, and strong and courageous and always borne me up. You've been a tower of strength!"

"That's it, Margaret, that's it! Keep it up! I know it's overdrawn, but I like it too. And just to think all those years have passed since you and I walked down that aisle together into life, and now our boy is attending a grand wedding and taking part in it. I'd like to see it, wouldn't you? He'll tell us all about it when he comes back."

"Yes," said John Saxon's mother, and drew a little fleeting sigh. "And then, some day, he'll probably be walking down an aisle on his own account. And oh, I hope he'll get the right girl—!"

"Of course he will!"

"And that you and I can go to the wedding," finished the sweet old breathless voice hurriedly.

"We'd go to John's wedding if we had to cut down the orange trees and sell them bit by bit for kindling wood. We'd go if we had to *walk!*" said the father rising and reaching out his hand to her. "Come, Mother, it's time for you to be in bed. John's finished this wedding and gone to his train. It's midnight, and to-morrow he's going to see the great doctor man. We'll go in now and pray for John!"

Mary Elizabeth arrived at her own home, looked eagerly among the mail lying on her desk and felt a distinct pang that there was nothing there that she could not immediately identify. It seemed reasonable to suppose that if he wrote a letter as soon as he got on the train it might have reached here by the time she did, and her heart went down with a dull thud and seemed to touch the foundations of things.

Maybe he wouldn't write at all. Maybe this had been after all only an incident with him, and now it was a closed incident although her heart bounded up once more and told her firmly that that couldn't be so! After all she had been hearing from Sam about him, he just couldn't be that way. It was impossible!

With her heart on the rebound again she sat down and gathered up the rest of her discarded mail and went through it. Nine invitations. She threw them down on the desk. They didn't seem to interest her, no matter what they were. Several bills, those didn't bother her. Bills never had. Yet it did come to her with a strange pang that there were people in the world who had hard work to meet bills when they arrived. John Saxon was a man who had always had to be careful. To think of his pawning his watch and precious books to send that little child to be cured. How wonderful of him!

There were racy letters from several of her girl friends

telling of their social engagements, of their triumphs and disappointments. They all seemed flat to her just now. Perhaps by and by she would be interested in them again, but now her heart was on the *qui vive*. Was it possible that a few hours in the company of one stranger had entirely queered the flavor of other life for her? Ridiculous!

She reached for the last letter in the pile, Boothby Farwell's. She recognized the handwriting at once of course. He had a pride in doing everything he did precisely, and perfectly. His handwriting was no exception. It was almost like copperplate. The address on his letters was always intriguing because of that perfect writing. Yet she found herself drawing a weary sigh that she must read that letter and face the problems that it would inevitably bring to light.

She still had that gorgeous ring in her possession. She had promised, half reluctantly, to wear it while she was away, and test herself out. He had hoped, she knew, that it would help her to a decision. He had thought, she was sure, that she was merely playing with him, and that she certainly meant to marry him in the end, and she felt he was growing weary of the delay.

She had gone away to Europe twice to get away from his insistence and his persistence had almost brought her to think that perhaps she might yield in the end. If she had not felt so she would never have consented to take the diamond away with her. She had taken it more to please him than with any real idea of keeping it. He had counted greatly on the beauty of that stone, she knew. He was proud of it. And indeed no man could show his devotion more flatteringly than by presenting the woman of his heart with a remarkable stone like that. Perhaps she had even been a little pleased herself at the thought of wearing it, of trying out the idea that it belonged to her.

And she had worn it but one short hour! What would he say if he knew?

Then she opened the letter and read.

There was a smug assurance about his sentences that had never struck her before. Perhaps she had never really taken him seriously until now. Perhaps the wearing of his ring for that one brief hour had given her a new vision of what he was and what it might be to live out the rest of her days by his side.

He seemed to take it for granted that all was settled between them, now that she had consented to wear his ring, at least to receive it for consideration, for that was all he had at last persuaded her to say. And now he wrote as if she had actually become engaged to him! She was astonished how it annoyed her.

The letter was about their plans for the future. That is, he was announcing to her when they would be married, and what they would do, where they would go, and how they would live. It would seem that he had thought out every detail and had no idea of asking her to suggest what she would like. His was the last word in everything, his taste, his wishes, his likes and dislikes.

And then she suddenly saw something that had not been plain to her before because she had not been thinking much about such things, and that was that she did not, could not, never had loved him at all. She hadn't even been considering him from that standpoint. In fact, love had not figured in her thoughts with regard to him. It had all been a question of whether he would be pleasant to get along with, and one whom she could rely on to act according to the code of her upbringing. She hadn't been very sure a few days ago that there was such a thing as love, and that if there was, whether it was something to be seriously considered when one was thinking of marrying. Very young uncontrolled natures might indeed fall into what they called love, a sort of wild idealism that took hold of unanchored souls, but never of well-trained sane people who could look ahead and plan for the future.

Now she saw that she had reckoned without knowledge, and that new knowledge had come to her hitherto untried soul and given it a vision that changed everything.

That one brief walk down a church aisle, those few, sweet, deep sentences, red hot from a strong true heart, had changed her whole outlook on life. She suddenly saw that it made all the difference in the world whether you loved a man or not if you were going to marry him. There might be other weighty matters to consider, but that was the first, and must be paramount to all others. And she saw that if she loved Boothby Farwell this letter would thrill her—or would it? She read some of the smug dictatorial sentences over and considered them in the light of possible love between them and they still sounded almost selfish and utterly conceited. Oh, he told her in very fine English that he loved her, that she had been his ideal woman for a long time, that it was a great satisfaction to have the matter settled at last, and that now he might begin to put his mark upon her, and enjoy her.

It seemed as if she were a new car, or an exceptional kind of yacht that he had been purchasing, and that he were setting forth the price that he was to pay. She was to be taken to the ends of the earth to see all the things he enjoyed seeing, and then they were to settle down where *he* had always wanted to live, and do the things *he* liked to do, and *she* was to *like* them.

Then her mind ran away from the words her eyes

were reading, back to last night, to precious words that had been spoken in her ear in desperate haste, the dear feel of arms about her that hungered for her, the look that she had felt meant lovely deference to her in all ways possible!

Then there was another thing she began to understand, and that was that when a man loved her that way and she loved him, her utmost desire would be to please him and not herself, and that any true marriage would be that way, each desiring most the will of the other. Strange that one brief evening with a stranger had taught her all that!

At last she cast Boothby Farwell's letter aside, carelessly, gathering it up with her other letters and stuffing it in a drawer. In the morning she would send back his ring. That was a foregone conclusion!

Stay! What had his letter said? That he was calling at eleven in the morning to go with her to look at an estate he had thought of purchasing, and they would lunch in town together afterwards.

Well, then, the ring must go back to him earlier. She did not want to look at estates, and she did not want to argue questions of matrimony with him any more.

So she seized her pen and a sheet of paper and wrote large:

> *Dear Boothby:*
>
> *I tried your ring for a little while, but I found it far too heavy for my hand. I couldn't live up to it. And the truth is, Boothby, I find I don't really love you enough to marry you, and so we'll just call the whole thing off if you please.*
>
> *Sorry I can't ride with you in the morning but I have another pressing duty which includes lunch, but thank you for the kind thought of me. And I hope you won't*

hold it against me that I hadn't thought about this matter of love before, for it really seems quite important you know. So I'm returning your ring by Thomas who has instructions to give it into your hand direct.

Always your friend and sincere well-wisher,
Mary Elizabeth Wainwright.

Then Mary Elizabeth sealed her letter, put the ring in a lovely white kid box, enclosed both letter and ring in another worthy box, addressed her package in that same firm large writing, set her alarm clock for an early hour, and went to bed to dream she was walking down that church aisle with John Saxon.

9

SAM Wainwright woke early the next morning and began to consider his prospects for the summer. He felt very sure that something more must be done, and done quickly, or his mother would manage it somehow that he would go to the sissy-camp after all. He had had one-night victories before that had turned out the wrong way next day. But what to do was the question?

Of course he might write to Jeff, but Jeff was a long way off by this time, in fact no one knew yet where Jeff had gone. Silly thing, that, going off from everybody just because you had got married. He wouldn't do that when he got married, if he ever did, he'd stick around and have a good time.

And like as not Jeff would be too busy getting acquainted with Camilla to answer him right away, even if he knew where to write, though Jeff was always pretty good about knowing when things were important. Well, he'd write. He'd get up pretty soon and write just a line or two anyway, and likely Dad would know where was a good place to send it. Jeff would tell Dad. Dad knew how to keep his mouth shut.

His next best bet, he decided, was Dad. He would get Dad off by himself and tell him some more about that camp. Tell him plenty. Tell about the gambling that went on there, that would get Dad's goat. Tell him about some of the songs they sang and the stories they told. Tell him how that poor fish that thought he was the camp manager was off with a lot of fool girls all the time and didn't pay any attention to what the fellas were doing. Tell him you could get by with anything. Those things would open Dad's eyes.

And then he'd tell Dad about Mr. Saxon's camp, how different it was. He'd tell him to ask Jeff about it.

He lay still a long time thinking what he would say to Dad, thinking how the Florida camp had cemented the boys together in a bond of friendship that never could be broken, thinking about the camp fires and the singing, and the prayers, and suddenly his eyes grew large and thoughtful and he arose from his bed, and went down on his knees. God knew about the camps, both of them, and if God wanted him to go to the sissy-camp of course he had to go, but personally he felt sure God wouldn't approve that camp at all. So he put the matter before God in his most earnest way, and then, with a cheerful face he arose and began to dress rapidly. He was no longer worried about his summer. He felt sure that his prayer would be answered. He meant of course to do all he could to help answer it himself, but he had confidence that God would look after the rest for him, and he went down the stairs whistling softly, knowing that his father usually ate breakfast early and went to town before the rest of the household was even awake.

His father looked surprised when he walked into the dining room. He lowered his paper and greeted him with a smile.

"Thought mebbe I'd go down ta the office with ya,

Dad," he said genially. "Thought mebbe ya might miss Jeff a little, and I could take his place, run errands ur something for ya."

"Why,—ur—yes, Son, that's a fine idea!" said Mr. Wainwright pleasantly. "But—aren't you afraid you'll be bored to death by business?" He regarded his son with a puzzled grin of surprise.

"Well, I guess it bores you sometimes too, doesn't it?" said Sam accepting hot biscuits from the waitress. "I suppose ya can't stop doing things just because they bore ya! I think it's time I began ta learn some things about the business, don't you?"

"Well, Son, I hadn't thought of it in just that way yet. I thought at your age you might take a little more time at doing what you pleased before you got into the grind of business."

"Aw, you can't begin too young," quoth Sam. "I'd like it if you'll give me a job down there for a while, that is, till Mary Beth needs me. I could go with her for a little vacation p'raps and then come back and work again till school. I can't see just hanging round."

"Well, Son, suppose you come along down with me this morning anyway and we'll talk it over. I like your spirit at least."

"All right, Dad. Thank you. I'll like that a lot," and Sam ate his breakfast in grave silence letting his father finish the paper, and then together they went out to the car and drove to the city.

It was a pleasant ride for both of them and Sam managed adroitly to put a picture of both camps before his father which opened his eyes not only to the camps and their respective managers, but also to the fact that this boy Sam was no longer a wriggling writhing youngster with no thought for anything but play. He had thoughts, good original ones, and wanted to do things with his hands. His father realized that there was a wistfulness in his funny off-hand casual remarks that held a hidden appeal for a new kind of sympathy, a yearning for understanding that he could not get from only women.

Sam talked a little about Mary Elizabeth too, and how she had been "such a good scout" and was interested in boy things, and finally his father said:

"So you'd like to go down to the shore with your uncle's household a while when your mother goes to the mountains, would you?"

"Sure I would!"

"All right, we'll fix it that way if your cousin really wants you. But, Son, don't get up an argument with your mother. Just you hold your tongue and grin, and we'll fix it."

"Okay!" said Sam with satisfaction, and followed his father up to the office.

All that morning he stuck to his father gravely, sitting silently without wriggling, and doing eagerly any little errand his father found for him. He proved himself keen and attentive when he was allowed to look through the files for some papers. Of course he didn't know that they were not important papers, and that his father was merely trying him out, but perhaps he was just as careful as if he had known. Somehow Sam had a new motive in his life, a motive that made it seem worth while to do everything you had to do in the very best way you knew how.

During the whole morning while Mr. Robert Wainwright was engaged in important affairs, there was an undercurrent of interest in that quiet stubby boy over there, his freckled face so earnest over the filing cards he was working with, his brow drawn in a puckered frown as he laboriously copied names and addresses from the filing cards into a neat list. When he brought it at last for inspection his father was surprised at the neatness of the work, and the clear legible writing. There was going to be character in that hand a little later. There was character and strength of purpose in the freckled tip-tilted nose and clear brown eyes. There was something else, too, his father saw. A clear vision and balance that he was sure had not been there a short time before. Could it be the result of that Florida camp? He must look into that. He must cultivate this son. It would help to ease his loneliness about losing the other son.

And yet he had not lost Jeff! He was going into business with him as soon as he returned from his wedding trip, and they would see each other every day. Well, he would take both sons into business. He would gradually work Sam in little by little whenever he felt the urge for work. And as for that camp the boy disliked, he must see that Clarice didn't try to press that any more. The boy was old enough to choose a few things for himself.

"We'll go to lunch together, Son," he said to Sam in a low tone and together they walked out of the office, Sam swelling proudly and holding his shoulders up squarely. His father eyed him proudly too. He was a well set-up lad, and would be as tall as Jeff when he reached his age. He watched the light play across the speaking face of the boy, and a tender mist spread over his eyes. Sam, little Sam, growing up!

For a week Sam stuck close to his father, and his mother almost forgot she had to worry about him. He hung around the office making long lists of names from old files. The lists were unnecessary to the business of Wainwright and Company, though he did not know that. But his father felt they were necessary to the study and development of his youngest son, and the lists went on, each one written a little better than the last, and bringing a quiet word of praise to the writer, and Sam was content.

When there was nothing to do Sam fell into the habit of pulling out a little book from his pocket and sitting engrossed in it until there was need for him.

One day his father asked him what he was reading and he said he was learning some scout stuff, and when his father looked over his shoulder he saw he was studying the third chapter of John's Gospel.

"It's just some stuff we all promised Mr. Saxon we'd learn," he explained.

When Robert Wainwright went home that night he delved into the bookcase and finally brought out a rusty little old Bible in very fine print and retiring to his own private room read the third chapter of John's Gospel through considerately.

"It's extraordinary!" he said aloud to himself as he closed the book. "Something's got hold of that boy. I wonder if it's the same thing that struck Jeff? That Saxon must be unusual."

10

THE mail that brought John Saxon's letter to Mary Elizabeth arrived at eleven o'clock, but Boothby Farwell arrived at ten. The matter of the returned diamond had not deterred him in the least from his purpose of taking Miss Wainwright out to see the estate he wanted to buy. The fact that she had declined he did not take into consideration.

When he was announced Mary Elizabeth paused, turned from her mirror where she was putting on her hat and looked dismayed. Then a determined look came into her eyes.

"Tell him I am dressing for an engagement, and I can spare him only a moment, but I will be down as soon as possible," she said to the maid. Then she turned about and faced herself in the mirror again.

Since she had wakened very early that morning she had been trying to convince herself that she was done with the incident of the wedding night. She would probably see no more nor hear no more of the strange ardent lover whose impetuous courting had so swept her off her feet, and the accounts of whom since had been so intriguing. She must get him out of her mind, and to that end she must fill her mind full of something else absorbing. But a firm conviction had been growing that Boothby Farwell was not what she wished to fill her mind with.

She had hoped that the return of the ring, and the accompanying note would have kept him away. Failing in this she had hoped to get away before he could possibly arrive, but details of the household had delayed her, and now that he was come she was too frank and honest a nature to slip down the backstairs and leave word that she was gone. She must go down and face him.

Since she had to go down it would have been so much easier to have gone with her mind filled with the thought of another man. But having convinced herself that there was no other man for her, she must be consistent. So she faced herself in the mirror a moment, made a little wry face at herself, then hurriedly hunted out her gloves and purse and went downstairs.

She entered the room where her would-be lover waited and essayed to take the initiative in the situation, to get the upper hand from the start.

"Good morning!" she said breezily. "I'm sorry to have to disappoint you. You got my note in time to save your coming, didn't you? Thomas said he delivered it."

"I did," he said stiffly rising and standing before her with a judicial air, "but of course I couldn't accept any such decision as that and I came at once. I feel that you do not understand the gravity of the situation. You are no longer a child to play fast and loose in this way. Of course I know you did not mean that sweeping declaration, and I came at once. I feel that I have a right to demand that you put aside all other duties and engagements and talk this thing over with me. It is a matter that concerns both your happiness and mine, and you have no right to trifle with it, flippantly telling me that the ring was too heavy. What nonsense! A stone that cost a fabulous sum! A ring that a queen might be proud to own!"

His eyes were hard and cold. Mary Elizabeth suddenly had a revelation of what it would be to be tied to him for life and be under his condemnation. A spot of color flashed out on either cheek and there was battle in her eyes. She drew herself up to her full height and regarded him coldly but sweetly.

"That's exactly it, Boothby, I didn't feel up to the stone. I had no intention of being flippant about it. The ring is perfectly gorgeous of course, and I am duly honored that you had the thought of placing it with me. You will recall that when you handed it to me you said that you wanted me to take it and try it out. Were you being flippant when you said that? I was but answering you in the same vein. But indeed, Boothby, I was most serious when I returned it. I wore it but one hour and it gave me some very serious thoughts, and I found it stood for more than I was able to give."

"Nonsense!" said the man sharply.

"No, it is not nonsense," said Mary Elizabeth, "it is fact. I looked the matter quite frankly in the face and I've told you the truth."

"How ridiculous, Elizabeth,"—Boothby Farwell had always called her Elizabeth. He said it was more distinguished than Mary Elizabeth—"You have always liked me, you know you have. You have shown by your manner that you were very fond of me."

"Yes," said Mary Elizabeth with a dreamy look in her eyes, "I've been very fond of you. I still am. But that's not enough when you are talking about marriage. I don't know that I shall ever marry."

"That's absurd of course," said the man with great annoyance in his tone, "I'm sure I don't know what you're holding off for. If you've anything in mind suppose you state it."

"Why, I hadn't anything in mind," said Mary Elizabeth innocently, "I'm not trying to play a game."

"But you've never talked this way before, Elizabeth."

"Perhaps not," said the girl dreamily, realizing that a new door of experience had opened during the last two days and given her a vision of what love and marriage might mean under the right circumstances, "but you must remember I've never promised to really think it over seriously before. That was all you asked me to do when I accepted the ring on trial, and I kept my promise. I thought it over very carefully, and—well, I knew I couldn't. I knew you were just a friend—a very nice friend of course, but just a friend—and you couldn't be anything more."

She lifted sweet earnest eyes to the cold annoyed ones that were searching her face, and the man of the world found something baffling in her.

"Sit down," he said, a harsh note coming into his voice that was usually so smooth and oily and satisfied. "We've got to talk this thing over seriously."

"I'm sorry," said Mary Elizabeth, "I told you I had other duties to-day!"

"Sit down!" he said imperiously. "This is a matter of life and death!"

"That's it," said Mary Elizabeth, "it isn't to me, you know. I just couldn't feel that way about it!"

He bit his lip vexedly and let his eyes be gimlet-wise, boring down into her half contemptuously, most impatiently, to see if he could discover the cause of the sudden defection in this girl who heretofore had merely laughed his gravity away, and gaily introduced other themes. He had always felt sure of her. Could it be that there was really something coming between them? He quickly reviewed the men who were her friends.

"What do you find wrong with me, Elizabeth?" he asked at last in the tone one uses to a naughty little child who has to be soothed to bring it to reason. "What do I lack that you find elsewhere? Whom else do you know who is better prepared to make life one long delight? I can buy you anything in reason, and can gratify your every wish."

"I'm not sure that you could," said Mary Elizabeth earnestly.

He stared at her astonished.

"What—just what do you mean?"

"I'm not sure that I know what I mean," she looked at him speculatively.

"What have you in mind that you want that you think I wouldn't give you? I have yachts, two of them, considered by many to be superior to most boats of their kind now in existence. I can build you a home anywhere we like." (Mary Elizabeth noted the "we.") "I'm even considering a plane—"

"Yes," said Mary Elizabeth, pleasantly, "but you see I have more or less of those things now, or could have them if I chose, why should I get married to get them? Besides, I understood it was you that I was being asked to marry and not things."

"Then what is it, Elizabeth?"

"It's just that I can get along all right without you. I've tried it twice now, going off to Europe for months, and it didn't bother me a bit. I don't see why one should get married unless there's something more than just that. Of course there might be people who felt they had to marry, or were justified in marrying, for other reasons, say, if they were lonely, or needed someone to take care of them, for instance. But I'm never lonely, and I could take care of myself very well, even if I didn't have Dad and a host of loving family. It's just that I don't see marrying unless there's something more than that."

"Are you trying to make me sentimental?" he asked half savagely. "I'm sure you're not a child! And I've already told you that I have the very highest admiration and regard for you, and you certainly know that when I have attempted to caress you you have always held aloof."

Mary Elizabeth suddenly rose with her cheeks flaming and a firm little set of her lips and chin, but behind her hazel eyes there was a flood of light that made her seem suddenly illuminated. Boothby Farwell watched her half startled. She was more serious than he ever remembered her to have been before.

"Please, Boothby," she said gravely, "we won't discuss this any more, either now or at any other time. I have given you my answer."

He stood with his eyes upon her, almost savagely. It seemed incredible that she was actually refusing him. This must be just a whim. He had a high estimate of himself. Also, many women had spoiled him.

He lifted his chin haughtily.

"You can't keep this up interminably," he reminded her. "You must make a final decision! I won't stand for everything!"

She looked at him astonished.

"This *is* final!" she said, and then her eyes alight again she added, remembering when those words had been spoken to her, "This *is final!*"

He turned away from her with an offended air.

"Very well!" he said and his voice was like icicles.

He walked to the door, and then turning toward her again said,

"You can let me know when you return to sanity again! Good morning!"

"But," she said, and there was almost a lilt in her voice, "this is *final*, and I'm sorry if I ever made you think it would be otherwise. I just didn't understand myself before!"

He went away then without another word, his eyes averted from her. He wanted her to understand what his scorn would be for one who turned from the advantages he could offer the woman he married.

She felt it. She understood. But in her heart were ringing those words she had just said, those words another had said before her.

Final! Was anything ever final? Were John Saxon's words, his kiss, a final thing that was to change her life and make her thoughts belong to another?

She stood there where Boothby Farwell had left her, with a wondering light in her eyes and a glorious color in her cheeks, and it was well that he did not return to further question her for he would surely have asked her if there was someone else for whom she cared. But he did not return and she presently heard the dull thud of the front door letting out an outraged caller, who yet had by no means given up.

A moment more and Mary Elizabeth realized that the maid was coming down the hall. Quickly she closed the shutters to her soul and put on her gay accustomed manner.

"The mail has come, Miss Wainwright. I thought perhaps you'd like to look it over before you go out."

"Thank you, Tilly," said Mary Elizabeth swinging around with her heart in a sweet tumult and taking the handful of mail.

Tilly disappeared discreetly, and Mary Elizabeth tripped up the stairs to her room and fastened her door before she sat down to examine those letters. Oh, if it should be here! Oh, if it shouldn't! Of course it wouldn't be. She had settled that in the small hours of the night. That was merely a closed incident!

It was there! Right on the top! She knew it at once even though it was a plain envelope and she had never laid eyes on his handwriting before. It was there, and the very handwriting shouted at her soul as she touched it and gazed upon it!

II

MARY Elizabeth drew a deep breath and settled down to read her letter. Her eyes were very bright, she felt her lips were trembling. Her hands were trembling too as she held the pages of the letter, and devoured the words with her eyes.

There was something about his handwriting that seemed strong and satisfying, like himself, and her heart leaped up and rejoiced as, the words of the letter fitting with her memory of him, her vision of him ran true to form.

How that "My dear—!" thrilled her, as if she were again in his arms, his lips on hers. And then her heart began a song that lasted all through the letter, lilting on its lovely way through the precious sentences.

In all her favored life Mary Elizabeth had never received a love letter like that. Such delicate admiration, expressed in phrases that a poet might have used! Such exquisite melody of love! What a man this was who had crossed her path and flung his heart down at her feet without warning! Who or what was she, to have won this great prize from life? But no, it was nothing she had won, it was a gift come straight out of the blue and her heart stood still with the glory and the wonder of it.

But it was a mistake, of course, she told herself as she paused to look up and blink away the happy tears that came and interfered with her vision. He did not realize how superficial she was, how small and trifling, how gay and earthly. He never would have picked her out if he had known. Already her love was humble and she had put him high upon a pedestal. She had never met a man like this one before. Her men friends were all among the class who had no set purpose in life. They were rich, they had no need to work. They did not need to worry even about amassing more wealth, but only how to spend what they had. Their interests were to acquire better polo ponies, to race their yachts for more silver cups, to ride higher in the air, or drive a better ball over a fairway, or across a net; their only cares were to escape the cold in winter, the heat in summer, and to buy their way out of all labor or waiting or unpleasantness of any sort. Even to acquire the woman of his choice none of them would humble himself, or go seeking through literature or art or music for the words and colors and lilt to tell of it. Therefore she thrilled and thrilled to his words, and bright tears dimmed her eyes.

Perhaps though, she thought, this was the only real love that had ever come her way. Perhaps real love was always humble, always thinking more of the other than of self? She put that by to consider later and went on with her letter.

But when she came to that bit about laying his lips upon hers and holding her close she had to close her eyes and rest her head back in her chair, and let the joy and wonder of the thought flow over her like strong gentle waves of water that bore her spirit up and floated it away into a bliss she had never known before. His lips upon hers! His arms about her! Ah! But this was too beautiful, too wonderful to last!

The telephone interrupted. She looked at it like an intruder and let it ring on. She could not be interrupted now, and presently it hushed its clatter and let her go on.

There were words and phrases that stood out as she read slowly, "Years together!" Could it be possible that anything so heavenly could come to her as to have years together with a spirit like his? "Your eyes spoke to my eyes!" Was that true? Did she answer the look she had seen in his eyes when she first lifted her own and saw that strong bronzed man standing like a young god beside her cousin Jeff? The color deepened in her cheek as she acknowledged to herself that an involuntary message had gone forth in her glance and the acknowledgement made her heart beat the faster.

"I love you, love you, love you!"

She bent her head almost reverently and laid her lips on the words, as if she were drinking in the sweetness of their meaning.

"Eternity"! How long was that? She had never before had occasion to think in terms of the ages, but now it seemed good to do so, even necessary. For a thing as precious as this must last forever!

But when she came to the sentence that said there were things that she should know at once her heart stood still with fear, and she hesitated to turn over the next page lest a spectre should await her there which would destroy this new found joy. So near to that word "eternity" she could not bear it.

But when at last she turned that page and found him telling of his poverty and struggle she drew a breath of relief and a tender smile came upon her lips. Why, these were all things she knew already, through Sam's boyish tale, and they were precious. They only made him more dear. And his people! Why it wouldn't matter, would it, about his people? He was the one that mattered. And she would love his people no matter what they were just for his sake, wouldn't she?

She drew in her breath as if it hurt when she read of the idea of his coming to her, and again sharply when she thought of him struggling away in sun-drenched Florida, alone in an orange grove battling against such enemies as belonged to orange groves. Struggling alone. A wild, sweet, futile thought came that she would like to go and help him.

There was another page to turn when she came to that last thought which should have come first because it was paramount to everything else in his life. She drew in a long, slow, sore breath of pain before she turned the page and came upon God! God, standing there in her room looking down upon that letter, knowing what was in it, having a right to know, and to come between her and this marvelous lover of hers! God, watching her! And she *didn't know God!*

It was not that she resented His being there, or that it astonished her, what John Saxon said, for she had heard all about it from young Sam, and it had rather pleased her. It seemed a unique part of this winsome man who was so strong and so sweet and so tender, and yet so true. It was not entirely that it frightened her, to have this Christ of John Saxon's standing there in her room, judging her, whether she were fit for His man. It was that she had suddenly become so small in her own eyes, and so useless, so far away and utterly worthless. It was as if His presence there watching her quietly as she read that letter, were judging her and setting her away back where she belonged, so far away from John Saxon that she could never, never catch up with him, and she found herself wondering pitifully about his disappointment in her when he found she was not what he had thought. All those lovely things he had said in the letter about her, how she wanted to live up to them! How she longed to be his equal mate. And yet she felt she could not be because she did not know his God.

A long time she sat there staring at his name as signed to that first part of his letter, unable to go on because she had to stop and let his Christ search her life from beginning to end and show her how very small and useless it was. Full of just nothing but trying to please herself, that was all!

At last she roused to see what was after his name.

Then suddenly her heart which had felt small, but happy in spite of its smallness, went down, down, down, with a thump till it seemed that it could go no farther. What was this he was saying? That he had thought her another girl! That he was blaming himself for having made love to her? Oh, the bitterness of humiliation that she had come to this, had grasped for this bright bubble of a dream and now saw it melt and fade away because it belonged to another!

For at first she did not see that it was her name, her honorable name, her wealth and position that had frightened him. She only saw that name of Camilla's little absent friend whose place she had taken. Helen Foster! All that priceless love belonged to another? She sat speechless, humiliated, and stared!

Well, hadn't she known that it wasn't the thing to pick up a strange man that way? She had realized at the time that a Wainwright couldn't do a thing like that! That a Wainwright according to tradition must meet a man formally, must know him well, and his position and eligibility, before she allowed him to speak of love to her. Yet she had not only listened, but had taken a part in it actually asking him if he wasn't going to kiss her good-bye! How her cheeks burned with shame. How the kiss that he had given, and—yes,—she had more than just *received,* scorched sweetly, bitterly on her lips, and she buried her face in the beloved letter and let hot tears flow down and wash away the sting. How that Helen Foster whom she had never seen had come and taken away her joy!

But it came to her that she had not yet finished reading the letter, and she lifted her face and read on, till she came to the place where he said: "I love you, Mary Elizabeth! I write your beautiful name reverently, Mary Elizabeth! How wonderful if I might someday say, 'My Mary Elizabeth'!"

Then suddenly the joy bloomed out again and her heart began to leap. His love was hers, after all, not that other unknown girl's. He had never seen her. He did not want to see her. He had set his love upon herself, Mary Elizabeth, as soon as he had seen her, even before he had spoken to her! And all that was worrying him was her wealth and position! What foolishness! Wealth and position! What were they? She arose to her feet. She broke into smiles! She felt like singing.

She lifted shy eyes to where the vision of John Saxon's Christ had seemed to stand, as if she would question whether she might rejoice, she, Mary Elizabeth, pampered daughter of wealth, who had wasted her bright days on nothings instead of getting ready to mate this wonderful man of God. Would John Saxon's Christ let her have this precious jewel of love for hers? Could she ever walk softly enough before Him to be half good enough for a man like that?

She laughed out gently, a little apologetic laugh. She, Mary Elizabeth, seeking to be religious! She didn't even know how!

Presently she sat down again and read the letter over

slowly, this time taking in every precious turn of sentence, till she felt as if her lover were beside her. He loved her, yes, he loved her! She had to get used to it. She had to let it sing itself into her heart and her life. She couldn't sit right down and answer that letter. It was too sacred a thing to do. It would take time to think out the answer. Could she ever put upon paper what she felt toward him? She had no poetry at her command that could fittingly reply to his.

The telephone broke in upon her meditations again, and with sudden premonition that Boothby Farwell might be asking if she were yet returned, she gathered her precious letter into her handbag and fled, sending the maid up to answer the telephone and say that she was out. By the time the maid reached the telephone she was out at the garage starting her car, joy singing a high paean in her heart, joy smiling on her pleasant lips. She wasn't just sure where she was going now, or what she wanted to do, but she felt that somehow she had got to get away where Boothby Farwell could not reach her until life had taken on a more definite outline. Perhaps she *had* been laughing down a sunlit way ever since she had begun to grow up. Perhaps she *had* let people take too many things for granted. Could it be that she had unintentionally allowed Boothby to take too much for granted? He seemed to think she had. Perhaps she would have to write him a note pretty soon and ask his pardon for playing around so long when she was not serious. But that, too, would require thought, and she was too much shaken by her own new joy to think out what to say just now.

She decided to wheedle her father out to lunch with her some day soon and talk over the possibility of opening the old shore cottage.

She turned her car downtown, and went singing on

her way. And presently she laughed out loud at herself again, for the words she was singing were:

I know a fount where sins are washed away,
I know a place where night is turned to day!

Mightn't that be a reminder to her that even she might find that place some day and get her life changed so that it would more possibly fit into the life of the man who loved her, and who yet was bound to put his Christ first?

Second to Christ, only! In a way, a rather wonderful way, that was probably a great honor!

12

"WHY, no," said Mary Elizabeth, over the very delicious luncheon she and her father were eating together a few days later in the quiet old-fashioned restaurant on a back street where he usually went at noon, "no, I don't see why it would need doing over. I want to open the house just as it is. I thought I'd like to be there, where I can remember Mother. I'd like to have the same furniture and the same arrangement and everything. I thought maybe you'd enjoy coming down nights, or at least week-ends. You always liked the sea."

Her father looked at her quizzically.

"You don't realize," he said half sadly, "that things deteriorate, especially by the sea, and that they get very old-fashioned. What do you think your fancy friends that you will gather about you will think of being invited to a shabby old place like that?"

"Well, in the first place," said Mary Elizabeth, "I don't intend to have any fancy friends down there. That's the very thing I want to get away from. I don't want week-end parties, nor a mob of people. I want to have a quiet homey time. I thought maybe you'd like it."

Her father's face softened.

"I should," he said his eyes resting tenderly on her bright face, "but you wouldn't like that long you know, and what's the use fixing up an old seashore cottage for a few days' experiment?"

"I don't mean a few days, I mean all summer," said the girl eagerly, "and I don't want to fix much. Don't you keep it in repair?"

"Oh, somewhat," said the father thoughtfully. "The roof doesn't leak, and I had it painted last fall. There's a man of course who keeps up the grounds to a certain extent, too, but you've forgotten how utterly out of date the old ark is."

"No, I'm sure I haven't forgotten," she said, "I always loved it, that white, white building with the lovely fluted columns standing among the pines with the sea at its foot."

"Yes, it was considered very fine when I built it, when you were a baby and your mother was with us!" He sighed heavily, and looked thoughtfully down at his salad without attempting to eat it. "But you've forgotten, Mary Elizabeth, that none of your friends go to Seacrest any more. It isn't the thing to do. They will laugh you to scorn when they hear of it."

"Let them laugh!" gurgled Mary Elizabeth gleefully— "Why tell them about it? We'll just casually disappear, and when it leaks out where we are the summer will be nearly over. Don't you see it will be fun?"

"It sounds that way," said her father cautiously, "but I'm sorely afraid you'll be lonely and wish you hadn't tried it. However, I suppose we can leave if you don't like it."

"We?" said Mary Elizabeth eagerly. "Then you'll go, too?"

"Why yes, of course, if you want me. I wouldn't miss

an opportunity like that. But remember I may not be able to come down every night, though I'd enjoy it sometimes. It would be like the old days."

Mary Elizabeth looked as if she wanted to jump right up from her chair and embrace him though she didn't. She only sat eagerly and outlined her plans.

"Better take some of your friends down with you, first, and see how the old house looks. That will probably cure you," said her father with another sad little smile.

"No," said the girl, her eyes shining. "I'm only taking Sam. He and I get along famously, and when we've looked things over I'll report. Do I need to take a carpenter and a plumber and an electrician down or can I find them there?"

"Find them there, of course. That's the fair way to treat a place where you own property anyway, employ local men. But I should say you'd better take some servants along."

"Not till I've seen it," said the girl firmly. "Just Sam and I are going first to look things over. Uncle Rob said he might go, though I don't think Aunt Clarice liked it very much. She has a pet camp where she wants him to go, and he hates it."

"I see. Well, if you think Sam would be happy going with you I'll call your uncle up and ask him to see that he goes to take care of you. How is that?"

"Fine," said the daughter, giving him a loving look. "I think we'll start to-morrow morning. It's only a two-hour drive isn't it? I've almost forgotten."

"About that!" said her father. "Better have the car gone over before you leave, and don't run any risks."

"I won't," said the girl with shining eyes, "and Dad, please don't inform anybody where I've gone or what we're going to do. I've got a special reason for asking."

He looked at her keenly an instant.

"Of course not," he said. "You're not running away from anybody, are you?"

"Not anybody that matters," said Mary Elizabeth with a comforting smile, "not now that you've promised to go along."

"All right, little girl. And if you decide to really carry out this scheme you'd better leave an order for the telephone to be connected."

Mary Elizabeth's next move was to call her uncle's house on the telephone and ask for Sam.

Fortunately Aunt Clarice was not at home. The housekeeper answered.

"Mr. Sam's went down to the office with his father this morning, Miss Mary," said the woman. "He mostly goes with his father, lately."

So Mary Elizabeth with a question in her eyes called up her uncle's office.

"Uncle Rob," she asked crisply, "is Sam there? And if I come down to the office could I see you and him for five minutes? I'll promise not to stay longer."

"You'll be welcome, Mary Beth," said her uncle, "and you can stay as long as you like. You always had good sense."

So Mary Elizabeth went to her uncle's office, and was welcomed eagerly by both the old and young Wainwright.

"It's about Sam," she said with a gleam in her eye for both relatives. "Is Sam working regularly in the office now?"

"Well, he's been helping me out the last few days," said his father looking at the boy with a twinkle and a grin, "because why, Mary Beth? Did you wish to offer him another position?"

Sam grinned at his father's grave tone.

"Well, I wanted him to help me out for a few days," said the girl, "but I wouldn't want to take him away from a regular job."

"Well, I don't know but I could spare him a while if it's anything important. How about it, Sam? Can you help your cousin out?"

"Sure thing!" said the boy with embarrassed eyes.

"Well, I'm driving down to the shore to look the old cottage over for Dad, and I'd like a man along," said Mary Elizabeth.

"H'm!" said her uncle comically. "This is the first time I've ever known you to be short a man, Mary Beth, and I wouldn't want to see you in a situation like that. But are you sure there isn't some more eligible man?"

"I'd rather have Sam, Uncle Rob, if you can spare him."

"Of course I can spare him if you really need him. When do you want to start?"

"To-morrow morning early, if that's not too soon."

"Well, Son, speak up, will you go?"

"Gosh, yes!" said Sam with a look of delight in his face.

"Then I would advise you to go home early, boy, and get your fishing tackle and your bathing suit together. You might need them in between helping." Uncle Robert gave a wink toward Mary Elizabeth. "How long are you staying, Mary Beth?"

"Probably only two or three days now. It depends on how I find things, and what needs to be done. Are you still willing I should take Sam down with me if we decide to stay there this summer? Dad thinks he'd like it. He'll come down week-ends anyway. Perhaps you'd come with him sometimes?"

"Sure, I'll come. I'd love to. It gets rather dull here in the city when your aunt is in the mountains. Yes, Sam an come if he likes. There won't be so much for him o do here in the office during the hot weather. I think ae can finish the lists he's making between trips," and he ;ave his niece another broad wink and a curious twist of ais kind pleasant mouth that looked sometimes so much ike his son Jeffrey's mouth.

"That's great! Then he doesn't have to go to camp?"

"No!" said his father. "I've put my foot down on hat."

So Mary Elizabeth carried Sam off in her car and anded him at home to pack, and went back to her own preparations as gleeful as if she were only thirteen herself.

The next morning they started like two children on a picnic, Mary Elizabeth reflecting wickedly that she would be away when Boothby Farwell called that morning according to a note she had received the night before, and her maid was instructed to say only that she was away for a few days. So she would not be followed, and she would have time to examine herself and find out just where she stood. For Mary Elizabeth had not yet answered John Saxon's letter, and that was one of the things she meant to do when she got to the shore. It had seemed to her that there in the stillness and beauty and freedom from her world she could more properly answer that letter, and her soul was impatient to find out just what she was going to allow it to say.

The day was fair and lovely, neither too cool nor too hot, a rare day, a June day at its best. The roads were good, and the way open with little traffic.

By common consent the two travelers talked but little ill they were out in the open country, with only a little clean village by the way now and then.

"I had a letter from Mr. Saxon," volunteered Sam at ast, settling comfortably back with his eyes ahead for a

startled rabbit that might spring out of the scrub oa
along the way.

"Did you?" answered Mary Elizabeth coolly with n
sign of the start the announcement had given her sense
"How is he? Did he say?"

"Naw! He doesn't talk about things like that. H
doesn't talk about himself. He was talking about us fella
He's writing to us every little while, every week, maybe
If we do the work he sends us and answer him, then w
get another letter."

"Work? What work are you doing for him?"

"Why the Bible lessons he sends. We're taking
course, see? He sends us a new one as soon as we get th
first one worked out."

"That sounds interesting," chirruped Mary Elizabeth
"I'd like to see them. Has he sent you any yet?"

"Oh, sure! This is the second one I have."

"Did you bring them along?"

"Course! I expect to do a lotta studying while I'n
down here, that is if you think I'll have time."

"Why, of course," said Mary Elizabeth. "There'll b
heaps of time. We just have to give orders to men an
things like that, and then wait around and see that the
do it. I'd like to do some studying myself if you thin
I'm not too stupid. I never knew much about the Bible.'

"Aw, quit your kidding!" said the boy.

"I mean it," said Mary Elizabeth. "I never studie
Bible at all. I'd like to see if I could understand it. You
see I've never had a scout master to teach me."

"Well, ya can read my papers. I guess you can under
stand 'em if I can."

"All right, we'll try. Now, how soon do you thin
we'd better stop for lunch? I asked the cook to put us u
a lunch. I didn't seem to remember any very inviting
place to stop along this road. She put some lemonade in

one thermos bottle and some milk in the other so we can have cold drinks without stopping, and Father says there's a nice place to eat when we get there, so we're sure of a good dinner tonight."

"Gee! Aren't we having fun?" said Sam.

The old Wainwright summer place stood up a little from the shore, a fine old colonial house, spacious yet simple and lovely of line. Its lawn ran down incredibly near to the sea, and its outlook was clear to the skyline, though it was partly surrounded by great pines, and other imported trees, which in the time of the house's greatness had been the wonder of the resort. The white fluted columns which had been kept painted every year, still gleamed out among the dark pines, almost like marble, and the stately piazza across the front, the lovely fantail window over the front door, the high iron grille that surrounded the place were in perfect repair, and the lawn kept trimmed as if it were in use. The place stood out among the quieter, smaller homes as a great estate of a bygone day, quaint and restful and almost awe-inspiring in contrast to its rows of bungalow neighbors, which had crept up nearer and nearer to its greatness as fashion receded from the resort, and tales of its wealthy owner became a mere tradition in a quiet, comfortable, but unsmart straggling town. Thus early in the season, there were few summer residents, only the winter inhabitants who stayed there because they had no other place to go, and because it was cheaper to stay there and vegetate than to migrate. It was almost like visiting a deserted village, as they drove down the wide main highway that wound around behind the Wainwright estate, locked in behind its massive iron grill.

"Oh, Boy! Isn't this great!" sighed Sam in delight. "No boardwalk! No dolled-up people cluttering the beach. We gotta beach all to ourselves! I was never down here. Why didn't we come before? Why don't all of our family come down ta this place and stay all summer?"

"Well, I'll bite, why?" asked Mary Elizabeth boyishly, her eyes taking in the beauty of the sea spread before her, the plumy pines, the gleaming of the white, white mansion set up on a slight eminence.

"I guess it's because there wouldn't be any chance ta dress up and show off!" said Sam thoughtfully, studying the scattered humble cottages in the near distance.

"Well," said Mary Elizabeth, "perhaps you may have hit the nail on the head. But how would you like to get out, Sam, and see if you can open our gate with this great, big, old, funny key?"

Sam accepted the key with delight and scrambled out to try the well-oiled lock which the caretaker kept always in order, and presently they were driving in along the graveled winding way, skirting the house till they came to the front, where the trees were cut away to show the sea in all its broad blue and gold beauty, under a perfect sky.

Mary Elizabeth stopped the car and sat looking off at the wonder of it all, and even Sam kept still and took it all in.

"Gosh, I don't know what they'd want of any prettier place than this!" he said at last with a sigh, "they" meaning his mother who was the general that managed all their family migrations.

"Yes," said Mary Elizabeth, "I've been almost around the world, Sam, and I don't remember anything prettier than this. And listen to those pines, boy, they are whispering in perfect rhythm with the waves down on the shore! I suppose they've got used to it, being together so much all these years. Especially in winter they've nothing else to do but practise, and it must be magnificent to listen to their harmony. There must be some grand music in a storm. Sometime I'm coming here in a storm just to hear it!"

"Oh, Boy! Say, I'll come too, then!"

"All right! That'll be a compact. Now, shall we go in?"

But just then there appeared a man walking around the path that skirted the house, his cap in his hand deferentially.

"Is this Miss Wainwright?" he asked. "I had a wire this morning from Mr. Wainwright saying you was coming. I hope you'll find everything in order, Miss. We've always tried to keep it as though the family might come in any minute!"

"Why, that's wonderful!" said Mary Elizabeth beaming at him. "I wish we had come before! You're Mr. Bateman, aren't you? Father said you would be here. You have the keys?"

"Yes, Miss, and you can call me Frank. It's easier to remember."

"All right, Frank, and this is Sam Wainwright, my cousin. You'll be showing him all around and telling him about everything, I know."

"I had the windows open, Miss, all morning. And you'll find everything all right. My wife Susan was over getting out fresh linen. She thought you might want her to get you a bit of dinner to-night. She's a fine cook, if you think she can please you?"

"Why, that would be lovely," said Mary Elizabeth interested at once, "if you think she would. Sam and I had our lunch by the way, so we wouldn't want anything before six I should think." She glanced at her watch. "Tell her just something simple will do. We don't want anything elaborate. And how about a place to stay to-night? Is there a hotel open yet?"

"Not any hotel in Seacrest, not yet. We haven't but

one in the town left now, and it went broke last fall. I don't know if it will open at all. The rest are all standing idle, with their shutters down like so many of the dead. But we thought, Susan and I, that perhaps you'd be staying here in the house. We could make you comfortable. We've been using the servant's quarters ourselves you know, so the house isn't to say closed, nor damp. We've had some part open to air most every day."

"Well, I should say there wouldn't be anything better than that," said Mary Elizabeth looking around with delighted eyes. "I would rather stay here than anywhere else, wouldn't you, Sam?"

"Sure thing!" said the boy, grinning his delight.

"Well, we thought you might, so Susan made up two of the rooms, and she'll be glad to be of service in any way. She used ta be lady's maid to a senator's wife before I married her, so she ain't to say ignorant exactly."

"Well, that's wonderful," said Mary Elizabeth, her eyes dancing, "but I don't need a maid. We're going to live simply here. But I'm quite sure everything is going to be lovely. Father said you would tell me about things, and whether any repairs were needed."

"I shouldn't say so, Miss, I've tinkered up anything that was out of the way myself. But you can see when you look around."

So Mary Elizabeth entered the large, old rooms shrouded in memories of a bygone generation.

Big, wide rooms with fine white matting on the floors, and many comfortable willow chairs and couches, with cushions of faded but fine texture. Quaint, old pictures on the walls, some of them very fine, done by artists of renown. Long, sheer curtains at the windows, floating in the breeze. Mary Elizabeth looked at them in wonder.

"Are these the old curtains? I would have thought they would have dropped to pieces."

"Yes, they are the original curtains that were up when we came here to take care o' the place. But Susan she took care o' the curtains. She kept them washed and folded away where they wouldn't mold nor rot, and now and again she's done them up to have them ready in case some o' the family came back. She wanted it to look like home for them."

"And now we've come," said Mary Elizabeth. "I'm glad! And it looks so nice. It seems just as it was when I was a child."

"Well, we figured you might like it," said the man with a pleased grin. "We didn't get all the curtains hung yet, of course, but we went to work as soon as the wire came this morning, and we got all downstairs, and two bedrooms done. I'm glad you like it. Now I'll call Susan."

Susan came in a clean blue gingham dress, with her hands wrapped embarrassedly in her white apron, and her face shining with welcome.

"It's wonderful, Susan," said Mary Elizabeth. "I came down here expecting to find things all run down and needing a lot of repairs before we could be comfortable here, but it seems everything is perfectly all right and doesn't need a thing done to it."

"I'm glad yer pleased!" said Susan, her face shining with pleasure. "I been hoping ye'd come some summer. It seems such a nice pretty old house."

"It is!" said the girl looking around with loving eyes. "I love it here! I don't know why we never came before. But we're staying here this summer. My father will be down week-ends sometimes, and as often between as he can spare the time."

They went over the house eagerly, Sam as interested as anybody.

"Say, this is a swell joint!" he said.

But Sam didn't waste much time in the house. He took possession of the room allotted to him, hung up the things he had brought with him, jammed himself into his bathing suit and was off down to the beach.

Mary Elizabeth went about in a daze of bliss. It seemed somehow as she trod the old halls and went into the rooms that had once been dear and familiar, as if her own mother had left the impress of her sweet spirit there, and by and by when Susan left to prepare the evening meal she took out the letter of her stranger-lover and went to her mother's own room to read it over again. It gave her a sense of confiding in her mother, reading it there where she could remember sitting on a little footstool beside her mother, playing with her dolls.

Somehow the letter took on new sanctity, read there. She could fancy telling her mother all about it, what the stranger-best-man had said going down that aisle, what had happened all the evening, and his farewell at the station. It seemed, read in the light of a mother's eyes, as if John Saxon would bear the scrutiny, and have a loving mother's approval.

Sometime she would tell her father all about him, but not yet. Not just yet!

The summons to dinner came while she was still sitting in her mother's big chair by the window looking out between the pines to the sea, dreaming.

She had seen Sam come dripping up from the sea and vanish into the house, and now she could hear him clattering down the stairs, hungry from his swim. So she tucked her letter away into safety and went down. To-morrow, or perhaps the next day, she must answer that letter. She hadn't yet felt ready to answer a letter like that. There were so many things to be considered about it. But soon she must answer it. She must not wait too long! It was as if the content and wonder into which his letter had led her were a spell too precious to be broken, a dream from which she was not ready yet to wake. And she felt instinctively that to answer that letter was to make more definite one way or the other this marvelous thing that had come so unexpectedly into her life. For the time she was so lifted out of the conventions of life that she feared to get back into them by the formalities of correspondence, lest she might lose some part of the wonder that had touched her soul. Afraid lest facing facts, Wisdom might step in and forbid the joy that was welling up inside her.

So she put it off, the writing of that letter, from day to day for three days more, going about as in a lovely dream, allowing her mind to frame tender phrases that hovered on her lips in a smile and made her so lovely that even Sam looked at her and wondered.

The second morning there came a letter for Sam, forwarded from home. And there were also letters from her father and uncle for Mary Elizabeth, her father giving directions for certain modern improvements in the way of plumbing to be installed in the house, for renovation of the old stable into a garage, and for several minor repairs and changes to be made in the house before he came down.

From her uncle came a brief note telling Mary Elizabeth that her Aunt Clarice had gone to the mountains with a friend, and that therefore Sam was at her service as long as she wanted him, but that she was to return him to his home whenever she grew tired of his company. Sam could be in the office with him a good deal, and would get along well enough, if he grew troublesome to her, or she was bored with having a child about.

She looked up from these letters to find Sam at her feet sprawled on the upper step of the piazza, absorbed in a letter of his own. She watched him for a moment for there was an eagerness in his quietness that interested her.

"Did you get a letter from your mother?" she asked, wondering if the matter of the camp were still hovering in the offing.

Sam looked up with a bright face.

"Gosh, no!" he said. "It's from Mr. Saxon! He's sent the new Bible lesson for this week! Gee! I gotta get ta work!"

"Oh," said Mary Elizabeth with a heightened color in her cheeks, "is he—back at home—again—yet?"

"Oh, sure!" said Sam. "He's back. He's been working in the orange grove all day the night he wrote this. Wantta read it?" And Sam handed up the letter into her hungry hand.

It was just a brief simple letter, as if an older brother were writing to a beloved younger one, yet the girl's eyes lingered on every pleasant word.

> *Dear Sam:*
> *I got back home last night late and have been working in the grove all day, so haven't had much time to write, but I made out the lesson for this week on the way down and enclose it. Am anxious to know how you got on with the first lesson, and shall hope to hear from you soon. If you find the work too hard let me know. I'm hoping it interests you as much as it has me to get it ready for you.*
> *Your friend in Christ,*
> *John Saxon.*

What a friend for a boy to have! What a tie to claim, "in Christ"! Mary Elizabeth felt a passing pang at the sure strong bond that bound them, and gave a half envious smile at the boy as she handed it back. There was no disturbing separation between those two, it was all settled. It was a friendship, a fellowship, that nothing could break. There were no disturbing questions to settle.

"This looks like a corker!" said the boy lifting his eyes from the other paper he held. "Wantta see it?"

Mary Elizabeth accepted the other sheet and ran her eyes down at the startling questions, the strange symbolic abbreviations, and her eyes grew large with earnestness.

"It looks—" said Mary Elizabeth searching for the right word, "it looks—rather—startling! I'm afraid I wouldn't know how to go to work to answer those questions."

"Aw, the references'll answer those," said Sam easily, "only sometimes ya do havta use yer head. How'd it be if I get my Bible and show ya?"

"I'd love it," said Mary Elizabeth fervently. "But— have you a Bible with you? I don't know whether there would be such a thing about this house or not."

"Oh, sure! That's part of it. We fellas always carry our Bibles wherever we go. We all got small ones that don't take up much room fer traveling!"

Sam tore up the stairs three steps at a time and returned with a small limp Bible of surprisingly supple and diminutive proportions, and sat himself down on the upper step again.

"Now, Mary Beth," he commanded, "you read out the questions and references and I'll look 'em up and read 'em!"

So for nearly two hours through that long bright morning the two sat on the piazza and studied the Bible together. Questions grew out of the first question, and Sam found he had to go back to foundation principles and give some of the instruction that had been given to him during his winter in the Florida scout camp with John Saxon, but both the young teacher and the learner were deeply engaged in the study, so that they were surprised when the lunch bell rang to discover that the morning had fled.

Bright-faced, the boy got up from the step and tossed back his sandy hair that matched his golden freckles and grinned at her.

"Gee! I was going crabbing this morning, but I guess it doesn't matter. Anyhow I'm glad I got this lesson worked out. It's lots more fun having you do it with me. I wish I had somebody all the time. I hope I didn't bore you."

"Why, I think it's wonderful!" said Mary Elizabeth. "If you don't mind I'd like to study it every week with you,—unless—you think Mr. Saxon—might mind. This isn't a secret organization, is it? This Fellowship of yours?"

"Not on yer life!" said Sam. "We're out ta get everybody studying we can. I'll tell Mr. Saxon I got a new recruit."

Mary Elizabeth's cheeks flamed.

"Well, perhaps you'd better not, just yet, Sam. It might make me sort of embarrassed, you know. I'd rather wait till I learn a little more. You see I don't know so much about it yet. Just keep it to yourself awhile, Buddie."

"Okay!" agreed Sam cheerfully and grinned as if he understood. And so they went out to lunch.

After lunch Sam went with Frank Bateman out in his boat for a little crabbing and later to watch the hauling in of the deep sea nets.

But Mary Elizabeth sat on the porch and faced her future.

13

THE day that Mary Elizabeth finally wrote her first letter to John Saxon, Sam had gone off to the Inlet with Frank Bateman. They had taken a lunch and Mary Elizabeth had the day before her uninterrupted.

She had been invited to go along, but had declined on the plea that she had letters to write and would go another time. So quite early in the middle morning she took her writing materials and established herself in a great steamer chair where she could look out across the vista of pines and lawn and see the wide, blue sea and sometimes catch a glimpse of a great wave curling high and breaking in foam on the white sand through the lacework of the iron grille that surrounded the estate.

A long time she sat with pen in hand, gazing afar where a little white toy of a boat tossed on the blue horizon, trying to decide how to begin. She wasn't just sure how much of her heart she was willing to reveal in that first word she would put upon the paper, but at last she began to write:

Dear Breath-taking One:

I have been waiting a few days since receiving your letter, trying to get my feet down to earth again after being up in the clouds with you! For you must own you were unexpected to say the least.

You see you had the advantage of me, you having been looking for me a long time, you see I am afraid the traditions of my family had prepared me for a more conventional form of prince, less interesting, less eager, more calculating! That was what I was brought up to expect in a lover. My highest dreams had not dared snatch at such a romance as you flung to me so unexpectedly coming down that aisle.

And so I've had to get my bearings, and my breath, before I answered you.

Not because your letter did not also carry me away again, but because I sensed that this was the gravest, most serious thing that would ever come into my life, and I must not write this lightly, gaily, as I have always taken all things in life so far. I wanted to weigh every word of my reply, and be sure I answered you as you had a right to be answered. Your letter meant too much to me, to be answered on the spur of the moment.

So, I have come down to Seacrest, to an old summer home we have had a good many years, where we used to come when I was a child, when my mother was living. It seems more like home than any other place on earth now, with memories in every corner, and the blue sea stretched out before me. It seemed to me a place where I could be still enough to think, and alone enough to talk with you.

I brought my young cousin Sam along, whom

you know. But he is away crabbing for the day, and I am alone with you.

If I were a painter I could make you see where I am sitting looking over toward the sea. If I were a musician I could make you hear the melody the waves and pines are making in such perfect rhythm. If I were a poet, like you, I could tell you how the sea and sky and pines, and the perfume of the roses growing over the porch, and the quiet of the big old house behind me, full of dear memories of the past, are combining to make a haven for me where I can talk to you, this first time, as I did not feel I could back in the city.

But I am neither poet nor painter nor musician, only a gay girl who has gone about like a butterfly tasting of this flower and that all over the earth wherever a bright bloom called me. Never before have I come face to face with a great love and a great wonder and been able to call them mine. Therefore I approach the matter with deep reverence and heart-searching.

And now, *I* have the advantage of you! For you seem only to have found out about my financial and social position and the possible traditions that belong to the family of Wainwright; while I have been learning much of your inner life from one of your most devoted admirers, my young cousin Sam, who seems to be remodeling his life after the pattern which you have given him.

You cannot know what it has been to me to learn of you in this way, out of the mouth of a guileless child who adores you. And the more I have learned the more I am filled with humility and awe to know that you should have put your love upon such a one as I.

You have been blaming yourself for the beautiful thing which you did, in confessing your love, because you think that perhaps I have more money than you, or a higher social rank in this world!

But don't you know that such great love as you have to offer far outweighs any such differences as those? Just material differences! And anyway, if I give you my love wouldn't any wealth and position I might have be yours also, just as any other asset I might have, such as hair and eyes and smiles and the like?

And you have tried to humble yourself for matters of that sort! But I, far more, for another reason!

Why, John Saxon, you made me feel for a few paragraphs that you were sorry for what you had done, that you repented having told me of your love. You made me jealous of that poor other girl—Helen Foster, whom neither of us has ever seen—until I read on farther, and found your love again, and that healed the hurt. But it made me know as I read on, that it was my place to be humble, not yours.

Because you have something that makes a far greater difference between us than wealth or station. You have a God, and I don't know Him! And I'm afraid He doesn't approve of me!

It is not that I mind being second to your God. I would count it a great honor to be so near to God as that. But John Saxon, beloved stranger, I'm afraid He wouldn't want me there! He wouldn't think that I was worthy to be near to you.

In fact, ever since your letter came, I have felt your God standing near me, looking through my soul, and I feel so small and shamed and utterly undone, I need to hide somewhere. I never knew a God before, not so near. I never thought about God before at all! And *you* are *His!*

You see now, don't you, that it is not money, nor family, nor position that should separate us, but your God!

I feel that perhaps you know this already.

But I love you, oh I love you, John Saxon, beloved stranger! I never loved anyone this way before. I never knew there was such love!

And you have said that you will pray for me!

It seems to me that I shall go reverently all my days, just because you have made mention of my name to God.

Mary Elizabeth

14

ONE morning a couple of days after Mary Elizabeth sent off her letter to Florida, she and Sam were sitting on the piazza deep in their Bible study. It was nearly eleven o'clock and they had been down to the beach since breakfast having a good long swim and a run up the beach to the lighthouse and back, with another dip for a finish. They were feeling tired and quiet and ready to sit down in the coolness of the piazza and rest.

They had been doing this intensive study for three days now and it was a question which of the two enjoyed it most, for it had developed that Mary Elizabeth asked just the questions that the boy needed to bring back to him knowledge acquired the last winter in the Florida camping class, and he brought it forth in his most original boy manner, yet clearly, so that it was like a revelation to the girl to whom heretofore the Bible had been a sealed book full of dead sayings that meant nothing.

Mary Elizabeth had ransacked the house for a Bible, and had found one most unexpectedly in possession of Susan, the caretaker's wife. Susan had two, one that she had earned in Sunday School as a child, reciting certain Psalms, and another with big print. She loaned the one with big print to her young mistress with great delight that she had something worthy to lend. So Mary Elizabeth was equipped with a Bible if not with the knowledge to enable her to find its different books. Sam had to put her through a course in the books of the Bible before she was able to hunt out references. It was amusing to see how patient and eager Sam was as a teacher. He felt it was great of Mary Beth to companion with him this way. She was as good as a boy, any day, and a "lot better than some fellas!" he told her gallantly.

This exclusive feminine fellowship might not satisfy indefinitely. Doubtless there would come a time when he would hunger and thirst for a good rousing game of baseball. But for the present to the lad who was accustomed to frustration of his many plans by a too-anxious parent, and ensuing loneliness, it seemed for the time being bliss.

They were deep in the mysteries of a perplexing question on John Saxon's lesson list, the answer to which was to be found among half a dozen Bible references, and required careful thought and consideration of various phases of the subject, when suddenly the honk of a loud and arrogant automobile horn close at hand broke the stillness startlingly, and around the curve of the graveled drive which circled the house there swept two costly sport cars gleaming smugly in chromium wherever chromium could find an excuse to be, and filled with a noisy company of young people in smart costumes. The foremost car was driven by Boothby Farwell!

"Oh heck! What's this?" exclaimed Sam half rising from the step and dropping his Bible on the piazza. One could almost see his hair bristling like a cat's at sight of a dog in the offing.

Mary Elizabeth looked up in dismay with a blankness in her gaze as she stared unbelievingly at her unwelcome guests. Now, who had invaded her quiet when she had taken so much pains to hide her going? Boothby Farwell, of all people!

And he had dared to bring the whole gay bunch of her old associates from home! Cissy Ward, Tally Randall, Jane Reefer, Rita Bowers, Anne and Maude and Whitty Gensemer! She recognized them one by one, the dismay growing in her heart and face as she rose hastily from the steamer chair leaving her open Bible where she had been sitting, and came forward to greet her uninvited guests.

How in the world did they find out where she was? Surely her father had not given her secret away!

But here they were and there was nothing to do but receive them, though she felt like a child whose doll had been broken and her tea party shattered.

"Well, isn't this unexpected!" she said as she tried to summon her inbred courtesy, and some degree of welcome into her face.

"How in the world did you find out where I was?"

This last question to Boothby who took her hand severely, possessively and gave her a look of reproof.

"Bribed old Tilly to tell where they forwarded your letters," answered Boothby promptly and a little curtly. "Just what was the idea in running away like that? A game of hide and seek, or some similar child's play?"

"I came down to look the old house over and see what repairs it needed," answered Mary Elizabeth coolly, with a steady impersonal look at her former lover and no heightening of her color.

"Well, it's about time you came back again then," he said with a contemptuous glance at the house of other days. "What's the idea of repairing this old barracks anyway? It's a waste of money, I should say."

"It happens that we don't feel that way," laughed Mary Elizabeth. "Won't you come up on the piazza? I think we can make you fairly comfortable, even if we are a bit antiquated. Sam, can't you bring out a few chairs?"

Sam greatly resembled a cat up a tree with its back arched, but he slowly unbristled and went into the house after chairs, giving a baleful glance backward at Boothby Farwell, the perpetrator of this intrusion into his Eden.

"Oh, don't bothah!" said Boothby Farwell, looking about contemptuously, "we're not going to stay here of course. We came to get you and take you up the coast to lunch. Get your hat and come on. Or perhaps you don't need a hat?"

"Sorry to disappoint you," said Mary Elizabeth sweetly, "I couldn't possibly leave. I have a man coming to do some electrical work and I have to be here all the afternoon. He may come any minute now."

"Send word to him not to come then, you simply must go with us! We've come all this way to get you and you can't disappoint us that way."

Then the girls began to clamor, and the other men.

"Oh, come on, Elizabeth! Don't be a flat tire!"

But Mary Elizabeth stood her ground firmly.

"I can't possibly go," she said. "You'll have to get out and take lunch with me. I have a maid here who will be delighted to have some one to serve. Come up and sit down and cool off. There's really a wonderful view of the sea here, and we'll have a pitcher of lemonade at once. Sam, dear," she gave her young cousin a ravishing smile that reduced him to her abject slave again, "could you ask Susan to make us some lemonade?"

"We've something better than lemonade, in the car,"

said Boothby coolly, "and none of us are thirsty! We've just been drinking. We came to get you."

"Oh, I didn't know!" said Mary Elizabeth with a twinkle at Sam. "No lemonade, then, Sam. We don't need it!"

Sam grinned and took his seat on the step again, gathering up his Bible as calmly as if it were a spelling book.

"What on earth are you doing?" asked one of the girls coming up the steps and looking at the Bible curiously.

Mary Elizabeth looked at her guest as if she had not noticed her before, she caught also a glimpse of Sam's lowering countenance, and then she said brightly:

"Why, my cousin and I were doing a little studying together."

Cissy Ward flung a curious glance at her in turn and then picked up the Bible from Sam's knees and gave it a comprehensive scrutiny.

"Oh," she said lightly, "is this your spelling book? Tally, can you spell Methuselah?"

"Not me!" shrugged Tally lightly with a wicked little gleam in his handsome reckless eyes. "I couldn't even pronounce it."

"You're mistaken," said Mary Elizabeth in a clear voice that they all could hear, "that isn't my speller, it's my A B C book. I've only just begun on my alphabet, but if I live long enough I mean to get so I can read it and understand it. I never took a course in the Bible and I thought it was about time."

They all focused their eyes on her. Cissy was flicking the leaves of Sam's Bible through carelessly. Tally had picked up the Bible that Mary Elizabeth had left lying in her chair, examining it comically as if he meant to analyze it and dissect it. The other young folks were climbing out of the car and coming up the steps. They ensed that there was a distinct situation and that Mary Elizabeth was dominating it. They had wondered a little why Boothby who was usually so exclusive in his invitations had invited them all to come along after Mary Elizabeth. Now they were sure that something had gone awry between him and Mary Elizabeth, and she most unusually was holding out against him. They were not quite sure what part they were to play in this one-act drama but they entered gaily into it, determined to get as much fun out of it as possible, and incidentally stir up the chief actors in the plot to reveal the point of the whole matter. So Cissy, who stopped at nothing when she was out on a riot, suddenly held Sam's precious Bible aloft in her thumb and finger, and shouted in a high shrieking voice:

"Listen, boys and girls, I've found out what's the matter with 'Liz'beth! She's turning religious and we'll have to snap her out of it. This book's evidently at the bottom of it, and we'll have to burn the book! Who'll build the bonfire, boys and girls? Here goes the book! Catch it!"

But just as Cissy Ward was about to fling the offending Bible out over the steps Sam sprang into the air catching his precious Bible in one hand and Cissy Ward's extended arm in the other, setting her down hard on one of the porch rockers.

Sam looked almost grown up as he turned angrily upon the astonished girl.

"That's my Bible!" he declared in a clear ringing voice that had lost its boyish treble and seemed almost manly in its accent. "If you wantta play horse with Bibles go getcherself one of yer own ta use, and don't take mine. I guess they have some back in the city stores!"

Mary Elizabeth looked at her young cousin startled. She opened her mouth to say something to him about his behavior and then closed it again. Instead she quietly stepped to Tally's side and took her own borrowed Bible firmly away from Tally's careless hand. Then turning to Sam she smiled and handed him the other Bible.

"Buddie, will you just take these in and put them away? They wouldn't be understood here," she said calmly, and then turned back to her surprised guests.

"Won't you all be seated?" she said with grave courtesy. "We have plenty of room and lunch will be at half past one. What can we do to pass the time? Would you like to take a swim? I think I can rustle up enough bathing suits. They may be a little out of date, but I'm sure that won't matter for once."

Sam disappeared with the Bibles and then reappeared quietly and kept in the background, ready to do his cousin's bidding. She noticed him several times, sitting easily on the railing of the piazza with one foot swinging lightly back and forth, his eyes gravely off on the distant sea where a little boat went curtsying across the horizon. Once his eyes met hers and a look flashed between them of perfect understanding, and she was sure that unless something outrageous happened Sam would keep further words to himself. He was angry, but he was under control. She pondered this the while she tried to play the part of courteous hostess, greeting her guests as if nothing unpleasant had happened, getting the right seat for each, giving a gay little word here and there in answer to their own protests that she would not go with them up the shore. Sam and she understood each other and Sam would stay by and help her out in everything even though he fairly hated every one of the guests.

Presently she excused herself to speak with Susan, and Sam appeared at her side suddenly as she arrived in the butler's pantry.

"They're only a bunch of unbelievers!" said Sam in a low tone. "You don't need ta mind!"

She gave him an astonished look, and then her face broke into smiles.

"That's right, Sam," she said, "let's try to remember that. I don't really know just what you mean by unbelievers, but we'll take that up when we have more time. And meantime, if Susan needs anything could you take Frank's bicycle and go for it?"

"Sure thing!" said Sam eagerly. "Watcha want?"

"Well, I thought maybe some of those lovely big strawberries with white insides. And some fresh fish. I'll see what Susan says."

"I'm right here, Miss Wainwright," said Susan appearing excitedly from the kitchen, a long streak of flour on her rosy cheek. "It's all right whatever you want. I mixed up some soda biscuits as soon as I saw the cars drive in. I thought maybe you would want to ask 'em to stay."

"Oh, that's nice, Susan. I'm sorry it will make you so much extra work. Couldn't Sam get that little Ivy girl you had over here the other night to help you?"

"I already sent Frank to tell her, and he's bringing the fish. If Mister Sam would get me the strawberries and cream? There's sponge cake. That'll do for dessert. Will fried fish and hot biscuits and a tomato and cucumber salad do for the main course, and iced coffee for the drink?"

"Wonderful, Susan! That will be great. Isn't that going to be too much for you to accomplish?"

"No indeed, Miss Wainwright! I love to have company. And how about the table?"

"We won't set the table," said Mary Elizabeth. "We'll serve lunch on the porch. When Sam gets back with the berries he can bring out the two nests of little tables, and you can show him where to find the linen doilies to put on them. Then you get out the knives and forks and spoons, and glasses and napkins and put them on a tray and he'll look after fixing them on the tables, won't you, Buddie?" She gave her cousin a loving look, and Sam's eyes were full of devotion.

"Sure!" he growled hoarsely.

"Then, Susan, you can bring the fish in right on the plates. Pass the rolls and butter. Fix your salad on little plates that won't take too much room, and will Ivy help serve? Then I think that'll be all right. Fine! Call me if you want me. Sorry I can't come out and help."

"Oh, Miss Wainwright my dear!" protested Susan smiling. "We don't need more help. That Mister Sam is a perfect angel."

So Mary Elizabeth went back to her guests and Sam departed on the borrowed bicycle, thinking scornful thoughts of the interlopers, and in particular despising the man Boothby Farwell. Now what did Mary Beth want with a chump like that when there were men in the world like John Saxon?

"Now," said Mary Elizabeth arriving back on the piazza with all the gaiety and most of the zest of former days, "we're going down and take a swim before lunch. Girls, come upstairs with me. Boys, go down those steps at the end of the piazza, turn to your left and open the door under the back piazza. You'll find a row of bath houses and plenty of men's suits in the chest near the shower. Make your own choice. We girls will meet you at the beach in ten minutes. See who'll be there first!"

The girls trooped off gaily and Mary Elizabeth led them to an upper row of bath houses off the upper back piazza, and there was much fun and laughter getting arrayed in the old-fashioned bathing costumes.

"Girls, I've found a peach!" cried out Cissy Ward.

"Black with sleeves to the wrist and a full kilted skirt. And stockings to wear with it, black stockings, as I live! Bloomers, too, that come to the knee. I'm wearing this one, girls, and I'll be sure to drown, and all the rest of the crowd will have to dive for me and bring me up. Just wait till you see me. Here's a sunbonnet too! What luck. The vintage of eighteen seventy-five!"

The morning passed quickly, Mary Elizabeth having a time of her own, which became almost a race, trying to keep herself in a crowd so as not to let Boothby Farwell isolate her for a private lecture.

She was relieved indeed when the bell rang loud and clear from the front porch as a signal to them to come back and dress, and they swarmed back through the hot sand, laughing and shaking briny drops from their voluminous garments, all talking at once, all except Boothby Farwell, who was trying to show Mary Elizabeth how hurt and angry he was.

15

BOOTHBY Farwell tried to walk back with Mary
Elizabeth but she eluded him three times and dashed
ahead to speak to somebody else and at last he gave up
and sulked behind the crowd.

When they all were dressed and back on the piazza
again they found there were little tables scattered about
and pleasant chairs beside them, enough for everybody.
The tables were set with spotless white linen squares, and
everything needful in the way of dishes and silver. There
was a plate of salad, cool and inviting, at every place.
Mary Elizabeth gave a sigh of relief. Susan and Sam had
done wonders.

They were no sooner seated than Sam marched in
with a tray of plates, the appetizing odor of fried fish
spicing the air and whetting appetites already keen by the
plunge into the sea.

Big reserve platters of fish and quaint linen-lined
baskets of hot biscuits appeared as soon as there was need
of them. Pickles and cheese went the rounds, and approval ran high.

"Say, this is great! You can't take Elizabeth off her

guard! She's always prepared for an unexpected crowd!" They called out for more butter, and to have their glasses of iced coffee replenished again and again.

Sam, going about with trays and pitchers, waiting gravely upon the guests, had the air of an elderly host who disapproved of the company but nevertheless desired to stuff them to their capacity. After the superstrawberries and cream and sponge cake were finished with more iced coffee, the little tables disappeared as if by magic, and Sam was seen to saunter by in a brilliant red bathing suit going in the direction of the beach.

"What about a little drink, Tally?" called out Boothby Farwell as Sam stepped noiselessly by the piazza on the thick turf of the lawn. Sam grinned on the off-side of his mouth. Only Sam knew that there was no drink. He had carefully investigated while the crowd were in bathing in the morning, had dextrously opened each bottle stowed in the cars, and sent the contents gurgling harmlessly down the drain behind the house, filled the bottles with good honest water from the hose faucet, cleverly replaced the stoppers, and gone on his way rejoicing in silent revenge for a lost morning. He had silenced his conscience by telling it that he did it so there wouldn't be any funny business to annoy his cousin, in case Tally Randall took a little too much. Sam was a canny lad. And so he stalked sternly down to the water, dived out into the waves and planned to be a good way from shore and duck under if anybody came after him to visit a just punishment upon him.

But it happened that Tally and Boothby returned from their visit to the car with empty hands.

"There's been a mistake in that case of liquor," announced Boothby in annoyance. "They must have given us a case of bottles that were not properly inspected. I can't understand it. There's nothing but water in the rest of them. I can't understand it. The bottles we opened on the way down seemed all right, didn't they, girls?"

"They certainly did!" clamored the girls. "Hasn't somebody been tampering with them?" They looked at Mary Elizabeth. "How about it, Mary Beth? What kind of servants do you keep about the place?"

Mary Elizabeth hid a startled look in her eyes with a smile.

"Absolutely impossible!" she said. "Frank and Susan are ardent prohibitionists. And nobody from outside could get in the gate without ringing the servant's bell." But Mary Elizabeth's eyes rested meditatively on a bright spot of red darting among the white-crested waves.

"Well, we'll have to report this when we get back to the city," said Boothby with annoyance. "They certainly must have made a mistake and given us a broken case. That makes it very awkward. We can't get anything worth drinking this side of Allenby's Lodge, and that's quite out of our way. We'll have to be starting pretty soon if we must go that far. Come, Elizabeth, change into something for evening and come with us. We're not going to let you off. We've had a royal time and a delicious lunch, but we came down to get you and we don't mean to leave you behind! Get down to the basement and give your orders to your electrician if you must, but make it snappy! We ought to be moving out of here in half an hour if we mean to make the Crestmont Inn in time for an eight o'clock dinner, and we oughtn't to be later than that for there are special attractions there all the latter part of the evening that we don't want to miss."

Mary Elizabeth recalled her eyes from the bobbing red bathing suit and set her lips sweetly but firmly.

"Sorry to disappoint you," she said, "but it is absolutely impossible. I have other plans!"

Boothby Farwell flashed her a look of displeasure, but his firmly set lips showed he had no intention of giving up, and presently he asked her to show him about the house and grounds. The whole company started out together to wander about the lovely grounds, which though not extensive, had a sweet quaintness about the shaded walks and neatly kept drives and garden groups of perennials that at least made it an excuse for a walk.

Mary Elizabeth tried to make this an affair of the whole company, but in spite of her Boothby Farwell drew her away from the rest and made her sit down on an old rustic seat which had a view straight to the sea. He began to urge her once more to marry him, even taking out that gorgeous diamond and begging her to let him place it upon her finger. But something seemed to have changed within Mary Elizabeth's mind. The ring no longer drew her. The prospect of a leisurely life of pleasure in Boothby Farwell's company, drifting about the world wherever an attraction was offered, no longer seemed to her possible even of consideration. Finally she looked at him steadily, giving him that clear, frank gaze that she so seldom gave to any but those who knew her well.

"I can't marry you, Boothby, not *ever,*" she said. "I'm sorry you feel the way you do about it. I'm sorry I didn't know sooner myself, although you'll have to own that I never gave you encouragement. But I know that I shall never change about this and I wish that you would promise me to put the whole thing out of your mind finally and never speak to me about it again."

The man looked at her sternly, deeply offended.

"You are going a little too far, Elizabeth," he said sternly. "I have come a long way to-day to get you, and you refuse to go with me. Now you are trying to put off our marriage again and the time has come when I must refuse you. I insist that you come out in the open and acknowledge our engagement, and that you set a near date for our marriage. I am not willing to be played with any longer."

Mary Elizabeth was white with annoyance, and there were dangerous lights in her eyes.

"Engagement?" she said in astonishment. "There has never been any engagement between us."

"You wore my ring!" challenged the man.

"For one brief hour," said the girl. "I am not sure it was even so long. I put it on as you asked in the letter you sent with the ring, as an experiment to see how it would feel to wear it. That was what you asked. I never really expected to wear it longer than that evening, but I did as you requested, put it on and tried honestly in my heart to think how it would seem to have it belong to me, with all that it would mean if I should accept it. And I found—" Mary Elizabeth's eyes softened with a memory that still seemed like a fairy dream—"I found that it was quite impossible. As soon as I was back in the car I pulled off my glove and removed it. Boothby, you and I were never engaged and you know it perfectly well. You know that I have always refused to even consider such a thing. We have been friends. Just good friends. But if you will not put this thing out of your mind, if you still go on insisting that I shall marry you,—well, we shall have to cease to be even friends."

"Nonsense!" said the man with a sneer on his lips. "You don't mean that! You don't suppose for a minute that I am going to take this seriously!"

Mary Elizabeth lifted her chin a little and looked at him haughtily, her lips closed in a thin, firm line. She said no word but there was battle in her eyes. Before her steady gaze the man's cold eyes shifted almost uneasily at last and he said, his tone still angry:

"You act exactly like a kitten playing with a costly crystal ball."

"You being the ball?" asked Mary Elizabeth, and suddenly laughed, uncontrollably.

The man's face flushed angrily.

"Or else," he added with a sneer on his lips, "like a naughty woman who is playing with another man!"

At that Mary Elizabeth flashed him a cutting glance of scorn.

"That will be about all!" she said coldly, and got up to go.

"No, that is not all, Elizabeth!" said the man as if he had the right to rule over her. "I do not propose to give you up to any other man, no matter who he is, whether lover, friend or husband. I always get what I want and I never give up what I choose to keep. You will find it will not be easy to get away from me. And there are more ways than one to carry out that promise. Everyone has a weak spot somewhere."

Mary Elizabeth looked at him for a moment and a procession of emotions swept over her speaking face, the final look being utter contempt. And she said, in a clear cold voice:

"If I had needed anything further to make me know that I would rather be lying dead than marry you, you have furnished it in that remark!" And Mary Elizabeth marched definitely away from him and went into the house.

The other guests were gathering again to the piazza, sitting about smoking, laughing, beginning to be a little bored and quite thirsty, but Mary Elizabeth was in the house telephoning to a carpenter. They could hear her quite distinctly from the booth in the hall, where she had purposely left the door open a crack. She was arranging with the carpenter to come and adjust the garage door, and to be there early the next morning. They ceased their indifference and looked at one another inquiringly. They looked out toward the rustic pergola where their hostess had been seated but a moment since with Boothby Farwell and found nothing but a rustic seat smothered with summer roses. Boothby Farwell was not in sight. He presently came around the corner of the house from the direction of where the cars had been parked. He was frowning, his eyes still filled with fury.

"What has become of Elizabeth?" he asked one of the girls.

"She just went into the house," said Cissy watching him curiously. "She seems to be talking to a carpenter. Isn't she going with us?"

But just then Mary Elizabeth came out, a cool little smile on her lips and in her eyes. She had gained control of herself again, but she did not look at Boothby Farwell as he stood there cold and forbidding, eyeing her with retribution plainly written on his handsome face.

"It is time we left," he said haughtily to his party. "Get your belongings. Tally and I'll have the cars around here at once! We haven't any time to waste if we want to be up the coast in time for the performance!"

He turned on his heel and marched around the house out of sight.

"Of all the grouches!" cried out Cissy. "Do let's hurry and get the dear baby a drink! That's what's the matter, of course! He won't rest till he's had all he wants! Liz'buth, aren't you really going with us? Oh, why not? You'll miss the time of your life. Come on and be a sport! I've got two evening frocks along, if you haven't your togs down here. I didn't know which I liked best so I brought both. You can have your choice! Come on and play the game!"

Mary Elizabeth gave them a bright little enigmatical smile and shook her head.

"I really couldn't," she said cheerfully, "though it's darling of you to be so generous."

"You better run along, Cis, and get your hat or Farwell will bite when he sees you're not ready!" admonished Tally, whirling his car around the corner of the house and coming to a noisy stop.

There was a scurrying of feet up the stairs, a quick powdering of noses and adjusting of smart, silly, little hats, all the girls talking at once, pitying Mary Elizabeth, gushing over the nice lunch and the swim, and then a fluttering downstairs again, a clamoring and laughter as they adjusted themselves in the cars.

But Boothby Farwell did not come up on the porch again. He did not bid his hostess good bye, nor say he had had a good time, not even in the modern patter of the day did he do the courteous thing. He stood dourly in the driveway assisting the ladies into the cars, but he did not once turn his eyes toward Mary Elizabeth until they were driving away and then he turned and gave her such a look of menace and hate as she would not soon forget. It was like a threat.

But Mary Elizabeth kept her lovely color, the shine of her eyes, the serene smile of her lips, until the cars had swept away around the curve of the drive, out the big iron gate, up the coast road, and disappeared like two wild specks in the distance. Then she suddenly dropped limply in one of the porch rockers, put her burning face down in her cold hands and began to laugh.

She laughed until the tears began to come, and then, lifting her face to brush them away she became aware of a stubby young figure in a wet, red bathing suit, with dripping hair and a look of terror on his face.

Sam was standing on the grass beside the path and regarding her with deep anxiety. Mary Elizabeth looked at him and began to laugh again.

"Sam," she said when she could speak, *"what* did you do with the gentleman's liquor?"

Sam looked sheepish and slowly began to grin.

"Put it where it can't do any harm!" he said laconically.

"Where, Sam? Where did you put it?"

"Down the drain!" he said, eyeing his cousin keenly to see if she was going to make him confess and apologize.

But Mary Elizabeth was laughing again. Somehow she had to laugh or cry and she chose laughing. For Boothby Farwell had managed to unnerve her, as she knew he knew he would.

Sam stood still and regarded her with a half fearful little grin. He wasn't just sure of this cousin since those "city bums" as he chose to call their recent guests, had been here. He couldn't tell just how much Mary Beth thought of that poor fish Farwell. Maybe she was engaged to him after all, as his mother had once intimated, and if that was so he was done with her. A girl who could have Mr. Saxon for a friend to go and get engaged to a rotten egg like that Boothby Farwell, well, if she was he would go back to the city to-morrow. He wouldn't stand for it, not a minute!

But he had seen a look of weariness and defeat in her eyes when she looked up through her laughter, and he sensed that something had happened more than he knew. He felt troubled for Mary Elizabeth. He was there to protect her, and what could he do?

So he stood on one cold foot after the other, beginning to shiver a little now. A strong sea breeze was coming up and he was turning blue around his mouth and his teeth were chattering, but he stood there puzzling what to do.

Then Mary Elizabeth looked up again, saw him there and stopped laughing.

"You're a dear!" she suddenly said earnestly. "But you are catching cold, Buddie, run up and change quickly and you and I will take a run together on the sand and get the day out of our system!"

So Sam hurried off to his room, and in a very short time appeared reasonably attired, his hair giving evidence of having received what is known as a lick-and-a-promise, but his face full of eagerness.

They had quite a run on the sand and came back shining and a bit breathless.

"Did you get the afternoon mail from the box, Buddie?" asked Mary Elizabeth. "Dad said he was going to write me about that electrical work."

"Why, no," said the boy, and sprang away to get it.

He came back with several letters in his hand and eagerness written all over him.

"Oh, gee!" he said. "There's one for me from Mr. Saxon. That'll be the new lesson. Won't that be great! Now we can do some of it this evening, can't we?"

"We surely can," said Mary Elizabeth looking up from her own handful of mail and giving a wistful glance at the address on Sam's letter, then turning back to her own and sorting it over, hoping there might be one for her also, though she knew there had been scarcely time since she had written.

They settled down on the piazza to read their letters, Mary Elizabeth lifting a furtive glance to the boy at her feet in his usual place on the top step. She watched his face change from bright eagerness to dismay. Then he suddenly exclaimed:

"Oh Gosh! *Good night!* Read that, Mary Beth!" and springing up he cast his letter in her lap and dashed away up to his room.

16

WITH consternation in her eyes and a great fear clutch-ing at her heart Mary Elizabeth stared after the excited boy. He leaped up the stairs three steps to a bound and banged his door after him. Then she picked up the letter and began to read:

Dear Prayer-Partner:

I am writing in great haste to ask you to help me pray for my dear mother who is very critically ill. There are no doctors left in our vicinity whom I can trust, all the specialists have gone north, and not a nurse to be had. I have to be doctor and nurse and housemaid, for Father has broken his ankle and is able to do very little to help.

Humanly speaking there is no hope for Mother, though if I had my old doctor-teacher here from New York, of whom I have told you, I feel certain he could save her for us, for I saw him perform just such an operation as she needs and save a woman's life.

But I know that with God all things are possible, so I am calling on all you boys to pray with me that if it be God's will He will let her live a little while longer.

You will understand, I am sure, why I cannot send you the lesson just now.

Feeling comforted because I know you will be praying with me,

Your friend,
John Saxon.

Mary Elizabeth read the letter through twice that she might not miss anything. Then she put it in her lap and sat looking off at the sea, but seeing a little house in a Florida grove, and a man carrying a heavy burden of sorrow and doing everything alone.

No, he wasn't alone, either! There was God! His God! Mary Elizabeth wished she knew God. How she would pray!

But not knowing God, what was there else that she could do? John Saxon had not yet had her letter when he wrote this one to Sam. It might not reach him till to-day. If he had to go to the post office for it he might not get it even then. He had not asked her to pray. Perhaps he suspected she did not know how. And anyhow, until he got her letter he would not know whether he had the right to call upon her. His letter to her had made it plain that he was not counting on her now that he knew who she was.

But, oh, there must be some way she could help! Doctors and nurses were what he needed! Money could bring them to him in a few hours by airplane! Perhaps he would not like her to help that way, but one could not stop on a matter of that sort when a life was at stake! She sat several minutes thinking rapid thoughts, making quick plans, unhampered by any question of cost. Then she got up and tiptoed upstairs to Sam's door, intending to tap and ask him to come out, but when she reached the door she found he had banged it so hard after him that it had not latched and had sprung back again. It was open several inches and she could see Sam kneeling beside his bed, burrowing his nose into the pillow and praying in a half-audible murmur. He evidently thought himself shut in alone with God.

"Oh, God! You promised! Anybody who abides could ask what he would and you'd do it. Mr. Saxon does that. You know he does! I'm not much at it, but I'm reminding you of your promise. Do it for him won't you? Make his mother well! And you said if we ask in Christ's name you would do it for His sake! I'm reminding you! I'm not much good to you myself. I snitched those bottles and threw out that stuff. I hated those folks too! But do it for Christ's sake, please—!"

The pleading voice was smothered in the pillows again and Mary Elizabeth tiptoed away to her own room with a mistiness in her eyes.

Mary Elizabeth sat a long time listening to the stillness in the house and thinking out a plan that had come to her with breath-taking vividness. Dared she?

She leaned her head back and closed her eyes thinking out the details, weighing possibilities. Perhaps he would not like her to meddle. Perhaps the plan was on too large a scale. And yet, if God were going to answer that prayer He would have to do it through some individual, wouldn't he? But she! She was in a rather anomalous position. It might hurt John Saxon unnecessarily, as if she were flaunting her wealth and influence. Could it be done without her? She turned the question this way and that, all the time feeling more and more that the time was short, and knowing that somehow she was going to do it. And then she thought of the boy, and after a moment called him softly.

There was silence for a moment and then she heard a

stirring, and presently he came in the dusk of the hall and stood by her door.

"Did you call, Mary Beth?" he asked in a subdued tone.

"Yes, Buddie! I've been thinking. How would you like to help answer those prayers?"

"Oh—Boyyy!" came the answer in a long-drawn-out wistful voice.

"Come here and sit down." She drew a low hassock near the window and he came and sat in the shadow, but his whole attitude was eagerness.

"I think we ought to get a doctor and a nurse down there just as quickly as possible, don't you?"

"Sure! But how could we?"

She was still a minute and then she said,

"Sam, if you had a lot of money what would you do with it?"

"Why, take a doctor and a nurse down there in an airplane," answered the boy without an instant's hesitation.

"Exactly!" said Mary Elizabeth with a quick breath of satisfaction. "Well, I'm going to give you the money. He wouldn't probably take it from me. I'm—rather—a stranger—you know, but if you did it that would be different. You could say when it came to the questioning that you had some money that you were free to use, see?"

"I see! Oh gee! Mary Beth, you're a peacherine! Oh gee!"

"Well, Buddie, we've got to work fast! Sickness doesn't wait on time. The first thing is to get the right doctor. I don't suppose you know who that doctor was that he mentions, do you?"

"Sure I do!" said Sam, on the alert at once. "He told us a lot about him down at camp. Told about his operations and all that, and how he had learned more from him than any other teacher in medical college. His name is MacKelvie, Martin MacKelvie. But the college would be closed now, it's vacation time."

"Still, it oughtn't to be so hard to trace him if he hasn't gone abroad. That's a rather unusual name."

Mary Elizabeth was writing the name on a pad from her bedside table.

"Now, Bud, do you know the directions for getting there? Were you ever at Mr. Saxon's house?"

"Sure thing," said Sam eagerly, "so was Jeff! He stayed down and worked with Mr. Saxon after camp a lot."

"Well, write out the directions and everything you know while I go telephone New York."

Mary Elizabeth hurried down to the telephone booth and did some pretty good detective work for the next half hour. She was rewarded by discovering that Dr. Martin MacKelvie was at his summer cottage on Lake George. A little more clever work assisted ably by the telephone operator, and Dr. Martin MacKelvie was on the wire.

Sam was just outside the booth listening, his heart in his eyes, and Mary Elizabeth will perhaps never feel a thrill more triumphant than when the doctor's vibrant voice spoke, "Dr. MacKelvie speaking."

Mary Elizabeth caught her breath and tried to steady her voice.

"Dr. MacKelvie, I'm a friend of John Saxon who once was in your class at medical college. Do you remember him?"

"I certainly do!" came the ringing answer. "One of the best men I ever had the honor of instructing."

Mary Elizabeth drew another breath tinged with relief and went on eagerly:

"John Saxon's mother is very critically ill in Florida.

He feels that you could save her life. We're taking you and a nurse down in an airplane to-night if you'll go, and we'll gladly pay whatever fee you ask. Will you go?"

"What's the matter with her?" came the crisp keen question.

"We don't know. He spoke of an operation he had seen you perform. That's all we know about it. He is out in the country on his own, and the best doctors have all gone north. He said there was no one near whom he could trust."

"Yes, I'll go!" came the answer after an instant's deliberation. "If John Saxon wants me I'll have to go, but I won't charge him a cent."

"That's all right, Doctor," said Mary Elizabeth with a ring in her voice, "we want to pay it for him."

"We'll talk about that later. How soon do we start and where do I meet you?"

"As soon as we can get a plane. I'll telephone at once and make arrangements. Wouldn't it be better for the plane to pick you up? Where shall I tell them to come?"

A few minutes more of careful directions, telephone numbers exchanged, and the matter was arranged.

"Will you get a nurse, or shall I?" she asked.

"I'll look after that! I'll be ready inside of an hour. Let me know if you can't secure a plane and I'll see what I can do."

"Oh, I'll get a plane," said Mary Elizabeth with a lilt in her voice. "I know a pilot in New York. I'll call you again as soon as I get him."

"Oh, Boy!" said Sam softly, out in the hall. Then he tip-toed into the dining room and suppressed the dinner bell that Susan was about to ring, while Mary Elizabeth called up the flying field. Now, if her man was only there!

Fifteen minutes later she came out of the telephone booth triumphant.

"He says he'll go. He gave orders to have his plane ready inside half an hour. I heard him. Now, Sam, we've got to work fast. I'll have to call Dad and Uncle. Do you want to go? Will Uncle Robert stand for it?"

"Do I wantta go?" echoed the boy. "Do I *wantta* go? But I don't know about Dad. Do we havta tell him?"

"Yes, we have to tell him, Buddie. I couldn't take that responsibility. Perhaps we'd better get it over with before we eat."

So Mary Elizabeth went into the booth again and called her home, getting her father on the wire.

"Dad, I'm taking a doctor and a nurse in an airplane down to Florida to-night to a very sick friend. You don't mind, do you?"

"Why can't the doctor and nurse go by themselves?" asked her father.

"Because, they can't! There are circumstances that make it impossible. The sick friend is poor and might not accept the help if—I—didn't go and engineer it. Dad, I haven't time to explain. It's a matter of life and death and I *must* go. The woman will die! I'll write you all about it."

"Whose plane are you going in?"

"Cousin Richie Wainwright's."

"Oh, well, that's different. Why didn't you tell me that before? All right, but wire me the minute you land?"

"Yes, Dad. And Dad, I'd like to take Sam. Do you think Uncle would mind? He's crazy to go."

"Well, ask him. I don't know what he'll say. You say there's a nurse going along? And who's your doctor?"

Mary Elizabeth answered his questions and then called her uncle.

"Uncle Robert, I want to ask you something very particular. I hope you'll say yes. I'm taking a doctor and nurse down to Florida to a sick friend to-night. Cousin Richie is taking us in his big plane. I'd like to take Sam with me for company if you are willing and he's just crazy to go."

Sam held his breath for the answer as he stood by the open door of the booth and waited for his father to consider. After a moment's hesitation he answered:

"Why, yes, I guess he can go, Mary Beth. A boy loves that sort of thing, I know. But Mary Beth, tell him if he wants to write to his mother—she's in the mountains, you know—tell him to address his letter all right and then send it to me to mail. She's rather shy about airplanes you know, and there's no need to stir her up. And Mary Beth, wire me when you get there. Let me speak to Sam a minute!"

Sam with a trembling hand took the receiver and spoke in a serious grown-up voice.

"Yes sir?"

His father gave him a few general directions, bade him take care of his cousin and do just as she told him. He answered "Yes sir!" "Yes sir!" "Yes sir!" in that grave, awed tone, and the matter was settled.

They hurried through their dinner, packed their suitcases, and drove to the nearest flying field to await Cousin Richie and his plane. After arranging about the care of the car during their absence they sat in it and talked in low tones, Sam going back over John Saxon's stories about his wonderful doctor-teacher and friend, and Mary Elizabeth listening eagerly.

The moon rose and touched the flying field with silver sheen, filling the heavens with glory, and Sam sat quietly looking up into the sky trying to realize that in a few minutes now he would be sailing along above in that sea of silver.

And at last, sooner than they had dared to hope, they saw the lights, and heard the humming of the great bird that was to carry them away on their errand of mercy. As Mary Elizabeth sat there watching it arrive she marveled that the intricate arrangements for this journey had been made so quickly and so easily. There were a thousand and one little things that might have happened to spoil it all. The doctor might not have been found, he might not have been willing to go, Sam might not have remembered his name. Some other doctor might have been difficult in more senses than one, and might not have been acceptable. It was just a miracle that all had worked out as it had. That was it, a miracle, an answer to prayer! Then there were such things as answers to prayer! She would never again doubt that.

Mary Elizabeth liked the doctor's face at once, and the nurse was a quiet elderly woman, who, it developed, often went with the doctor when he was called to very critical cases. She had gentleness and tenderness, and strength and firmness written in her face, and the very look in her gray eyes gave Mary Elizabeth confidence.

The doctor asked a few questions, some of which Sam had to answer because he knew more about John Saxon's affairs than any of them. Then at the doctor's advice they settled down to rest.

But Mary Elizabeth, as she gave a look at the world below sailing in its silver sea, and then closed her eyes, turned the page into the next day and the problems she would have to meet when she reached Florida.

And Sam, though ostensibly resting, did not take his eager wondering eyes off that silver world below him until they actually dropped shut with sleep, and then as he slipped off into slumber there was a prayer upon his young lips.

"Oh, God, keep her alive till we get there. Oh, God, show the doctor what to do, and save her life if it be Your will—!"

17

IT was after one o'clock when Mr. Robert Wainwright turned over for the thousandth time in his bed and stretched out his hand for the telephone, calling a familiar number with a sort of sheepish sound in his voice.

"That you, Sam? Well, I couldn't sleep. Sorry to wake you up but I thought it would be better now than to wait another hour or so. I was bound to do it before the night was over."

"Yes, all right, Bob," came the sleepy voice of Mary Elizabeth's father, "I got used to that long ago. As I remember, the night you were born you began waking me in the night—!"

"Shut up!" said Robert Wainwright. "You couldn't remember that far back. You know I'm only a year younger than you are. And besides I shall wake you if I like. I intend to keep on waking you up whenever I please the rest of my life."

"Yes, Bob, I know I couldn't expect anything else. What is it this time?"

"Well, it's that pest of a Mary Elizabeth of yours. Whatever is this mad scheme she's got up now, and pulled my Sam in with her? Where has she gone anyway?"

"Why, Florida! Didn't she ask your permission? She said she was going to."

"Yes, she asked it and I said yes, he might go, but somehow since I got to bed I got to thinking how Clarice would feel about it. She'd think of that awful wide sky and so many mountains to fall on and die, and all that bunk you know, and I decided he'd better take the morning train back to the city and stay with me till she got back."

"Too late, Bob, they left half an hour ago. Mary 'Liz'beth phoned me just before they started."

"Yes, I found that out!" snapped his brother, "at least I was afraid I had. I called up that shore cottage of yours where they were supposed to be stopping and nobody answered. Don't you keep any servants down there to answer the phone?"

"Why, yes, there's the caretaker and his wife, but they likely sleep in the far corner of the house, and there isn't any extension. But it's too late, Bob. They've gone, and I wouldn't worry. Mary Elizabeth promised to wire as soon as they arrived. And if you just turn over and snatch a nap or two the wire will be here and the thing will be over. You can write Clarice he's gone to Florida. She doesn't need to know how he went. In fact you don't need to say anything about it for a few days, she knows he's at the shore, why not let it go at that? Go to sleep, old man. It's only a few hours now till they arrive."

"Yes, but a lot of things could happen in a few hours!"

"There always could. Even if he was at home things could happen."

"Yes, but Clarice would blame me!"

"I don't see that. He's half your son. Haven't you a

right to let your half go planing? He's old enough to enjoy it. That's the kind of things boys like."

"Yes, that's what I figured when I said yes," moaned Sam's father.

"Well, figure it again. Richie's along. No flier has a better record than Richie. He'll look after them."

"You're sure he went?"

"Absolutely. He called me up and said he'd look out for them."

"Well, that's different. But all the same that Mary Elizabeth of yours is a wild, erratic child and ought to be spanked."

"Absolutely! Try and do it!"

"What started her off on this wild goose trip?"

"Some old lady dying for want of a special operation, and Mary Elizabeth seemed to think the people wouldn't let the doctor in or something unless she went along. Sam seemed to be mixed in it too, somehow, some friend of his. Saxon's the name."

"Saxon? Not anyone belonging to that friend of Jeff's? Not the best man of Jeff's wedding?"

"Might be. How should I know? Mary 'Liz'beth didn't have time for details. She seemed to think your Sam was even more essential than the noted doctor they raked up."

"H'm! If it's John Saxon then I guess it's *my* child that needs spanking, though yours was a party to it. She humors Sammy too much. He seems to be able to get anything out of her he wants. Look at the way he wheedled her into keeping him away from that lady-camp his mother wanted to send him to! But Sammy is just gone daffy about John Saxon!"

"*John* Saxon!" said Mary Elizabeth's father. "She said it was a woman!"

"Perhaps it's Saxon's sister," said the brother Robert.

"Likely somebody she knew in college. This Saxon is an intellectual fellow I believe."

"What kind of man is this Saxon, anyway? Is he down there *now,* do you suppose?"

"I wouldn't be expected to know that," said Robert, "but he's an A number one lad all right according to Jeff. Jeff thinks he's the finest fellow he knows. That's why he chose him for best man."

"H'm!" said Mary Elizabeth's father thoughtfully. "Rich and conceited like all the rest I suppose. I declare I wish I could hide Mary Elizabeth away from them all. I haven't liked any of 'em so far, but I suppose a mere father is not expected to interfere in such matters any more. There's that Farwell, I can't stay in the room with him he irritates me so. Thinks he's the only authority on any subject you happen to mention, has a way of looking at you as if you hadn't a right to exist, thinks all people over his own age are in their dotage."

"Just so!" assented Uncle Robert. "I wondered what you were thinking about to tolerate that intimacy. If it were my affair I'd read the riot act to Mary Beth, even if she *is* twenty-one. I wouldn't have it! That fellow is a puppy! I could tell you some things—well—not over the phone, but I will when I see you!"

"Oh, yeah? Think I don't know a few myself? But the thing is how to get rid of him? I've taken her to Europe with me twice hoping to shed him, and what does he do but trot along, or come afterwards!"

"Why don't you talk to her?"

"Well, you know Mary Elizabeth's a chip off the old block. She's like the rest of us. She likes to run her own affairs. I was afraid I might only make her stronger for him if I said anything against him, although she knows I don't like him. At least—she ought to know. Man! I wish I knew where there were some real men. I'd like her to meet a few. I begin to think your Jeff is the only one left I know, and I wasn't so sure of him a while ago. But he seems to have settled down for sure now. What's he going to do? Going to take him in with you?"

"That's what I've planned to do, and he seems to think it's about the best thing he knows."

"Well, that's great, Bob! I wish I had a son to come in and lift the burden off my shoulders. But now, how about this Saxon fellow? If he's down there and my girl's gone down, I suppose I'll have to begin to worry about him. What's he doing down there this time of year anyway? Did the sister or whoever she is get sick and they couldn't come back north when everybody else did, or what?"

"Oh, they live down there I understand. They have an orange grove."

"You don't say? I don't see why anyone would stay so far south in the summer. What's the idea?"

"Well, I don't really know much about it, but I've surmised they couldn't afford to travel around and they've just settled there."

"What's the matter? Lost their money? What was it? Investment or Real Estate? Don't tell me they were Florida boom people!"

"Nothing of the kind, Sam, they never had any money to lose. As I understand it Saxon's father is a retired minister or doctor or something professional, I'm not sure just what. They're nice people, Jeff says. But you needn't worry about Mary Elizabeth. This young Saxon's poor as a church mouse and has his own way to make yet so he's out of the running so far as Mary Beth is concerned."

"I don't see why," said Mary Elizabeth's father, "not if she took a liking to him. She's not a gold digger, and after all she's got plenty of her own. But I'm not so sure

I wouldn't like him all the better for being poor. Money's what's spoiled most of the young men to-day. They've had too much of it, and they don't know what it means to have to get down to hard work and earn it the way you and I did. I guess it's a mistake to hand over a lot of money to your children before they've cut their eyeteeth. Your Jeff was an exception."

"Yes, Sam, our children are always exceptions. However, you're bearing me out in what I used to say long ago. Clarice always thought I kept Jeff on too small an allowance, but I felt with all that money coming to him from her father when Jeff would come of age, and all I would naturally leave him, he needed to get a little experience before he had the chance to handle it."

"Well, you certainly did a good job of bringing him up," said Jeff's uncle heartily, "and I guess I can trust Mary Elizabeth, too, to use good common sense. And don't you worry about Sammy. It'll do him good to be on his own a while. Anyway, you were going to send him to camp, what's the difference?"

"Yes, I suppose so," said the troubled father, "only Clarice makes such a fuss about airplanes, and if anything *should* happen she'd never let me hear the last of it."

"Well, nothing's going to happen. Just make up your mind to that, Brother. Get to sleep now and get a little rest and by the time you wake up it won't be long till a telegram comes. I suppose we're a couple of old fools!"

"What! Couldn't you sleep either?"

"No, blame it!" laughed Mary Elizabeth's father, "but I'm going to now. Good night!"

18

BOOTHBY Farwell was exceedingly gloomy and silent as his party went on its way in search of amusement. When he spoke at all he was so disagreeable that presently the rest refrained from speaking to him any more than they could help.

At the first opportunity to quench their thirst, which by the time they had driven for an hour had become almost unbearable, the entire party indulged freely, Farwell drinking more deeply than the rest. When they arrived at the fashionable hotel a hundred miles up the coast which was their rendezvous he drank again and often during the evening. Also, he annexed a young woman of his acquaintance, Stephanie Varrell by name, whose startling artificial beauty was only rivaled by her daring conduct, and the whole party had a very gay time indeed. But during it all, and while he paid for most of it, and was a participant in all their hilarity, he was morosely silent, glowering at them and answering only when he had to do so with caustic sentences that might have been written with a pen dipped in vitriol.

Now Boothby Farwell was not a man who easily gave

up. He had been wont to boast that he always got whatever he really went after. The only question in his mind was whether he really wanted to go after Mary Elizabeth enough to make the effort. There would be ways to get her, of course. He considered several, as he sat at tables with the gay group he was entertaining. There would be weak places in Mary Elizabeth's armor. If money would not buy her there were other ways. Her family was a great weakness of hers, the pride of race. Just how to get her through her family was not quite plain.

But the family standards—ah—conventions! Even though she was fairly broad-minded for the times, her family were great sticklers for the conventions. They were almost Victorian in some things. Suppose, now, that one could plan to get Mary Elizabeth off somewhere in a lonely situation where she would be compelled to stay all night in his company? Would it not be likely that Mary Elizabeth's father would urge immediate marriage?

But how to get her away, even after the plan was made? Mary Elizabeth was a young woman who knew her own mind and who did what she wished to do.

He drank a great deal that night, and when he finally piloted his gay and irresponsible party back to their homes again he was keyed up to almost any measure that would reduce Mary Elizabeth to his terms. The next day he studied his plan again and finally got into his high-powered car and drove back to Seacrest alone.

It wasn't conceivable that Elizabeth would refuse to see him, nor that she would not accept his apologies for anything that might have been done to annoy her yesterday. It could easily be blamed on some one else in his party. He would have no trouble in persuading her that everything disagreeable he had done had been because of his state of mind, because of his frustrated love for her. For after all Mary Elizabeth Wainwright was a gentle, kindly soul and did not like to hurt people. Perhaps he might even come to confessing a weakness or two, a little sentiment, which wasn't his natural line. It might even be that she was holding him off playing for something of this sort. He had been going with her for so long that perhaps she felt he had come to take things too much for granted. Well, he could give her sentiment, romance, if that was what she wanted. He knew how. He had had large practice in the past, before sentiment and romance walked hand in hand out of the picture of modern times.

As he drove along in the brightness of the morning he was making shrewd sinister plans. He would try romance, make violent, desperate love to her, and if that failed then he would be abject before her, touch her pity, until she would finally promise to go and take a last ride with him before he left for parts unknown to solace his broken heart.

Once get her in his car, and out of the town where people knew her, and his car would do the rest. He knew a lonely place where they could be stranded for the night while he pretended to work on his car.

The devilish scheme grew in his mind as he tore along the highway, bearing south and east, arriving at Seacrest an hour sooner than he had expected.

As he came in sight of the Wainwright estate, its tall plumy pines shut in by the handsome iron grille, he was reminded of the last time he had seen it, when he had had a vision of an imp of a boy in a bright red bathing suit striding down to the beach.

He was instantly on his guard, instinctively slowed down his speed, and considered. He must reconnoiter.

It would not do to come on that kid. He was uncanny. He would suspect something perhaps and make trouble!

So he traveled cautiously about the town, approaching the Wainwright place from different angles, but saw no sign of anybody about and the vista of the beach was free from bathers. No red bathing suit loomed on the prospect.

He had to ring at the entrance gate, however, as all the approaches to the house were firmly locked with formidable chains. It annoyed him to have to ring for entrance. He was full of impatience. Now that he was here he was anxious to carry out his plan at once. As he sat in his car awaiting admission he told himself he must proceed cautiously, with a friendly attitude as if nothing had annoyed him at their last meeting. Elizabeth had always been friendly enough if approached diplomatically. He must remember that and not lose his temper. But once get her married to him and he would break her will and stop her gay independence! He set his lips together in a thin, hard line, and a glitter came into his eyes. He was certainly going to enjoy breaking Elizabeth's will, and putting her through training, once he really had her fast!

But when Susan arrived a little hurriedly because of having waited to put on a clean apron, he learned that Elizabeth was not there.

"They've gone!" said Susan with perhaps a bit of satisfaction in her voice, for she recognized the man and the car, and she had not liked the man. She thought he was not a gentleman.

"Gone?" said Farwell blankly. "You mean she is out? When will she return?"

"No, sir, she's gone away. I couldn't say when she's coming back. She said she'd let me know."

"When did she go?"

"Night before last."

"Oh! You mean she has gone back to the city, to her home?" What a fool he had been not to try her home first. Of course she wouldn't be likely to stay long in a little backwoods place like this.

"I couldn't say, sir," said the well-trained servant. "She didn't tell me her plans. She just went away and said she would let me know when she was coming back."

"Well, surely you know whether she is likely to come soon."

"She might and then again she mightn't, she didn't say."

"That seems very strange," said the man giving her an ugly look. "I suppose you are holding out for money, but I'd have you to understand that I shall report this to Miss Wainwright. Perhaps you do not know that I am going to marry her. But here, take this, and give me her present whereabouts, or her address or something, or it will go hard with you later."

Susan drew back from the offered bill, and her chin went up angrily. She stepped back inside the gate and closed it with a click, letting down the bar that held it from intruders.

"I've no address to give you, and I don't want your money, no matter who you are. I know my duty and I'm doing it. I'm earning my money. I don't take it in bribes. I have nothing more to tell you!" And Susan, tossing her head, walked indignantly away from the gate, and no amount of subsequent ringing of the gate bell could induce her to make her appearance again.

At last the man who always got his way turned his car toward the microscopic town of Seacrest and invaded the post office, confident that money would give him the lady's present address. She must have left word to have her mail forwarded.

But he discovered to his amazement that here was at least one honest servant of the government, for the little, round, sturdy postmaster shook his head.

"Can't do it, sir, it's against the law. If you wantta leave a letter here with her name on it I'll address it and forward it to her, but the law says I can't give out addresses."

He tried more money but the government official remained obdurate and at last Boothby Farwell shook the dust of Seacrest from his feet and departed at high speed for the city.

In the early evening, having attired himself for an evening call he arrived at the Wainwright home. But the butler said Mr. Wainwright had gone to New York and Miss Wainwright was away somewhere. When he pressed the old servant for more explicit directions, the old housekeeper was called upon and vouchsafed her young lady was spending the summer at Seacrest.

When Farwell said he had been to Seacrest and that she had left there, she shook her head.

"She's down in Florida somewhere visiting a sick friend," she said, "but I don't know the address. She had her cousin Sammy with her. Mebbe Mr. Robert Wainwright would know."

So, growing angrier and angrier, Boothby Farwell drove over to Robert Wainwright's home and rang the bell with vigor.

The second maid who answered the bell didn't know anything about the young master Sam's whereabouts and while she went to ask, Farwell lingered in the hall tramping impatiently up and down. Suddenly his eye was caught by a pile of letters on the hall table and right on the top was one addressed to Master Samuel Wainwright care of Dr. John Saxon, with a Florida address.

Farwell whipped out his note book and jotted it down before the maid's tardy return with word that nobody knew anything about young Sam, and got himself out of the house with brief courtesy.

His car shot out down the street toward his own apartments. Arrived there he sent for his chauffeur and gave orders that the car should be looked over and conditioned for a long drive, sent for his man, and finding him gone for the evening, himself filled a bag with a few necessities, scribbled a few directions, called up a few people and excused himself from a few engagements, and inside of two hours was on his way on the highway, under a brilliant moon, his car headed toward the south. As he rode he made his plans, definite, detailed and devilish. Little gadabout! Playing fast and loose with him! She needn't think she could escape him this way! He would get her, and get her good and fast.

He thought of her happy eyes with that starry look in them in which he had no part. It galled him to think that she could exist so easily without him. She was playing with a high hand, and thinking likely to bring him to her feet in utter subjection at last, but she would never do that! He would conquer her. And when he did he would take it out of her for every bit of trouble he had taken to find her and bind her.

Bind her! That's what he would do! Bind her and show her who was her master!

In the night, in the moonlight, as he shot southward, his eyes glittered with a baleful light. He was planning how he would woo her with something more deadly than diamonds. He would woo her and make her pay an hundred fold for all she was doing to him now. She had dared to put some other one's trifling interests above his, running away again from the honor he would have put upon her. No girl in her senses would really intend to do that permanently of course. She was just enjoying the game of tantalizing him. And this was now the third time she had done it. Once she had run to Paris with her father, once to Egypt with a party of friends. Now she was running to Florida in summer time on pretense of seeking a friend! A friend in Florida in summertime! How absurd!

And he would catch her, and carry her off, and make her pay, pay, pay!

And so, a Nemesis, he rushed on through the night!

19

A HOT, hot morning in Florida with a burning blue serene sky, relentlessly bright and hot after the blessed coolness of the night.

The sun looked down unflinchingly upon its ally the white, white sand, that burned back smilingly from every white hot particle of sharpness and radiated the shimmering heat waves which rose from the earth in visible quavering wreaths.

The long, gray moss hung straight and limp like an outworn, ancient garment, not a quiver of breeze to disturb its ghostly draperies. The orange trees only stood shining and bright in their glossy foliage, a few golden discs left from the winter work, a stray gracious blossom here and there filling the air with heavy musky sweetness, the hot, shimmering, still air.

Out in the town that in winter had been so gay and sumptuous, tall palatial buildings with hot red tiled roofs and picture palms towering above them stood with closed eyes, a dead place with all its gaiety fled. A wide, bright, lonely ocean stretching away to emptiness lay beyond.

Out in the empty streets where few humans remained to walk, little shadowy lizards slithered, and paused at the approach of any, to turn to background, motionless till the interloper passed. Out beyond the town to isolated little bungalows among the orange groves, narrow board walks, hot and strangely resonant, spanned the sand, and more little lizards scuttled in and out the wide cracks between the narrow boards so much like ladders set on stilts. Little blue chameleons lay basking on hot fences or neatly stacked piles of wood, their little white vests palpitating as they surveyed an interloper with their mild, intelligent, bright eyes, pretending by their very stillness to be only a bit of the fence, or the woodpile, changing their color imperceptibly to that of their resting place.

Not a cloud in the sky and yet before an hour it might rain a downpour, as if the very floor of heaven were drawn out to let fall a solid chunk of water that would cease as suddenly as it came and cause the steam to arise from all the blazing points of hot, white sand and hurry back to the clouds again, to get ready for the next downpour. It is a game they play, the clouds and the sun, in this hot, bright, intermittent, rainy season. Another hot, hot day like those intolerable ones that have preceded it! If it were not for the blessed coolness of the night it would be unbearable.

John Saxon came to the door and stared out at the bright shimmer of the world. His face looked old with anxiety, worn with weariness. It somehow seemed that strong and young though he was he had reached the limit. His eyes were too heavy to stay open. He turned and stepped back into the room and dropped into a chair, his head in his hands, his elbows on his knees. Tears stung into his eyes. Must he give up the fight with death, give up because he was not able of himself to cope with the disease? He groaned within himself.

"God, it is not that I will not give her up if You want to take her. It is that I must see her suffer when I know that she could be relieved if I only had the skill. Oh, God! Must she go this way?"

His soul was filled with anguish! Father, too, suffering deeply and unable to get about and help! It seemed as if everything had come upon them at once. The hard winter and the small crop of oranges, smaller of course because they had not had the money to put into fertilizers and cultivation for the grove. His father working too hard always! He recalled how he had found his father in the grove, nearly fainting with the pain of his broken ankle; how he discovered that the laborer who had been hired had failed them, and there seemed no other available, so his father had been going out as soon as it was light, and working without breakfast, because he feared to wake Mother if he stopped to eat, also Mother would have protested against his hard work. Mother and Father, saving and scrimping without his knowledge that he might have the more to pursue his studies! Oh, it was all a confused tangle! Perhaps he ought never to have tried to study medicine. Perhaps he should have stayed at home and cared for them and spent his days in cultivating oranges.

Yet they had wanted him to go into a profession, had urged and begged him to go! And everything had seemed so well planned. To make good with the great specialist would mean that in another year or so he would be earning enough to give his Father and Mother luxuries!

Ah! but he had not reckoned with sickness, and threatened Death.

All night long he had sat by his mother's bedside

giving her medicine faithfully, watching her pulse, her temperature, seeing the frail, delicate features drawn with terrible pain at increasingly frequent intervals. Frantically he had telephoned to doctors he knew in the north, not even counting the expense of long distance, searching here and there to locate someone to advise with him, and failure had been written on every attempt but one, and that one a fading hope, a last resort. All the others he had tried had been away where he could not trace them. This one he had little faith in, yet he dared not go another night through without advice. And this doctor had given him little hope, corroborating his own fears, suggesting a remedy that might ease the pain, but giving an impression of indifference toward the case, as if he had said, "Oh, well, she's old. It's time she died. Why bother?"

Yet John Saxon had telephoned for the medicine and when it came had given it faithfully, hanging on to the last shred of hope, yet knowing that the frail sweet mother was growing momently weaker. He suspected that the medicine was merely doping the patient, dulling her pain somewhat. He was fearful that she might slip away from them in a stupor now at any moment.

His father was still asleep, worn out with anxiety and pain. John Saxon had come away from his vigil by his mother's bed to get a breath of air, lest he fall asleep at his post, and now here he was sinking down in his chair, too tired for even the tears to heal the smarting of his eyes. Too tired and sore-hearted to even think.

Into the open doorway stole the sweet spicy odor of the orange blossoms from the trees about the house, just a faint little breeze stirring the hotness of their waxen petals, lifting a burnished leaf or two here and there, rustling the great banana leaves at the back of the house like the sound of silken skirts on ladies near at hand.

Silken skirts and orange blossoms! How that brought back the sweet, sharp memory of the wedding, and the girl coming with graceful tread up the aisle, looking at him with that glad, clean look in her eyes, the girl of his dreams! And how like a fool he had rushed out to secure her at once without even lifting a questioning eye to his Guide. He had dared to tell her of his love, without guidance, so sure he knew she was a Christian girl! And now—to find her a woman of the world, the world from which he stood pledged to live a separated life!

Ah! God! Was all this trouble, this fight with death for the saving of his precious mother, to show him that he must not try to walk alone and guide himself?

The heavy delicacy of the perfume stole upon his weary senses and brought a dream, flung it about him as if it were her arms, the perfume of her hair, the beauty of her features, her face against him. The thrill of her lips on his came over him with crushing sweetness. In fancy he let his face lie there against her sweet breast an instant, resting from his fearful weariness, drifting unconsciously into momentary sleep.

Outside the perfume drifted back stirred by honey seekers, and the drone of bees mingled with the distant caw of vultures hurrying in search of prey. The gray moss waved majestically, now and then a mocking bird struck a raucous note, the little chameleons skittered under and over the narrow resonant board walk, and John Saxon slept.

Slept and dreamed of walking down a church aisle with a wonderful girl beside him, breathed words of love hot from his heart into her listening ear, felt her small hand tremble on his arm, saw again the starry look she gave him, the breath of the orange blossoms, oh, how sweet it was, the drone of the bees like a lullaby! Her arms were about him, and he murmured in his sleep, "Mary Elizabeth! *My* darling!" and that woke him up!

Startled he lifted his bloodshot eyes and looked about the familiar plain little room so eloquent of home and mother and father. He rubbed the sleep out of his eyes and tried to get his feet down to earth. Then all his burdens descended upon him again. His mother! How long had he been asleep?

He sprang to his feet and stepped softly into the bedroom. There was no change! He turned from the precious fragile face, so like to a fading flower, and felt again the stab of pain. A glance at his watch showed it to have been but a very few minutes since he had come out to get a breath of air, and yet in that time she seemed to have drifted farther away. It was no use! He had tried everything and nothing helped!

He glanced over at his father, still asleep, and thought pityingly of how it was going to be for him if Mother went. He too was frail. Yet always so gallant! Such a pair of saints for parents! How blest he had been! What was poverty and sickness beside the loss of these dear souls? And he could do no more! If only there had been time for him to order medicines! His stock was so small and did not contain many drugs that might have at least helped! Oh, why had he run this risk for his precious mother? Why hadn't he been sure to have everything on hand that might be needed, here in this wilderness home, when everything within hailing distance was closed for the summer.

Ah, that was the trouble with his mother. She had spent too many long hot summers in this forsaken place. She had been happy, yes, and had never complained, but she ought to have gone north and had a change of climate, at least every other year. This tropical climate invariably got every northerner who did not have a change now and then.

He had seen it coming. He had noticed her growing frailer, saw how easily she tired, and he had said more than once that she ought to go north for a change, but she had always smiled and shaken her head and declared she was all right. She had always said she would wait till he was done with his studies, and then they would save money and go north for a summer together. Lately, just since he had come back from the wedding and had been telling them all about it, she had said:

"We'll go north for your wedding perhaps!"

And now—*and now*—!

His thoughts trailed off into sorrow, and tears filled his eyes again. He was all in! He must get another wink of sleep somehow or he wouldn't be fit to go on nursing. A glance at his watch showed there was still fifteen minutes before he must give the medicine again. Now while they were both sleeping he would just stretch out for a minute.

The couch had been put in the bedroom for his father, so that he and his dear companion need not be separated. John's own room was in the second story. He would not go so far away. He flung the cushion from a chair on the floor and lay down there. The perfume of the orange blossoms drifted in and wove their spell again, and the droning of the bees in the blossoms hummed with the music of his dreams. He slept instantly and profoundly, tired brain and weary body refusing even the golden walk down the aisle with Mary Elizabeth. Some severe sub-conscious conscience told him this was no time to dream dreams, while his mother lay a-dying! He had need for every faculty, and he must rest if only for a minute.

Yet perhaps the perfume and the memories were still

at work within that sleeping mind, for sharply he came to himself a little later, aware that the bees' humming was extraordinarily loud, they seemed to be coming toward the house in a body, they were almost at the door.

He sprang into action. It was time to give that medicine! Alertly he paused to listen. Those bees! He had never heard such humming! Was he still dreaming? He must not go to the sickroom until he was wide awake. He might make some mistake.

He stepped to the door and the humming increased and drew nearer. Lifting his heavy eyes he stared in amazement. Was he seeing things? Was he losing his mind? Surely just loss of sleep wouldn't do that!

He pressed his hands on his eyeballs and looked again. It seemed a great bird was flying low and coming straight toward him, and the sound was like the droning of millions of great bees.

And then all at once he was thoroughly awake and saw what it was, a great plane, flying low and evidently going to land on that big open space across the road that he had just finished clearing of stumps for his new grove before he went north to the wedding.

What in the world were they trying to land there for? Were they in trouble, had something gone wrong with the motor? He frowned. He couldn't go out and help them now. He couldn't leave the house. And they would make a noise and disturb his mother! Even just coming to the door to telephone for help they would make a noise. What should he do? He couldn't refuse help—yet—he couldn't have his patient disturbed. There was scarcely a shred of hope left, yet he couldn't give up that shred!

Mutely, anxiously he watched the plane, hoping against hope that it would go on. There really wasn't any place nearby where they could get a mechanic, if they didn't have one of their own. There were no supply shops. There wasn't even a gas station if they were out of gas.

Yet against his wish the plane came on, nearer and nearer, lower and lower, and now he could see that it was as big as the passenger planes that went overhead in the winter when the town was full of tourists. What could such a plane be doing here? Surely a man who could operate a plane like that would realize at this time of year that this locality was as barren of help as a wilderness! He must be in terrible straits to land here! Yes, he was unmistakably trying to land, circling about, reconnoitering, and the roar of the powerful engine was terrible in the hot bright stillness. It might frighten his mother if she woke from her stupor! If there were only some signal he could give them to go on! If he could only prevent them from landing there! He was frantic and helpless! It was not like the calm strength of John Saxon to be so unnerved, but the truth was he had had only snatches of sleep for the last four days, and he was appalled at the new danger that seemed threatening his patient.

Suddenly the engine was shut off and the plane drifted to a standstill exactly opposite the little house in the orange grove, in a direct line with the front door and the neat path of Bermuda grass that went down like a carpet to the white wooden gate. And then, as he watched, a person detached himself from the plane and came on a run toward the house, and he had a dim impression of others disembarking. He must do something about this at once. They must not be allowed to come to the house and make a lot of noise. Several people talking! It must not be! He would tell them there was critical illness here, and they must go on, even if he had to lend them his old flivver to go in.

He tried to think where to send them. It was five miles to a garage where any sort of mechanic could be found, or even makeshift parts of machinery. There was a new man over at the Lake, but he knew nothing of his ability. Still it was only a mile and a half away. Perhaps they could telephone for help. No, he must not let a lot of people come in to telephone. His mother would be startled.

He started down the path to meet the approaching boy, his hand up to hush him to silence should he start explaining in a shout.

But this boy did not shout. He came silently, with shining eyes and a solemn face as if he were performing angels' duty. And he came as if he were answering a far desperate call.

It was when John Saxon reached the little white gate and swung it open to stop the progress of his unexpected guest that he recognized the boy, and stopped short in wonder and astonishment and a growing relief. Here at last was someone he knew, someone who would understand, even though he was but a boy. Someone who could run errands if he could not do anything else! And John Saxon swung out into the road and grasped the hand of the prayer partner who had arrived so suddenly out of the blue.

"Sam! Dear lad!" he managed to say in a husky voice, and with a tone that one man might use to another deeply beloved.

"How is she?" Sam asked breathlessly. "Is she alive yet? 'Cause I got yer doctor and a nurse! They're right behind me! Did we get here in time? We started as soon as we could after the letter came."

"You've got a doctor?" John Saxon eyed the boy in

joyful wonder. Almost any doctor would be a help when he had had to go on his own so long, tortured with uncertainty, and mortally aware of his own inexperience.

"Yer own doctor! Doctor MacKelvie! Dr. Martin MacKelvie!" said Sam proudly, mindful not to let his voice rise. Both the doctor and the nurse and the two cousins had warned Sam about this. He must be utterly aware that he was in the presence of great danger. He must not startle a sick person.

John Saxon put his hands on the shoulders of the boy and looked deeply into the young eyes, and his own eyes were full of tears.

"Kid!" he said. "Oh, *kid!* I'll never forget this! It's a miracle! How you ever did it I can't understand, but thank God you've come!"

20

WHEN Mary Elizabeth awoke the morning after they set sail in the air all the world was roseate with an opal sea. Clouds like lovely pastel draperies were floating intimately and the earth showed below quite empty of human life.

And then it all came over Mary Elizabeth just what she was doing and she was appalled at herself. How did she know that her ministrations would be welcome? How did she know that they would not be resented as unwarranted interference? Just because the doctor and the nurse had assented to going, even a great doctor like the one she had secured, just because her father and her uncle had made no serious objection, and her cousin Richie was piloting his most commodious plane in his best and swiftest style was no warrant that John Saxon might not be angry at what she was doing.

After all, John Saxon was a stranger, an utter stranger, and the letter he had written her days and days ago, the contact she had had from him, might be repented of by this time, or forgotten. He might be angry that she had not replied to it sooner.

And now she was sorry that she had written so soon. It would be easier to face him, not having replied so frankly to him yet, than to go down there nosing into his affairs, daring to bring a nurse and doctor without his knowing it, and remember that she had told him baldly that she loved him. Him! An utter stranger! She must have lost her head!

She remembered how jubilant she had been last night when each step of the way had been accomplished so easily. She might have known it was all too easy. There would be a hitch in her plans somewhere. Either John Saxon would have telegraphed for another doctor and he was already there, and his mother better, or she might have passed away even before their expedition of relief had started. In either case how flat she would feel to arrive under such circumstances.

How clearly she saw that she should have wired her intention, or asked for permission, or at least sent him word they were on the way! Yet just as clearly she had thought last night that it would be better to come as an entire surprise. She had instinctively felt that he would never allow her to come if he knew beforehand, and she would never forgive herself if his mother died and she had done nothing to save her.

She went through an embarrassing dialogue between Dr. MacKelvie and the possible other doctor John Saxon might have secured. She met a withering glance from the keen MacKelvie Scotch blue eyes that she knew by instinct could glitter like steel when reproving. And how she would hate being disapproved of by him whom she had already begun to like, possibly just because she knew John Saxon liked him.

Then she took up that other possibility of Death having arrived before them. In that event she would be questioned. There had been little time so far, and she had to remember that the approval of doctor, father, uncle and cousin had all been given without a sufficient knowledge of the facts. She fairly cringed when she remembered that.

Suppose for instance that they knew that her sole connection with the sick woman whom she had turned heaven and earth to rescue was through a son whom she had never seen but once and who had proposed marriage on the way down the aisle at a church wedding? "Unwarranted interference" that is what her father would say, and her uncle would ask "What is HE to Mary Beth?" She could hear him now. She could almost hear the disapproval of Aunt Clarice's tone even from the mountains afar, when she heard about it. Not that anybody who knew would mean to tell her, but Aunt Clarice always heard about everything.

Suppose they knew she had written him a shameless letter telling him she loved him, when she hadn't known him but a few hours? Suppose they knew that she'd never even laid eyes on the sick woman for whom she was taking this wild extravagant trip?

Mary Elizabeth shut her eyes on the roseate and opal world below her and let these things roll over her. Yielded her thoughts to the prospect of the morning when she should arrive before this unknown lover not knowing how he had taken her letter. This lover who knew God so well, and lived in a world of spiritual things that she could not even understand.

And then panic took her. She could never, never be present at that arrival. She must not be part of the picture. Her presence would only bring mortification and misunderstanding to John Saxon. And certainly to herself! Before this strange doctor who knew John Saxon, and who thought of her—what did he think?

Before this unfamiliar nurse with her gray hair and keen eyes who doubtless had her thoughts also.

She arose precipitately and went forth to prepare her plans. She must get hold of Sam and wake him up and have a talk with him. Sam was her biggest asset. Sam believed in her and would do as she said. He would be true and keep his mouth shut. A pity to wake him up so soon but better to get the matter settled between them before others awoke and took a hand in making plans. This was her party and she meant to manage it.

But she discovered that Sam was up and wide awake, as perky as a robin. Sam was not missing a single rose nor opal of the world below him. Sam was looking down and his eyes were full of wonder and deep satisfaction, and also a kind of queer boy peace. But when she thought about it a second time she thought his eyes seemed as if he were praying, right out there in the clouds, watching God's wonderful waking world below him!

She conveyed to the boy her idea of arrival, that he should be the first to announce their approach. His eyes assented understandingly.

"And you'll make it appear that this was your expedition, because it would hurt him otherwise?"

"Oh, sure!" said the boy, like an experienced accomplice.

"And you won't say a word about me?"

Sam gave her a quick, startled look.

"Aren't you going to be there? Aren't you coming with us? I thought you were coming with us, Mary Beth! You *are* with us! You can't go back on that!"

"Oh, of course, but I'm going to keep in the background. It may not be necessary for me to go to the house. The more people there are the more embarrassing it will be for your Mr. Saxon."

He thought about this a minute and then he said, fixing her with troubled searching eyes:

"You'll come when it is necessary. You'd come then right away, Mary Beth?"

"Oh, of course," she promised easily. "If I am needed for anything."

"You'll be needed."

"Well, you'll remember what I said and keep me out of it if possible? I did this—for you—you know."

"Okay!" said Sam sturdily, and she knew he would.

And afterwards she had a talk with her grave gray-haired cousin Richie.

"I think it would be better if you were just to stop in the town and drop me off, Cousin Richie," she said. "I can be looking up accommodations for us all and hire a taxi or car to drive back and forth with."

Her cousin studied her silently a minute.

"What's the idea, Bess? Somebody you're afraid of? It isn't like you to get up an expedition and then cut and run and leave the whole business on your poor henchmen."

Mary Elizabeth colored up rosily in spite of herself and then was vexed.

"Not at all, Cousin Richie. I thought you would think that plan eminently sensible and showing foresight."

"On the contrary, it looks to me as if you were losing your perspective, and forgetting the main object of the flight, which is to save a life as I understand it. I've just been talking with your eminent doctor and I find he is anxious to lose not one more minute than is necessary. He evidently has some suspicions as to the nature of the trouble and he feels that time is a big factor. I think we'll just drop down there by the house as quick as we can."

"Oh!" said Mary Elizabeth with a sudden fright in her eyes. "Of course! I didn't realize!"

"And besides, Mary Bess, we've slept in this old ship one night, can't we stand a few more nights if necessary, to save a life? Speaking of foresight, I stocked up with eatables to last several days. We carry our hotel with us, remember, and if you ask me, I think you'll find it about the only stopping place open around our destination. This is summer, lady, and hotels have mostly moved north."

"Oh!" said Mary Elizabeth a trifle appalled. "Of course!"

Then she was still for some time trying to adjust her mind and her plans and her panicky state to this new point of view.

"I've been talking with the kid," went on her cousin. "He says there's a vacant field across the road from the house large enough he thinks for landing. I think we'll make for that."

"Yes!" said Mary Elizabeth, wondering what had become of her poise.

She looked up and assented to her cousin's plans, and managed her usual smile, but the fact remained that she was just plain scared at the whole thing.

It was not until the doctor came to her and began to ask questions again about how much she knew of the case and the circumstances, that she got her self-control back, and forced her thoughts into sensible every day grooves. This was just an emergency in which she was trying to save a life and she must not think of anything else. Romance and all that must be put aside. She must strain every nerve to help answer the prayer that Sam had made for John Saxon's mother!

Then the doctor looked her in the eye.

"If this is a case for operating," he said, searching her

face, "have you the nerve to help the nurse? I may need several hands to work quickly. Our pilot here has already offered himself. It may not be necessary, but can I rely on you if I have to?"

"Of course," she said simply.

"Ever present at an operation?" He was still searching her face.

"No," she said, feeling very ignorant and useless.

"Lose your nerve easily? Faint at the sight of blood?"

"Oh, no!" said Mary Elizabeth earnestly, realizing that it was only the sight of a certain young man who could make her lose her nerve. And she never remembered to have felt this panicky way before.

"All right, you be ready then if I call on you," he said, and began to instruct her in the common rudiments of being sanitarily ready to enter an operating room.

Then Mary Elizabeth ceased thinking about herself and her own emotions, and was filled with awe over the courage it must take to cut into a human life, even in order to try and save it. All the rest of the way she was thinking about that mother lying there dying with her desperate doctor-son doing his best to save her, until she wanted to cry out to the plane to go faster, and she tried to look down and count the miles as they sped on.

It was Mary Elizabeth who first began to notice the tropical trees, the tall pines with their draperies of moss, the palmettos turning their fanned spikes to heaven, the groves of dark glossy orange and grapefruit trees.

But it was Sam who finally guided the pilot to that wide vacant space, cleared of logs and stumps and offering no hindrance to landing.

The nurse had not spoken often. She was old in experience. Many words were not needed to adjust her to a given set of circumstances. That was why Dr. MacKelvie brought her on emergency cases, instead of a younger nurse. She asked Mary Elizabeth a few questions about the case, and when she found how little she really knew she just smiled gravely and said, "Oh, well, we'll find out when we get there."

But she was a woman of skill and courage and adaptability, one could easily see at a glance, and Mary Elizabeth liked her. She gave one a restful feeling of trust and assurance.

Sam recognized landmarks long before Mary Elizabeth did, though she had often been to that same beach, but never out in the direction of the Saxon home.

Gravely the boy sat beside the pilot and pointed out the way to go, and at last the great bird glided down and came to rest.

Sam did not need to be told when to get out. At the first possible moment his feet touched the ground and he started on a run. The doctor was not far behind, with his leather case, leaving the nurse to follow. These two, the nurse and doctor, were intent only on the case for which they had come. They did not look about them, nor apparently have a thought beyond the immediate danger they had come to meet, the life they had come, if possible, to save, and they hurried to the house exactly as if they had been there before and knew every inch of the way.

But Mary Elizabeth lingered, for she suddenly saw John Saxon standing by his gate, the crisp curls of his hair standing awry, his shirt open at the neck, his sleeves rolled up, a rumpled look about his garments and a haggard look upon his dear face so different from the handsome lover who had walked beside her down that aisle.

But suddenly she knew she was glad that she had come. She would not have stayed away for anything in life, not for fear of shame nor scorning. She would have come just to help him whether he wanted it or not. The fact that he needed it justified anything she had done.

Cousin Richie came behind her as she hesitated and helped her from the plane and together they walked over to the house, gravely, in silence. She was glad he did not talk to her. She thought that after this was over if there was anything left of her, she would make him know how wonderful he had been. But now her eyes were on the tall man standing at the gate, the man with weary eyes and lines about his mouth, lines of suffering. How dear, preciously dear he was to her! It was almost unbelievable that a stranger could in such a short time have become so dear.

He had not seen her yet. He was all taken up with the surprise of meeting his old professor. She could hear the ring of his voice, the very eagerness in this clear, silent atmosphere, even though she could tell his voice was hushed for the sick room near at hand. Yet in spite of that she could hear his words.

"This is great of you to come, Dr. Mac! If I had known where to find you at this time of year I wouldn't have dared ask!—" and then the two turned and took great strides across the road and into the house, their voices dropping lower, gravely speaking of the case, but the words could no longer be heard.

She was almost glad he had not seen her, though her heart was crying out hungrily for just one glance. She continued to walk slowly across the road beside her cousin, aware that he was watching her keenly and wondering about the good-looking giant who hadn't even seen her. She struggled to regain what she called her poise, looking with tender eyes toward the plain little house, that had yet so much atmosphere of home about it. She was taking in the beauty of the setting among the glossy dark trees, breathing the perfume of the hidden blossoms, getting glimpses of golden fruit. But most of all she was feeling the peace that seemed to hover over the place, even though the shadow of death might be approaching. She had a feeling that the inmates of that home were all ready for it if it should come, and would accept the sorrow that it might bring in sweetness and courage. How was it that she seemed to know so much about this stranger-lover and his family? Did love give one new perceptions?

They had reached the open door of the house now and were glancing hesitantly within.

The big cool room with its cheap, white muslin curtains, its comfortable but shabby chairs, its home-made book shelves filled with rows and rows of books, running all about the room wherever there was space, was most inviting, everything in perfect order, though the mistress of the house was laid low. John had kept it that way. There could not be many servants available, she knew, even if he had not stated in his letter that he was housemaid, nurse and doctor in one, for Mary Elizabeth had noticed as they were coming down that there were no houses, nor even shanties for any servant to come from, any nearer than the village. With appreciative eyes she took in the few bits of ornaments, the one fine picture, the photographs. There was culture and taste here. But of course she had known there would be. Her eyes were only corroborating what her heart had told her.

Hesitantly they lingered at the doorway, Mary Elizabeth and her cousin Richie, anxious eyes fixed on the open door where they could dimly see the outlines of a white bed. The doctor and nurse and John Saxon had gone in there and were consulting.

Cousin Richie had dropped upon a chair by the door, a straight chair, alertly as if he were ready for immediate action if it were needed. Mary Elizabeth gave him a grateful glance. It was as if he were an old friend of the family and understood. She noticed suddenly the dependable dear look about Cousin Richie. Of course he was a noted flier and had his name and picture in the papers all the time, and she was entirely familiar with his genial smile and his keen eyes and weathered face, but she hadn't noticed before that dependable look, that tenderness about his lips, that was usually masked in his merry smile. She was used to him probably, and of course it must have been there all the time and that was why she had turned to him instinctively when she needed the plane. Sometime she would tell him how he had made her feel. But now she was just grateful. She felt as if this was a sacred moment, while she was looking about for the first time upon the home of her stranger-lover.

Sam was standing out at the back door, having gone around the house to the pump he knew so well of old, to get himself a drink of "real water," he told her afterwards, but in reality to recover from his own emotions, and to get through the period of waiting for the doctor's verdict, into the time of action that would be sure to come afterwards. He stood there in front of a big banana tree, his profile outlined clearly against it, his eyes so grown-up and serious and his lips set in trembling determination, as if he had suddenly been required to take his place as a man, and he wasn't quite equal to it. As if this time of anxiety for his beloved friend were just too much for him.

Behind him the great banana leaves rustled and flapped like softly rustling taffeta skirts. Beyond him the long gray moss on a tall pine stirred slowly in the still air.

Mary Elizabeth, sitting in the same chair where John Saxon had dreamed of her but a few minutes before, felt the spicy air, heard the drone of the bees, and heard the marvelous stillness, such stillness as she had never experienced before, but kept her ears attuned to what might be going on in that inner room. Had they arrived too late, and was she already gone? It was strange that so many people could be in a room together and be so quiet about it. Her heart stood still with fear.

Then after a long, long waiting, when it seemed as if even the moss on the pine out beyond the window did not move, nor the banana leaves in the hot morning, when Sam's profile seemed a bronze statue, and even the bees ceased humming, the nurse came forth from the room as silently as a moving picture might have done and stood before them looking at them uncertainly.

"She's still living, but she's a very sick woman!" she said in her lowest professional tone, a tone that gave the words distinctly, yet left no sound over to echo beyond their own ears. "The doctor's going to try to operate, I think. The difficulty is the lack of proper light of course. But we've got to bring her husband out. He mustn't be in there of course. He's very frail! I'll get him into a dressing gown. He can walk with help. He just has a broken bone in his ankle. I wonder which chair we'd better put him in?" She gave the room a quick survey.

"I guess that's my job," said Cousin Richie smiling. "You fix him up and I'll bring him out. How about this chair? And those cushions will help prop up the foot. I know. I've had one. And I guess I can rig up a light. I have plenty of equipment in the plane."

"Oh, that's right," said the nurse relieved. "I'll tell them."

Then she paused before Mary Elizabeth who was listening mutely for something she could do. She felt so utterly left out.

"I wonder if you could fix a tray for the old man? Can

you make coffee?" She spoke as if she did not expect her to say she could. But Mary Elizabeth brightened.

"Oh, yes," she answered. "I used to make it a great deal in college. I had a percolator with me."

"There may not be any percolator!" remarked the nurse dryly. She had an idea that this daughter of a millionaire knew very little about real life. "Well, do your best. The doctor needs me. I must get some hot water going at once!"

Mary Elizabeth vanished softly through the door that obviously opened into the kitchen.

"Sam," she called softly, taking pity on the boy's dejected attitude, "come and help me, but don't make any noise."

The bronze statue came promptly and gratefully to life. He slipped off his shoes and entered the kitchen.

"What to do?" he asked alertly.

"We're getting a tray for Mr. Saxon's father. You'll have to help me find things."

"Okay!" said the boy, "I know where everything is. I been here a lot, ya know. Whatcha want?"

"Well, a coffee percolator if there is one."

"Sure there is. A toaster, too. They keep 'em here on this cabinet shelf."

He swung open a door and produced an up-to-date electric percolator. Mary Elizabeth seized upon it eagerly. She was exceedingly doubtful about her ability to make good coffee in any other utensil than an electric percolator. To achieve a tray for that cold-eyed nurse to pass upon was another thing that troubled her.

But she was reckoning without the knowledge of what an experienced helper she had called to her aid. She did not realize that her young cousin Sam was a far more seasoned cook than herself.

"The coffee's in that stone jar!" announced the assistant cook. "Ya put a heaper ta each cup, dontcha? And one fer the pot. That's what we did on the scout camp trip. The measuring spoon is in that drawer. There's the tray on that shelf. Better make enough fer our Mr. Saxon too, hadn't we? He looked as if he needed it. Though it's a gamble if he stops ta drink it if there's anything else he oughtta do."

Mary Elizabeth's cheeks flamed at the pronoun "our" but she assented.

"The napkins and the silver are in the dresser drawer in the other room. I'll get 'em!"

Sam dashed silently into the front room and returned with everything needful for a tray, and Mary Elizabeth's opinion of her own ability shrank perceptibly. How her education had been neglected!

Sam got out the toaster, produced two slices of bread, also the eggs. He volunteered to poach an egg for Father Saxon.

Between them in a very short time a tray was ready.

The nurse coming in to see if her big kettles of water were hot looked askance at the boy, and then gave an admiring glance at the tray. She couldn't have done it better herself, though she couldn't conceive why the young woman let a kid like that bother around her in the kitchen at a time like this. But when Sam, keeping a weather eye out for affairs in the other room, came silently in with the tray, carrying it carefully as any woman could, her grim disapproval relaxed. Sam could be quiet even if he was a boy, and he could carry a tray without slopping the coffee into the saucer. Neither was anything missing from that tray, salt, pepper, sugar, cream, spoons, butter, delicate toast. She gave up the idea of keeping half her mind in the kitchen during this campaign and put it on the operation. Perhaps this wasn't going to be so bad after all.

So Mary Elizabeth remained in the kitchen looking over her own possibilities and the supplies with a view to getting more meals later when they should be needed. Of course it had been arranged that the guests should eat and sleep in the plane, so far as possible, but there would be individual meals here at times, and she was the obvious one to look after them. How she wished she knew more about cooking! She could make delectable fudge over a gas hot plate, could brew a cup of delicious chocolate, fluffy with whipped cream, or coffee of just the right shade of amber, and she could scramble eggs to perfection on an electric grill, or mix a salad that a famous chef might have envied. But after that her culinary knowledge failed.

A glance into the bread box showed little more than half a loaf, and that of a texture which she judged to be homemade, for it looked wonderful, even if it was a trifle dry. Didn't they have baker's bread delivered daily out here? She stood aghast. How did people live afar from civilization?

Suddenly she perceived another wide gulf of separation between herself and the man she had so unwittingly come to love. She simply did not know anything of the life in which he had always lived. Neither spiritually nor materially was she in the least fitted to be his mate. For dimly she perceived that a man like this would go anywhere, do anything, answer any call that Duty made, unhampered by the limits of civilization. Could she adjust herself to that way of life? Could she ever learn all the things she would need to know in order to be fitted for any environment? The idea appalled her, yet intrigued.

Quietly she went about planning some kind of lunch for whoever would eat lunch in the disorganized household. Investigation of the store closet showed several rows of cans, canned vegetables and soups. A large porous earthenware covered tureen wrapped in a wet cloth, standing on a shelf in the open window, revealed a head of crisp lettuce, a few stalks of celery, a couple of ripe tomatoes, three green peppers and a little nest of raspberries in a lettuce leaf. They were all fresh and crisp. Was this strange dish a sort of refrigerator? Three curious looking objects also attired in wet cloths and hanging from cords in the open windows proved to be bottles of water, of milk, and of some kind of broth, probably for the invalid. And they were astonishingly cold! Could it be that people had to exist through hot days indefinitely without ice? Couldn't they *get* any ice at this time of year?

She stood appalled and looked at the bottles as if they were some strange magic, taking in what it must have been to live in primitive times, and what all her forefathers and mothers had gone through for mere existence. She was still looking thoughtfully at the bottles when Sam returned and explained them.

"Sure, that's the way they keep things down here. Ice is awful expensive to haul way out here, even when they have ice, and of course they don't have any even in the village this time of year. That's evaporation you know. You just havta wet the cloths every little while when they get dry. That useta be my job when I was out here visiting, that time when Jeff stayed here and worked."

"Jeff?"

"Sure! Didn't ya know Jeff came out here and helped Mr. Saxon in the grove, all spring?"

"No," said Mary Elizabeth thoughtfully, "I didn't know it. I'm glad he did." Then she turned away and looked out of the window at the flapping silken leaves of the bananas.

Sam presently brought her word of what was going

on in the other part of the house. Cousin Richie was rigging up a big light with a reflector. The doctor was getting out his case of instruments. Mr. Saxon was hollowing out holes in four blocks of wood to put under the feet of the bedstand to lift it high enough for an operating table. The nurse came in with a grave face and took the pans of hot water she had been heating. Everything was carried on in silence. It filled Mary Elizabeth and Sam with the utmost apprehension.

"How about Mr. Saxon's father?" whispered Mary Elizabeth to Sam in one of the awful intervals filled with silence.

"He's okay!" answered the boy. "The doctor told him he could help in the operation by eating his breakfast, so he ate it like a good child, and he's sitting there in the big chair now with his eyes shut and a smile on his lips. You oughtta see him. He's a prince! I guess he's praying! He's awful keen, you know, on Mrs. Saxon. 'Mother' he calls her, just like that. And she's a peach, too. Wait till you see her. Looks just like a piece of lace Mother has that she wears with a pearl pin. Her hair is white and her eyes are, well,—wait till you see her!"

Mary Elizabeth went on with hunting her condiments for the salad, her thoughts deeply occupied.

When the salad was finished she put it in a covered dish from the closet, wet a napkin and tucked it about and set it in the window, wondering if her crude arrangement would work as well as the other big tureen.

The nurse came out to put more water to heat and told them that the operation was about to begin. Mary Elizabeth asked if there wasn't something else she could do and the nurse gave directions about heating more water.

So there she sat with her thoughts, and nothing to do but put on more water when it was needed. Sam went and sat on the back steps under a big lime tree with the banana leaves rustling a melancholy tune. He had his elbows on his knees and his head bowed in his hands. She remembered his words about John Saxon's father, "He looks as if he is praying." What an extraordinary thing to have got hold of Sam, the wild young boy. And all from John Saxon's influence! Jeff, too! Jeff the easy-going, happy-hearted gay youth! Herself too!

And then Mary Elizabeth put her head down over her folded arms on the kitchen table. Perhaps she too was praying!

21

MEANTIME Mrs. Robert Wainwright had gone on the warpath.

She called up her home first, hoping that by this time her youngest son had returned from the shore and that she might be able to speak to him. She knew her power over him when she could get him to himself without his fond father by to alter her authority.

It was Rebecca, one of the oldest and most faithful of the Wainwright servants who answered the telephone.

"Is Sam there, Rebecca?" asked Sam's mother.

"No ma'am. He hasn't got back yet."

"You don't mean he's still down at Seacrest with his cousin, Rebecca?"

"Why, I couldn't say, ma'am," answered Rebecca with some hesitation.

Now Rebecca was one of the most honest of persons, and never had been known to tell an out-and-out lie, but she had figured it out with her conscience, or what she used for a conscience, long ago, that when she was asked a question that loyalty forbade her to answer, and she replied, "I couldn't say," she did not mean that she didn't *know* and therefore was unable to state; she meant that loyalty, or wisdom made it impossible to give an answer. In this case of course there was loyalty demanded either side of the question, for she knew quite well where young Master Sam was, but the old master had told her not to let *any*one know where he was gone, especially his mother, and particularly *how* he had gone. And in a case like this Rebecca's conscience always dictated that she should be loyal to the one whom she liked best to please. Rebecca's loyalty without question, was first to Mr. Robert Wainwright, for not only did he appeal to her as the one of the two most likely to be right and just to every one in everything, but also he was the one who paid the servants, and who slipped them a little extra sometimes, when there had been a special request of some kind, such as was now the case. Therefore Rebecca answered firmly a second time.

"Really, I couldn't say, Ma'am."

"No, I suppose you wouldn't know," said her mistress thoughtfully. "Well, has Mr. Wainwright come home from the office yet?"

"No, ma'am," said Rebecca briskly, "he told me he had extra work to-night and might be late for dinner. He said to have it a half hour later."

"Oh, then I suppose I can get him at the office. Tell the cook not to give Mr. Wainwright too many greasy things. I know he likes them but they aren't good for him this warm weather! Everything going all right? If Sam comes home soon you might tell him to call me up at once. Well, Good bye, Rebecca," and she hung up.

With a smile of relief on her lips and a glitter of triumph in her eyes Rebecca walked away from the telephone, well content. She had not betrayed her master's secret, and she had not told what she called a lie. Her answer had been discretion itself.

Then Sam's mother called up Mary Elizabeth's cottage by the sea, but it happened that the caretakers were off to a Sunday School picnic and she got no answer. As a last resort she called up her husband. As a matter of fact she didn't want to talk to him, because if she had anything to put over on the family he generally frustrated her efforts if he found it out in time. But time was a factor in what she wanted now, and there was nothing else to do. So she set her lips firmly and called him.

He was just about to go out to an important conference of some business associates, but he came obediently to the telephone and answered her fondly:

"Hello, Clarrie, is that you? I hope you're nice and cool up there in the mountains. It's hot as cotton down here in the city."

Mrs. Wainwright made a few caustic remarks about people who "preferred" to stay down where it was hot when they had plenty of money to go off for the whole summer and escape the heat, and then she came to the point.

"Where is Sam, Papa?"

"Why, Clarice, you knew he went down to the shore with his cousin!" said Papa Wainwright guardedly.

"Yes, but don't try to make me believe he's there yet! I know better!"

Papa Wainwright's heart took a flop. Had she found out where Sam really was? Had she found out *how* he went? *How* had she found out? This was going to be uncanny!

But he answered in a bland tone.

"Why, Sam loves it down there, Mamma! Hasn't he written you about it? He's been hobnobbing with the Life Savers, and he's been helping haul in the deep-sea nets, and learning all about the fish, and—and—"

Papa Wainwright tried to think of some of the other

things that Sam might be doing that his mother would think were perfectly harmless, but words were failing him. It wouldn't do to mention fishing or boating for she had always been afraid he would drown. But he didn't need to think of anything else just then for he was interrupted.

"But he would soon tire of those things, I'm sure, Papa, with no companions but Betty, and by this time she's got the house full of her crowd and wouldn't have any time for Sam."

"I think not," said Papa Wainwright gathering courage. "I happen to know that she didn't intend having any young folks down, at least not at present. She's just—*resting* you know!"

"What from?" snapped Aunt Clarice sarcastically. "She never *did* anything that I know of. She can't even *knit!* And as for contract bridge she can't keep her mind on it!"

"Well, at any rate," said her husband evasively, "Sam's all right. I just had word from him last night. I think you'll get a letter soon. I told him to write."

As a matter of fact Sam had written and enclosed it to his father to mail, and the father had mailed it that very morning. Now he regretted the home post mark that she would be sure to notice. She would think he was back at home again.

"That is, you see," he began again, "I told him to write you a letter at once and mail it to me, so I would know he had written, and I would forward it to you."

"Oh!" said the boy's mother graciously, knowing her offspring's dislike of correspondence. "Well, I'm sure I hope he does. It's very rude of him not to. But what I want to say is, that I've already tried to get him on the phone down at the shore and failed! So he must have gone somewhere." Her tone was suspicion itself.

"Oh, well," began the weary husband blandly, "I suppose then they've just gone off on some little trip or other. Mary Beth drives around a lot you know. Come to think of it they spoke of visiting some friend of hers sometime soon. They won't be gone long. I wouldn't worry. Mary Elizabeth is very careful."

"I'm not worrying, Papa!" snapped his wife annoyedly. "I wish you wouldn't always think I am worrying! Though it's a pity if you wouldn't do a little worrying yourself sometimes. But I want Sam. I want him to come up here at once. If he won't go to that perfectly wonderful camp where I wanted to send him, at least he's got to have some cultural influence about him before the summer is over. And I want you to find him by telephone or telegraph or something and send him right up here. There's a perfectly marvelous man up here teaching dancing and all the young fellows and girls are taking lessons, and it's high time that Sam had a little of that under circumstances that he can't help liking. You know I simply couldn't compel him to attend dancing classes last winter. He said it was 'sissy.' That's the answer he gives to everything I want to do for his education. And it's all your fault, Robert. You encourage him in that. And he's going to grow up a perfect gawk if something isn't done about it. You know Jeff used to dance so divinely, the girls were all just crazy about his dancing, and it's high time that Sam began to get into some shape. Next winter there will be the Junior dances in the schools, and it's time he went around and got to be a little civilized. There are some charming young fellows here at the hotel, just his age, two brothers from England among them, and they are so well trained, and so courteous! Just perfect little gentlemen! They wait on the girls so delightfully. It's really quite cunning, Robert. You would love to see them. And Sam has just got to come up here and get a little of this atmosphere or he'll grow perfectly wild!"

"Well, I'll risk it," said Sam's father shutting his lips firmly after his words so he couldn't be forced to swallow them. "I'd rather see Sam a fine strong boy with a little horse sense than have him made into one of your imitation little gentlemen, at his age. Clarice, you let Sam alone this summer and let him grow! You'll be surprised how much sense he's getting. He's going to be a lad to be proud of. And I'd rather see him with his cousin Mary Elizabeth for a little while longer before he gets to being so polite to the nice little modern imps that pass for girls to-day. Say, Mamma, where did you put those thin old Palm Beach suits I like so much for hot days?"

"Now, Robert! I told you I gave those away last summer! They weren't fit for you to wear. You looked like a rag-picker in them. They never had any shape anyway. I got you some nice light gray suits, why don't you wear them?"

"Because they're too hot, Clarice, and because I don't like 'em! Anyway, I've given them away. I didn't want 'em!"

"Robert! You didn't give away those lovely suits! Why, I paid—"

"Never mind how much you paid for them, Clarice, I'd rather not know. I've given them away and that's that! And I've got a conference right now, Clarice, and I've got to go! Good bye!"

"But Robert, wait! I want you to promise me that you'll telephone to Sam right away to-night and send him up to me by the first train in the morning!"

But Robert Wainwright had hung up and gone to his conference!

There was nothing for his wife to do but pour her

heart out on paper to her youngest son, and send it special delivery care of his cousin.

Boothby Farwell, on his way southward, having tested out the different kinds of liquors offered by the way, and evaded several detours that seemed more or less casual, finally shook his fist at a perfectly plain detour, about halfway down to Florida and plunged into forbidden roads.

"I'm doing this at my own risk!" he snarled at a workman who rushed up to him with a red flag trying to persuade him otherwise, and then put his foot on the gas and dashed on, bumping up and down over ruts unspeakable, getting all messed up in some fresh cement, and arriving with a dash just in time for a nasty bit of blasting through some rocks in the road bed, to avoid which he swerved to the side and brought up with his car in the embrace, as it were, of a great doughty truck of the working class.

Boothby Farwell himself was thrown forward on his knees and cut and bruised about the face and hands annoyingly but not dangerously.

When he recovered his wind and his senses he said a great many uncomplimentary things to the workmen who were doing their best to extricate his car from the clutches of the truck and to wash his wounds and bind them up. Silent workmen they were, angry at his bull-headedness, men who could say such things as he was expressing much better than he could, gazing at him in a kind of disgusted pity.

They pulled him out of his trouble, sent him in a little old rusty flivver, with one of their best linguists to tell him on the way to the hospital some ten miles away just what the whole gang thought of him, and to get a wrecking machine to bring what was left of his car after him, and then they dismissed him with contempt and washed their hands of him.

Farwell stayed in the hospital annoying the whole staff of nurses and doctors with his complaints, until parts could be sent for by telephone for his mutilated car. And at last, when it was patched up, he headed south again a sadder but no wiser man. He felt that everyone he met was against him and declared the liquor was growing worse and worse the farther south he went. Of course he could only judge by wayside inns, because he had no time to hunt hotels of distinction. He was already behind his schedule and his bird would perhaps have flown before he got there.

This thought annoyed him more and more until he reached the next large city and found a hotel. There he telephoned to Seacrest and tried to get the caretaker. But the telephone at Seacrest did not answer. Frank and his wife had gone to prayer meeting.

Somewhat reassured by the fact that there was no answer, but not yet relieved, he finally called up Sam's mother whom he happened to know was at the Mountain House where he wished himself at that moment,— but only if Mary Elizabeth could be there also.

"Good evening, Mrs. Wainwright," he said suavely, "this is Boothby Farwell. I wonder if you could tell me just when Mary Elizabeth and your son Sam are coming back from Florida?"

"Florida!" snorted Aunt Clarice. "What in the world do you mean? Who would go to Florida this time of year?"

"Well, I thoroughly agree with you, but that's where your son and Mary Elizabeth are, and I'm trying to find out how soon they are coming back!"

"Well, they certainly will return at once if I have anything to do with it, that is, if they are really there. I doubt it. Where did you get your information? I shall telegraph her immediately to bring Sam back."

"Don't worry, Mrs. Wainwright, I'm on my way down after them now. I'll have them back within a few days. I only called you to make sure that I should not pass them on my way. You see I have been delayed a little for repairs on my car. But all is right again and I am on my way. I hope to make Florida to-morrow sometime. But I was afraid they might already have left. You see I came down as a surprise, but I suppose I should have wired them I was coming."

"But I don't understand!" said Sam's mother now thoroughly aroused. "Did Betty tell you they were going?"

"No," said Farwell, "you see I was away for a few days. But it's quite like her, don't you think? She's so impulsive. However, she'll be all right, I'm sure. Don't worry. I'll let you know when we are starting back."

"Oh, that's so sweet of you, Boothby dear. I shall feel so comfortable about Sammy in your care. And I'm certainly ashamed of Betty running off like that without telling anybody."

"But she's quite used to doing what she likes, you know," said Mary Elizabeth's would-be lover. "What she really needs is some one to look after her."

"She certainly does," agreed Mary Elizabeth's aunt. "I've been hoping—"

"Yes, so have I!" said the man gallantly. "Well, I won't keep you, Mrs. Wainwright. I just wanted to make sure they hadn't started home. I thought you would be sure to know."

"But where are you, Boothby?" asked Mrs. Wainwright coming to her senses.

"Oh, just in a little town in Georgia. I'm on the regular highroad you know, and I'm bound to meet them if they start before I get there. I know Elizabeth's car, you know."

"Of course," said the agitated lady. "And please tell Betty that I want her to send Sammy up by the very first train after she gets home. I need him up here now. Tell her that."

"I will indeed, Mrs. Wainwright. In fact if you like I'll put him on the train myself when I get there and see that he goes directly up to you."

"Oh, that's so good of you, Boothby dear. And if there's any expense connected with it his father will of course take care of it."

"Oh, that's all right!" said Boothby Farwell, impatient to be done with the voluble lady. "I'll wire you when I find them. Good bye!"

"Thank you so much! But Boothby, you didn't tell me how you found out they were in Florida!"

But Boothby Farwell frowned and hung up. He didn't care to enter into that question.

Mrs. Wainwright, however, was greatly disturbed. She went and sat down to her delicate knitting again, but her mind was on the matter of her young son, and her niece. How had Betty dared take Sam off without permission? Finally she arose and sallied forth to a telephone booth and spent most of the rest of the evening trying to get her husband on the wire. Failing to get him, and being told that he was still in New York, she called as a last resort Mary Elizabeth's father, and after some delay got a servant who told her that Mr. Samuel Wainwright had gone to New York with Mr. Robert Wainwright.

Much vexed she hung up and went to bed early to consider how she might visit retribution on all the delinquents. Her husband was not at home looking after things as he ought to be. Her brother-in-law never did look after his daughter as she thought he ought to do and Mary Elizabeth had probably taken advantage of their absence and gone off on some wild tangent of her own. No telling but she would bring them up in Egypt with Sam yet. This really must be stopped. If there was no other way to do it she would have to go home in the heat and stop it herself, much as she hated to do so. She certainly would make her Robert understand a thing or two when she once got his ear again!

To make matters worse the next morning she received a loving letter from her husband postmarked New York, crisp and brief, telling of his sudden business call and saying he wasn't just sure how soon he could get home, but when she called up the hotel where the letter was written they said both Mr. Wainwrights had checked out.

Nothing daunted she tried home again, but received the same answer as the night before. Rebecca played off two stock phrases in her replies and got by nicely. "You don't tell me?" when her mistress announced she had heard that Sam was in Florida, and "I couldn't say, indeed ma'am!" when asked if she had heard anything about it.

Baffled but not discouraged Mrs. Wainwright retired to her room and missed a morning of bridge to write letters to her husband and brother-in-law, setting forth her ideas of bringing up children, and what she would and would not stand. But the Brothers Wainwright were taking a holiday. They were up in Maine on a rugged old farm, most of the time sitting on a rock in the shelter of great old hemlocks, where they used to sit as barefoot boys, fishing by the hour. They had stopped in Boston and bought new-fangled fishing tackle, and brought it along as an excuse for sitting there, but most of the time they were reminiscing, much to the annoyance of the fish who would have liked to be biting that lovely modern bait.

Mr. Robert Wainwright had dutifully written a nice loving letter to his wife and mailed it from Boston, and another from Portland, vaguely mentioning a business trip, and giving the impression of a swift return home. His wife's letter did not reach him for several days, and that not until he was actually back in his home city but his own letters had kept his wife from further attempt to create a campaign against Mary Elizabeth and Sam in Florida, if that was where they were.

Mrs. Robert Wainwright, realizing that she was wasting ammunition, went back to her bridge and awaited a telegram from Boothby Farwell which was so long in coming that one morning she awoke in genuine alarm and began to telephone again.

But that was days later.

22

MARY Elizabeth was startled from her position bowed over the kitchen table, by a sudden sense of someone standing by her side, though there had been no sound.

She looked up and there stood Miss Noble, the nurse.

"The doctor wants you," she said, in that almost inaudible voice that yet could be heard so distinctly by one close at hand. "Put these on!" She handed forth a long white gown and a white cap that would cover the hair entirely. "Make a solution of this tablet in water and wash your hands. Be as quick as you can, and *come!*"

The nurse vanished and Mary Elizabeth arose feeling her heart beating so hard that it seemed as if it would choke her. It was not assisting at a solemn operation that frightened her. It was that she knew she must be going into the presence of John Saxon.

She looked up and there stood Sam, wide-eyed, white-lipped, watching.

She put on the garments instantly. She took the tablet the nurse had left and washed in the solution carefully as the doctor had directed. Then she gave Sam a radiant smile. There was fright in her eyes, but there was a gallant light also. She went swiftly and silently into the sick room and stood beside the doctor. She did not look up. She did not see John Saxon, but she knew he must be there. She fixed her attention on the doctor and did exactly according to his low-voiced directions, and whether she was receiving a bloody instrument, and placing it in its antiseptic bath, or whether she was handing him another for which he asked, she kept her eyes directly on her work. She did not look up nor allow her thoughts to do so. And presently her thumping heart quieted and she was able to draw a long, still breath and go on with her little part in this tremendous business of life and death.

She did not trust herself to look at the patient lying there so white and still, she did not let her eyes wander to the details of the work that was going on, nor to think of who was in the room and what part each was taking in this solemn scene. John Saxon might be standing close beside her for aught she knew, but she would not let her mind wander to him. There was just one person of whom she was conscious in that room, and that was John Saxon's Christ, who seemed to be standing across from her on the other side of the bed close beside the sick woman, as if she were very dear to Him, and somehow Mary Elizabeth knew that He had been very close to this woman all her life, and in the event of her death it would be only going with One she loved. Somehow she knew suddenly that this mother had been part of the reason of John Saxon, why he was so different from all other men she knew.

Humbly she stood there and held the instruments, giving thanks that she was counted worthy for even that.

She heard the low spoken directions of the doctor to the nurse, she heard sometimes a word of explanation, which might have been given to John Saxon, but she would not let them lodge in her mind. She was intent on only one thing, doing what she was told to do, and doing it under the eyes of John Saxon's Christ.

As a matter of fact John Saxon hadn't seen Mary Elizabeth at all. It hadn't entered his mind that she was there, or could be there. He was just at the other side of the doctor, helping now and then. He might have seen the other white-robed, white-capped woman enter and take her place to serve, but it had not entered into his realization at all. The white figure on the other side there was just a shadowy helper whom the doctor had brought along. He did not look up nor see her face and she did not look at his. For the time she was set apart from thoughts of him. And John Saxon's eyes were on his precious mother, watching the hand of skill that was guiding the knife.

Now and again there would be almost inaudible sounds spoken between the two doctors, but it was as if they were in another sphere. Mary Elizabeth stood serving as if she were passing the first test under the eyes of John Saxon's Christ.

It might have been years that she stood there. Time seemed to have stood still. But there came an end at last. And still following directions she found herself out in the kitchen again washing her hands, taking off the white garments and folding them up, facing Sam white-lipped and anxious, and somehow she managed a little trembling smile for him.

"Is it over?" his eyes asked, and her own nodded.

Mary Elizabeth felt as if she wanted to cry, and yet there was a kind of exultation in her heart.

The door swung open silently from the front room and the nurse came in, a clinical thermometer in her hand.

"You'd better go over to the plane and lie down, Miss

Wainwright, you look white," she said in her professional tone.

Mary Elizabeth took a long breath and shook her head.

"I'm quite all right," she said proudly. "What can I do next?"

"Nothing, just now, except to be on hand. I've made her as comfortable as it's possible for her to be at present. Young Mr. Saxon is driving somewhere to bring ice and other things the doctor wants. Your cousin is with Mr. Saxon senior. If there were only something for you to lie on it would be good for you to get a little rest now so you would be better able to help when you are needed."

"I know where there's a cot," said Sam eagerly, and opening a door over in the corner vanished up a sort of ladder into a loft, presently descending with an army cot coming on ahead of him.

"That's fine!" commented Miss Noble. "I believe you're going to be a big help!" and she eyed Sam with surprise.

He lifted his eyebrows in a comical way behind her back, and then with his tongue in his cheek vanished out toward John Saxon's old flivver which was beginning to send forth a subdued clatter preparatory to starting.

"I've made some salad," said Mary Elizabeth to the nurse, and then thought how flat that sounded.

"You did?" said the nurse. "When did you manage that? That sounds good. I think it will be needed when everything settles down to quietness."

"Were we in time?" asked Mary Elizabeth suddenly, as if the words were wrenched from the aching of her heart. As if she could not wait any longer to ask.

"It's hard to tell that yet," said Miss Noble. "Her pulse is very weak. She may rally. I don't know. I don't think the doctor is very hopeful, but at least we've done all we could. It's a pity we couldn't have come a week sooner. She was almost gone when we arrived."

"Yes," said Mary Elizabeth sadly, "if we only had known!"

Mary Elizabeth stretched out for a few minutes on the cot until her frightened trembling limbs had ceased to shake, but her mind was on the jump now. She could not lie still.

It must have been two hours at least that John Saxon was gone but when he came back Mary Elizabeth had vanished from the kitchen leaving a pleasant meal set forth on the white kitchen table ready for any one who wanted it.

It was Sam who came after her, flying excitedly across the sand and mounting into the plane.

"Mary Beth! Where are you?" he called in a loud whisper. "Come on over! The doctor wants you!"

Mary Elizabeth was on her feet at once, her eyes filled with premonition.

"Is she worse?" she asked hurrying after the boy.

"Naw, she's just the same yet I guess. But they want you. The doctor says you can sit in the room a while and let the nurse rest a couple hours, and he and John'll rest too. He says to-night'll be the time they wantta watch her through, so they better get rested now."

Mary Elizabeth's eyes shone. She was to be allowed to help again! That seemed a great honor. And John Saxon would be resting and wouldn't be there. She wouldn't have to worry about what he thought of her coming.

"All right, Buddie, I'll just put on something suitable. I'll be ready in a second. You can run along. Maybe there's something you can do."

"Naw, I'll wait for you. I told them I'd bring you."

Mary Elizabeth slipped into a little white linen dress

and a pair of white tennis shoes and was ready. Sam regarded her with admiration.

"You look almost like a real nurse!" he said.

"Thanks! Is that a compliment?"

"Sure! They look awful neat!"

"So they do! But, Buddie, you didn't tell Mr. Saxon I was here did you?"

"Absolutely not!" said the boy. "He said a lot about how great it was and all that while we went after ice, and I wanted like the dickens to tell him, but I didn't. I let him think I had a legacy. I didn't say so, but I guess he thought that. Anyway he said sometime he'd be able to pay me back, but he couldn't ever pay what it was worth to him, and he told me a lot how he felt before we came, hopeless and helpless and all that. Gee, I guess we got there just in time. The doc told me he thought there was a *little* hope she might get over it!"

"Did he? Oh, how wonderful!"

"He said it wasn't sure yet, but he thought there was a chance. He told Mr. Saxon that! And he told Father Saxon that, too. But say, you'll never know how much our Mr. Saxon needed us. I wish you could have heard him!"

Mary Elizabeth's eyes were shining and something lifted her heavy frightened heart and bore her up. She looked about on the sand she was walking over and noticed for the first time the little wild pea vines with their cute little blossoms of white and pink and crimson like little imitation sweet peas, rambling all over the sand, a lacy carpet.

"Where is Mr. Saxon now?"

"He's gone up to his room to lie down. The doctor made him. He said they would have three patients instead of two if he didn't!"

"Oh," said Mary Elizabeth drawing a breath of relief, "that's good! That's a wonderful doctor!"

"He sure is!" said Sam. "Say, you oughtta hear how great he is. Mr. Saxon's been telling me about what wonderful things he's done, just like miracles!"

Mary Elizabeth entered the house shyly, relieved that John Saxon would not meet her just now, stepping softly through the front room where Mr. Saxon senior lay on an improvised couch apparently asleep, slipping into the dimness of the sick room like a wraith.

Nurse Noble came over and gave her directions, what to do, what to watch for, when to call for her if she didn't know what to do, and then Nurse Noble went into the kitchen and lay down on the cot.

It was very quiet in the house as Mary Elizabeth sat alone in a big quilt-lined rocker and heard the soft breathing of the sick woman.

For the first time she could see the outline of her sweet cameo face, the soft white hair curling into waves about her forehead. There was something fine and gentle and lovely in the face, something that made her understand John Saxon in his strength and sweetness better than she had done.

And presently, over there in the shadowy part of the room she seemed to feel again the Presence that had been there during the operation, and it was as if she sat there in that Presence and had her heart searched. She seemed to see that life had not been the gay, bright trifle she had always supposed it. It had a deep, true, serious meaning and there was a reason for everything that came if one could only get near to the Source of understanding.

She had heretofore classed people as rich and poor, good and bad, ignorant and cultured. But here was a different quality. Not just goodness, nor even culture and refinement, but something deeper, far more valuable. These people were set apart from all people of earth, it seemed. There might be others like them, but she had not come in their way. It might be possible for others, just common ones, to become this way, she wasn't sure. But with all her heart she wished she might belong in a class with them.

It seemed as she sat in the room with that Presence of John Saxon's Christ that she sensed that what made the difference between these people and all others was that they walked daily as in the Presence of this Christ.

The afternoon droned on in that wonderful quiet, with only the distant hum of the bees, the note of a bird high and faraway, and the perfume of the orange blossoms coming in the window as a little breeze stirred the thin, white curtain.

The patient was coming out of the ether and moaning now and then, speaking hazy little sentences that were almost inaudible. The gentleness of her tone drew Mary Elizabeth. She longed to be able to comfort her in the physical distress she knew she must be feeling. The little services she could render were so exceedingly small and inadequate to the pain she was bearing. Just moistening her lips occasionally, or wiping her forehead with a soft cloth.

But as the afternoon waned the patient's voice grew stronger, the accents more natural. She was coming more and more to herself, and the words she spoke were sane. It would not be long before she was back among them, if all went well, an individual again, understanding what was going on. Of course she was very weak, but she would presently be wondering who they all were who had arrived during her unconsciousness. There would be that to be reckoned with. And the father too! Mary Elizabeth had not met him yet. They would wonder who she was. They would not understand her coming, perhaps!

Her cheeks burned at the thought. How could she explain herself? She could not pass for long as just another nurse. There would surely come a time of reckoning, and what was she to say, to do? She realized that she had not foreseen this side of the matter at all. And she furthermore realized that it mattered very much indeed to her what these two thought of her, these gentle people who were the parents of her lover! So far, they probably knew nothing of her existence!

John Saxon didn't know she was here, either. She was sure he didn't. If he had caught a glimpse of her at all he had probably just thought of her as another nurse whom they had brought along! Was there any way she could just keep out of it entirely? If she went to Cousin Richie, perhaps, and told him a little bit about things—could she bring herself to confide the preciousness of it all to him? Would he understand? Would he help her to get away into the village till the patient was well and they could go back north, and she could meet John Saxon's parents in a regular way as such matters should be conducted? Would it take away from the sacredness of what had happened if she told it to Cousin Richie?

She sat considering, weighing one situation over against the other. Whether it were better to do that and keep out of it all, or just to face things as they might come? If she went away how could she explain it to the doctor, and that keen-eyed nurse?

And yet, how could she stay here and meet the questioning eyes of these dear people, the alien eyes, perhaps, of John Saxon, if he had already found out what a mistake he had made?

And then the little mother on the bed spoke out clearly in a new love-tone.

"John," she said looking up and away as if she saw him, "you're not to worry. I'll be all right. We'll just stay here in Florida till you're through with your studies. And when you're married, Father and I will come to the wedding! Father's promised me that! We'll save up our money and come!"

Mary Elizabeth held her breath. Had John told them about her? Or could it be that there was another girl? Perhaps someone he was engaged to? Oh, not that, not that! God, don't let him be unworthy, untrue! Don't let it be that he made love to me when he had no right!

Then instantly she knew that could not be. Of course there was no other girl! She would not harbor a thought unworthy of him! Whether she ever came to know him better or not she would always trust him utterly!

But the gentle voice from the bed was speaking again.

"John, you'll be careful to get the right girl! You won't take up with anybody who isn't worthy? I couldn't bear that, dear! Father was afraid you might be dazzled by some modern girl!"

Mary Elizabeth sat petrified, feeling that she had no right to be hearing this, yet unable to move. And it was just then she suddenly realized the presence of John Saxon in the doorway the other side of the bed.

He was not looking at her. He was looking down at his mother tenderly, oh, so tenderly! Mary Elizabeth caught a glimpse of his face and lowered her lashes before that sacred look. He had not seen her. If he had she realized that she was nothing but a nurse to him anyway. He came forward as silently as a shadow might have moved and bent over his mother.

"It's all right, Mother dear!" he said as gently as she herself had spoken. "I'll get the right girl or I'll get none! I promised you that long ago. Don't you worry!"

The sick woman brought her wandering gaze to rest

upon her boy's beloved features, and she seemed to recognize him and smiled, such a radiant look, showing the precious relationship between the two.

She put up her frail little hands gropingly and caught his hands.

"Dear boy!" she said, and closing her eyes slipped sweetly off to sleep again.

He stood there for some time holding her hands, not stirring lest he disturb her. Then softly laying her hands down, he stepped back and lifted his head, a tenderness in his face, a light of hope in his eyes. He looked toward Mary Elizabeth then for the first time, a smile on his lips that asked her indulgence, her understanding.

But the smile stopped midway in a look of utter surprise as he met the eyes of Mary Elizabeth, and he just stood there gazing at her in amaze, wonder and delight coming slowly into his face, yet with it a look of reserve that she could not quite understand.

Suddenly he came swiftly round the bed and stood beside her. She rose precipitately catching her breath in apprehension for what might be coming, longing for his nearness, yet fearing to meet all the questions and his possible disapproval. Fearing it more after the dialogue between himself and his mother to which she had just been a forced listener.

He reached down and took her two fluttering hands that were clasped on their way up to her heart, and he held them together in both of his, tenderly, like something precious, yet he did not take her in his arms.

"You!" he whispered looking down into her eyes with an unfathomable look, "so it was you all the while! You did this lovely thing! Oh, *my dear!*"

And then he suddenly dropped his head down upon her shoulder and stood so, his face against her soft neck.

She could feel his eyelashes and they were wet with sudden tears.

Then, without premeditation, just as a flower turns to the sun, just as a mother comforts her child, she bent her own head and touched her warm lips to his wet eyelids. There was something so precious about it that Mary Elizabeth felt almost as if it were a holy sacrament. It seemed entirely apart from the flesh, a thing of the spirit, and it seemed as if God were there, standing just a little apart from them.

Into the hush of that precious moment came the subdued sound of footsteps outside on the grassy velvet of the path. They entered the front room quietly, and were coming straight toward the sick room.

John Saxon lifted his head, looked deep into her eyes, then with a quick pressure released her hands and was on the other side of the bed looking down on his mother sleeping there so peacefully when the doctor and Nurse Noble entered the room.

23

MARY Elizabeth sped out of that room like a wraith, her cheeks fairly blazing, her eyes so bright that they would have blinded the eyes of any but a casual observer, though no one was looking at her. She fled to the kitchen, glad that Mr. Saxon senior was sitting with his back toward the bedroom door reading.

She was tidying up Father Saxon's tray that had been brought out after his noon meal when Nurse Noble came out to prepare a little cracked ice in a linen cloth for the patient to suck when she moaned for water.

"You're to go over to the plane and get something to eat," said the nurse. "Mr. Wainwright has it all ready waiting for you. The doctor and I have eaten. You'd better stay there and take a good long nap now. You seem to be a pretty good nurse. We'll likely need you in the night so you had better be prepared by some really refreshing sleep."

"How do you think Mrs. Saxon looks?" asked Mary Elizabeth.

"Why, she seems to be holding her own pretty well!" said the nurse briskly. "Of course I haven't talked with the doctor yet since he came back, but I could tell pretty well by his expression he felt well satisfied. Now you run along!"

Mary Elizabeth ran along. In fact she went out the back door, not to encounter anyone, and literally ran all the way over to the plane with a happy little song in her heart.

All through the ensuing hours, and in fact the first two days after the operation the little party of rescuers waited, tense and anxious, watching the fight between life and death. Hoping, praying, fearing and hoping again. But at last the doctor came out of the sick room and told them he thought the worst danger was over, and a great burden was lifted from their hearts. Later that morning Mary Elizabeth went over to the plane for something and Cousin Richie looked up with a smile.

"Pretty well satisfied with what you've done, aren't you?" he said with a grin. "Your doctor says he thinks the patient is going to pull through after all. He says when he got here he didn't think it was possible she would live through the operation, but she seems to have marvelous vitality."

"Oh, isn't that wonderful?"

"Yes," said Richie Wainwright, "it is! There's some satisfaction in having things turn out right. I'm glad you let me in on this."

"Oh, but, Cousin Richie, I think it is so wonderful that you were willing. I was so afraid to ask. I thought everybody would think me crazy. And I think it's great of you to hang around this way and help. I was afraid you'd have to go right back and take the doctor with you, and then what would we do if anything went wrong?"

"What do you think I am, Betchen, a quitter? No, I intend to see this thing through. And I guess the doctor does, too. He talked that way. You see it's fortunate that this is his vacation time and he doesn't have to hurry back to his classes. His patients, too, are mostly away on vacations, and he's got a young graduate doctor or something in the city taking his place. He means to see the little lady through to safety, I think. He told me if for nothing else than John Saxon he would do it. He thinks John Saxon is great. Says he's going to be a coming man, is as brilliant as they make 'em and good as gold into the bargain, and you don't get that combination in the medical profession any too often."

Mary Elizabeth's cheeks flamed annoyingly, and Cousin Richie watched her lovely face furtively, quite confirmed in his own surmises.

"How long have you known John Saxon, Bess?"

Mary Elizabeth dropped her eyes and busied herself with a handful of wild pea blossoms she had picked on her way over to the plane, picked them just out of sheer relief and gladness.

"Why, not so long," she said with a steady tone, aware that Cousin Richie was watching her searchingly. "He's a friend of Jeff's, you know."

"Yes, I know, but I was wondering—. How about the old lady? Know her well?"

"No," said Mary Elizabeth letting her voice trail off, "no, but I've heard a lot about her. Sam has been here before. He liked her a lot and he told me what a wonderful old couple they were."

"I see! Well, Bess, it was a good thought. It certainly was a good thought, and I'm glad you let me in on it."

"I couldn't have done it without you, Cousin Richie, and I don't know how I can ever thank you enough."

"I'll tell you," said the man of the world, "ask me again when you have some more angel's work to do. I'm no angel, but I can fly a plane, and sometimes that'll be worth while."

"I should *say!*" said Mary Elizabeth. "And I certainly will ask you again. I'll know who to depend upon. Oh, it's so wonderful that the doctor thinks she may get well!"

"Yes, it is! He says the only thing that's really against her is staying down here in the heat. He says if he could get her north into more bracing air it would do wonders. He says if she were up north in the right place we'd see a difference in her in a few days."

Mary Elizabeth turned a thoughtful look at him.

"I suppose it would be a long time before he would dare move her," she said speculatively.

"No, he seemed to think not," said Cousin Richie. "He seemed to think it might be only a matter of a few days before it would be safe to move her, provided we'd fly carefully and avoid rough weather. The trouble is, though, he thinks they haven't much money, and there seems to be no place where they could afford to take her. The doctor felt it out with young Saxon this afternoon, I believe. And then he says, too, she wouldn't go and leave her old husband behind."

"But why couldn't I take them all down to Seacrest?" said Mary Elizabeth breathlessly, her eyes shining. "Why that would be wonderful! I'm sure Dad would like it. He's always willing for anything I want, and the house is big enough to make two or three private hospitals out of it. There's a great big room on the first floor opening off at the left of the front door. Do you remember? And there's a bath connected with it, and then a little room back of it that we used to call the library. That would make a splendid suite for them. The back room would do for Mr. Saxon, or the nurse if she didn't have to sleep in the room with Mrs. Saxon when she got better. And there are rooms and rooms upstairs. Don't you think that would do?"

Cousin Richie did. He smiled. His words were having exactly the effect on Mary Elizabeth that he had hoped they would have.

"Go talk to the doctor, Bess, and then get the consent of that big bronze giant that rules things around here. If you can I'll stick around till your party's ready to return."

"Oh, Cousin Richie! You certainly are a peach!"

"He's a whole basket of fruit!" said Sam suddenly appearing on the scene. "Got any food, Mary Beth? I'm starved!"

But that was not the last time they talked over a possible transfer of the patient to a cooler climate for the summer. Mary Elizabeth met the doctor as she started back to the house a couple of hours later. He wheeled in the path and walked back with her.

"Your cousin Mr. Wainwright says you've got a house by the sea," he said. "Tell me about it."

Mary Elizabeth told, not forgetting the whispering pines and the rhythmic waves. The doctor listened and his eyes took on a faraway look.

"That sounds good," he said. "Where is this?"

Mary Elizabeth told him.

"I could come down there and look her over now and then," he said meditatively. "That looks good to me. We'll see how things go the next few days. I'd like to take her up with us. I don't see leaving her down here any longer than possible. She needs a change of climate at once. She's as frail as a breath of air, although she must have a marvelous constitution or she never would have got through the operation. But I have great hopes now."

"That's wonderful!" said Mary Elizabeth. "I can't ever tell you how splendid I think it is that you're willing to stay here a few days and look after her. I was so afraid you would have to hurry right back the next day."

"Child, I wouldn't do that!" said the doctor looking kindly at her. "I wouldn't do that to John. John's the best young man I know. I love John Saxon like my own son. If I had a daughter I couldn't think of any better future for her than to know she was going to marry John Saxon. Young lady, I don't know how well you know him, or whether you have other plans for your future, but if you haven't, just take my advice and get acquainted with John Saxon. You couldn't do better for yourself."

There was a twinkle in the doctor's eye and a grin on his wry old lips as he said it, but he gave Mary Elizabeth a searching look and she turned as red as a peony.

"Well, all right, Miss Wainwright," he went on returning to his formal voice, "you've relieved my anxiety very much. We'll try to work it in a few days. I'll have a little talk with Saxon as soon as the worst danger is over, and we'll plan to go north as soon as we can."

For the next two days the little group of people centering round that sick bed were busy and a bit breathless. Anxiety was still in all their hearts, fear lurked not far away, and there were constant ups and downs. Mary Elizabeth marveled that the nurse could stand it. For each set-back brought Mary Elizabeth to the point of utter discouragement. But the nurse went steadily on from hour to hour taking whatever came and never seemed to lose hope.

But there was one thing which troubled Mary Elizabeth, and that was a sort of veil, or wall, that seemed to have come between herself and John Saxon. She couldn't understand it.

All night long that first night after he had seen her, her heart kept waking up and singing with the thought of his head down on her shoulder, his wet lashes against her face. But when morning came and she saw him, while his face lighted with greeting, it still had an aloof look, as though he were glad that she was there, but he must not come nearer than a look.

At first it did not worry her because she thought that while his mother was so ill he could not take time nor thought for anything else, but when it went on all day, and all the next day, even though the doctor's word had gone forth that Mrs. Saxon was practically out of danger, his aloofness began to trouble her deeply. She could not forget it, no matter what she was doing, for almost it seemed that he was avoiding her, and what could be the cause of that? Certainly he had shown great delight that she was here! She just could not make it out.

Sam seemed to be a bit puzzled about their relation, too, for several times he made an effort to throw them together, all to no avail.

It was the morning that Mrs. Saxon seemed so decidedly better that John Saxon announced his intention of driving down to the village. But he did not ask Mary Elizabeth to go along. In fact Mary Elizabeth took particular pains not to be in evidence when he was starting so that he would not think he had to ask her, for by this time she was getting most sensitive and keeping as much out of his way as possible.

All this worried Sam who adored them both and wanted nothing better in life than to see them delight in one another's society.

Mary Elizabeth slipped away over to the plane until Sam and John Saxon should be done. There were things she could do over there to tidy up a bit, and when she saw them drive away she could go back and fix up the beds and the kitchen.

She got everything in order and was just starting back,

but she had gone only a few steps when John Saxon came across the road and confronted her. He was looking almost haughty, with his nice chin raised a little, the way he had been doing lately. Mary Elizabeth felt that he was hurt at her for having forced so much assistance upon him, but his eyes were looking straight into hers now as if he would see deeper than just eyes were supposed to see.

"Mary Elizabeth," he said, and his voice had a quality of demand in it that small boys' voices have sometimes when they are half puzzled, half angry, wholly worried, "did you ever get my letter?"

Mary Elizabeth's eyes opened wide in astonishment and the bright color flew into her face.

"Oh, yes," she said eagerly, "why of course I did! What do you mean? Didn't I tell you in my answer that I got it? You didn't think I would have written all that if I had never got it, did you?"

"Mary Elizabeth! Did you write me an answer?"

"Certainly!" said Mary Elizabeth a bit formally, remembering some of the things she had said in that letter, her eyes very starry, though her chin was lifted now a bit haughtily. If John Saxon didn't like what she had said she couldn't help it now, could she? But there must be some way to keep tears from coming into her eyes just at this critical moment.

"*When* did you write?" demanded the small boy in John Saxon, almost as if he had shaken her and told her to divulge the secret at once or she would have to suffer for it.

"A few days before we started down here," she told him shamefacedly, knowing now, quite suddenly, that she had waited far too long to answer a love-letter like that. "I couldn't write you sooner," she faltered. "I had to think things out—"

But John Saxon was gone.

Like a whirlwind he had dashed away again back to the house, leaving Mary Elizabeth standing there in the sand with the little pink and white and crimson pea blossoms creeping all about her feet on their lacy vines, and a great hawk over her head circling and looking down, wheeling, slanting, a big menacing shadow at her feet whenever he came between her and the sun.

There she stood and looked after him with sinking heart. He was angry then that she had kept him waiting so long for an answer! Angry! And she hadn't thought John Saxon could get angry. But now she saw that he had a right to be angry, and the tears welled up and rolled down her cheeks which had been so pink a moment before and had suddenly gone white. Would she ever, ever be able to atone for having waited so long before she answered that letter? For now she saw how her heart had really wanted to write that letter at once, and she had been holding back because the conventionality with which she had been born told her not to be too precipitate. And now he was angry, and her heart had told her all the time that he would be! What should she do?

Then while she was still standing there John Saxon's old flivver came racketing out the drive and down the road past her, and John Saxon, driving like a wild man, did not even look her way.

Right down there in the sand among the pink and white and crimson blossoms she dropped and putting her face into her hands began to weep, right where anybody might have seen her from the house if they all hadn't been much too busy to watch.

And when she had wept the tears all away, she suddenly lifted up her face and began to laugh. She had just remembered how like an angry little boy John Saxon had looked as he drove away, and he wouldn't be angry like that, would he, if he didn't *care?* And besides what did he mean, asking her when she wrote? Didn't he get her letter yet?

And now she understood and laughed the more.

Afterward when she had laughed a good deal of her worry away and got a bit of hope hung out in her eyes she laughed again at the puzzled glance there had been on Sam's good honest freckled face.

Then Mary Elizabeth got up and went back to the house to work.

John Saxon drove with all his might down to the village to the post office.

"I haven't been to the post office since I mailed that letter to you, kid!" he said to Sam who was with him, like a faithful dog, never speaking unless he saw the time was propitious, just sitting there waiting for him. "I haven't had time, I haven't had a chance to get away from the house!"

Sam looked at him with a puzzled frown, and wondered why that was so important. He kept on wondering while John Saxon went in to the post office and then he wondered some more when his friend came out with a handful of mail in his hand and his eyes happy as he looked down at the pile of letters he was carrying.

John Saxon handed Sam a bill.

"Run over to the store and pick out anything you think they need at the house. You know what is wanting better than I do just now. I'll stay here and read my letters," he said as he sprang into his seat already tearing the end off of one particular letter.

Sam caught sight of the writing on that envelope and knew his cousin had written it. Now, when had Mary Beth written to John Saxon? What did it all mean?

And what would Mary Beth write to John Saxon for? She hadn't known much about him till he told her!

Of course she had met him at the wedding, and likely it was something about that. Perhaps he had carried off her handkerchief or something by mistake that night and had sent it to her and she had written to thank him. That might be it. Probably it was something like that. Or else he was mistaken and that was just some writing that looked like Mary Beth's, some other girl perhaps. But that in turn made him uneasy. He didn't want any other girl but Mary Beth in John Saxon's life! It troubled him a lot as he walked through the hot sand to the grocery store and looked around for things he remembered they had needed. Cereal and sugar and butter. Raisins. Mary Beth had said she'd found a cook book and could make a rice pudding if she only had some raisins. Sam bought the raisins and a few other things that appealed to him, and sauntered slowly over toward the car where John Saxon was still absorbedly reading his letter. Sam stepped back into the store and selected a few more simple articles they could use, and kept a weather eye out toward the car till he saw John Saxon fold that letter and put it in his breast pocket. Then he came hurrying with his packages. Sam was discreet at times, almost uncannily so.

There was no mistaking the look of relief and exaltation on John Saxon's face on the way back to the house. Sam wondered and wondered. Perhaps after all the letter was from that new doctor he was going to study with. Still, no, his friend would tell him if it was anything like that.

Sam cudgeled his brains all the way home, but he kept his mouth shut, and when they arrived at the house, just as if he had been telling Sam all about it, John Saxon turned to him with a bright look and asked:

"Sam, where do you suppose Mary Elizabeth is? Would she be in the house or over at the plane? Would you mind finding her and telling her that I'd like to see her a few minutes if she can spare the time? Tell her I'll sit right here in the car till she comes."

Sam gave him one astonished look and then got out with a respectful "Yessir!" instead of his usual "Okay." *"Mary Elizabeth"* of all things! When had *he* ever called her that before? It was always a formal "Miss Wainwright" when he mentioned her at all, which had been but seldom.

Mary Elizabeth had been washing lettuce that she had picked in the shaded little garden that John Saxon kept close to the house for a few things that needed constant care to thrive. She shook the bright drops of water from the green leaves and laid them away in the porous earthen dish as Sam delivered his message. Then she looked up with such a radiant smile that Sam almost shielded his eyes from it, and said with a real lilt in her voice:

"Yes, tell him I'm coming right away, Sam!"

Mary Elizabeth came walking demurely around the house in her simple white dress with her sleeves rolled up above her elbows and her shining eyes looking down at the springy path of grass she trod.

She was trying to look casual and demure, as if she were coming out to take an order concerning something to be done in the house, but the smile on her lovely mouth belied her manner, and when she looked up and met John Saxon's gaze her face broke into radiance.

"Will you go somewhere with me for a few minutes, Mary Elizabeth? Somewhere where we can be alone? I've just read your letter. I hadn't been to the post office for days!"

Mary Elizabeth sprang into the car and settled down beside him, and the old flivver racketed joyously away down a sweep of sandy road that was seldom traveled, into a bit of scrub and hammock land, till they came out to a quiet shaded place with a glimpse of a little lake not far away, and there the flivver stopped.

Little creatures from the wildness scuttled about and sniffed, and cast curious bright-eyed glances from trees and ground, but John Saxon and Mary Elizabeth were not noticing them.

"Mary Elizabeth!" said John Saxon putting out his arms and gathering her close. "My darling!" He drew her head to his shoulder and her lips to his. And Mary Elizabeth lay close to his heart as if she had come home.

It was some time before they talked at all, and then the man, looking hungrily down into the girl's eyes as if he could not get enough of the sight of them, said:

"Mary Elizabeth! Why didn't you write sooner? I thought you didn't care! I thought you were scorning me and teaching me a lesson not to be so presumptuous!"

"I couldn't," said Mary Elizabeth, looking up into his dear face and softly smoothing the knot of the little old cotton tie he was wearing, as if it were costly silk and precious. "I didn't dare! John, I was afraid about your God! I was afraid He wouldn't think I was fit for you. I'd just found out I was a sinner. Sam made me see it. And I knew that something had to be done before I could ever be in the same class with you. I had to find out about that first before I wrote you."

He pressed his arms closer about her and touched her forehead and her eyes with reverent lips.

"Did you,—find out—?" he murmured gently as if the matter were too sacred to speak of aloud.

"I—think so. Sam said I had to accept Christ as my personal Saviour. I'm not sure that I know all that it means, but I did the best I could. I told Him I did! And the next day I wrote you my letter. I didn't feel that I was any more fit to be loved by one like you, but I had done the best I could, and so I wrote. But,—do you think your Christ will think it is all right for you to love me? I wouldn't want to come between Him and you in any way."

"Oh, my darling!" said John Saxon stooping to touch her lips once more with reverence, "My Christ *loves* you, don't you know that?"

"I don't see how He could," said Mary Elizabeth. "I've never paid the slightest attention to Him before! And I thought—well, I thought when you didn't look at me nor hardly speak to me that you thought I wasn't worthy, and you were sorry you had written me what you did when you didn't know my name."

"Oh, my blessed darling! I didn't know! I didn't understand!"

IT was on the way back that Mary Elizabeth told him her plan.

"Did you know we're going to take your mother up to my place at Seacrest?" she said.

He looked at her startled.

"Sometime," he said dreamily.

"Sometime *soon!*" said Mary Elizabeth. "The doctor says it may be in a very few days she will be able to travel."

John Saxon shook his head.

"You don't understand, dear," he said. "She would never consent to go anywhere and leave Father behind."

"Oh, your father is going too, of course! It wouldn't be any fun to leave him behind. He knows all about it. I told him last night and he was delighted. He said he had been praying for a way to get her out of this climate till the hot weather was over."

"So have I," said John Saxon sadly, "but I couldn't let you take all that burden on you. What will your family think?"

"My family think it's lovely. I wired Dad yesterday

morning when Sam went down to the village for bread and the answer came just now over the telephone while you were gone. He said 'The more the merrier. Give them my hearty welcome!'"

"Does he know who we are?" asked John Saxon grimly. His lips were set in a thin, firm line and Mary Elizabeth felt that this was going to be bad.

"You mean does he know that you are going to marry me?" asked Mary Elizabeth gaily. "Not officially yet, I'm leaving that for you to tell him. But I shouldn't be surprised if he suspects. He's a pretty canny man, my father is."

"Yes," said John Saxon still more grimly, "and you think I could have the face to go and ask the father of a Wainwright to give his daughter to a penniless man without a flicker of prospect for the future?"

"Why, yes," said Mary Elizabeth still gaily, "that is, if you still want to marry me!"

"I want to marry you, yes, God knows that, but I don't want you to be tied down to poverty, and I couldn't ask you, a Wainwright, to marry me a poor nothing, not until I was sure of a living."

"Forget that Wainwright business, will you?" said Mary Elizabeth crossly. "It's the first trace of snobbishness I've found in you and I wouldn't have suspected it. As if money made one person better than another."

"You'll find a father will think so."

"Not my father," said Mary Elizabeth. "If it did I'd disown him. However, of course," and Mary Elizabeth's chin went up a little proudly, "if you want to let your mother droop and die in this hot summer climate and want to send me off with a broken heart, and incidentally maybe knick a little crack out of your own heart, why keep your old pride!"

She turned her head away from him to hide the

tremble of her lip and the blinking of her eyes. Mary Elizabeth was not a crying girl, but she was tired and overwrought, and this man was going to be stubborn.

But John Saxon suddenly stopped his car and put his arms around her again.

"Mary Elizabeth," he said solemnly, "God knows I want to marry you, but I don't want to take any advantage of you."

"You already took advantage of me going down that church aisle," gurgled Mary Elizabeth from the shelter of his arms, "and now you've got to bear the consequences! Pride or no pride, money or no money, you're not going to stand aloof from me for months and years nor even weary weeks, until you've brought your bank account up to mine, for I won't stand it. You showed me what I wanted when you walked me down that church aisle, and now I can't be satisfied with any counterfeit. The men I used to know don't interest me any more. Please don't be difficult, John Saxon. I love you, you know. And you'll find that that will make all the difference with Dad, too. You see Dad loves *me,* and he's going to love *you!*"

They got back to the bungalow eventually, though they did not give very satisfactory accounts of where they had been. But everybody was too busy to notice much except Sam, and he kept his own counsel, and went around suppressing a perpetual whistle, grinning all to himself whenever he might not whistle for fear of disturbing the invalid. Twice he went off in the woods by himself just to whistle, he felt so glad.

There was another reason for whistling, too. Just that day the doctor had announced that if the patient's pulse and temperature stayed as they were for a couple more days he thought they could plan to take her away. That would mean that the horrible time of anxiety would be over. Sam drew a deep breath and said "Oh Boy!" out loud to the tall pines, palmettos and waving moss.

The doctor brought up the subject that very evening while he and the two Saxons and Cousin Richie Wainwright were eating a quiet family meal in the Saxon kitchen, with Sam acting as waiter and Mary Elizabeth doing a tasty bit of experimental cooking.

"By the way, John," he said genially, "I think it's imperative that we get that mother of yours away from this heat at once. How about starting day after to-morrow if she still continues to improve? Mary Elizabeth has invited us all to a wonderful place by the sea, and I think the quicker we get there the better. It will be a lot better for me, too. I need to run up to New York for a few hours and look after some matters, and of course after another week or so I'll only have to run down to the shore occasionally to look after her. You can do all that is necessary most of the time, and of course keep a watch on her. We mustn't stand any chances of relapse. It might go hard with her. What do you think?"

John Saxon looked at his beloved doctor with startled eyes, taking in the facts as the doctor put them, and realizing the good sense of his argument, but there was immediate trouble and anxiety in both voice and expression.

"I hadn't thought that far," he owned. "I didn't see how anything like that could be. It sounds wonderful of course, and Mary Elizabeth has been telling me, but I do not see how I could go. I didn't think I'd be needed. There is work here that I ought to be doing—"

"Certainly you'll be needed!" said the doctor brusquely. "I couldn't take the responsibility of the trip without you, nor of leaving your mother in her present condition, even for a few hours unless you were there. And your father is not able to take the responsibility yet.

You are the king pin of this expedition, young man, and you might as well make up your mind to let everything else go. Groves aren't in it when we're talking about life and death!"

"He's right, Son. Let the grove go. This does seem God-sent," said the father, turning his peaceful eyes earnestly on his son. Since God had given him back his beloved partner he felt that nothing else mattered.

"But Father, if we lose the grove—?" began John Saxon.

"I know, Son, but this comes first. And if—*when*—your mother gets well there'll be a way out of our difficulties somehow."

John Saxon looked troubled, and was silent through the rest of the meal, his eyes deeply thoughtful, and when they were finished he stepped out into the dark grove and wandered around among his trees, looking up to the dark blue above him studded with stars.

It was there Cousin Richie found him half an hour later,—just strolled around and stood beside him as if that was the most natural thing in the world to do.

"You've got a nice grove here," he said casually, as if groves were only incidental in the scheme of things.

"Yes," said John, "it will be if it can have the attention it needs. In a couple of years it will put Father and Mother in comfort."

"Well, of course, that's a thing to be considered, still I suppose it doesn't weigh against their health."

"No," said John with a sigh, "of course not. I don't just know what I ought to do."

Cousin Richie was still for a minute, then he said:

"Nice grove! I suppose the old folks are greatly attached to it, aren't they? They wouldn't want to leave it?"

"No," said John Saxon, "I don't think they are. But

it's all they have of course, and it would mean a big loss if it died out. They've often talked over the matter, and sometimes wished they had gone somewhere else when they were buying."

"They wouldn't think of selling, I suppose, would they?"

John Saxon smiled.

"You couldn't sell anything now," he said. "You could hardly give it away. People are not buying. We could never get our money out of it."

"*Some* people are buying. Some people think it is a good time to buy when things are cheap. What would you have to get for it to get your money out? Fertilizers, labor and all, I mean."

John Saxon thought for a minute and then named a sum that seemed so ridiculously low that Cousin Richie almost laughed aloud at how things were being thrown into his hand.

"I think I could get more than that for you," he said thoughtfully, "if you think your father would consider selling at all. I have a friend up in New York who is interested in real estate. You might speak to your father and find out if he would be interested. If you say so I'll call up my friend in the morning and see if I can get an offer. How many acres have you? How old are your trees?"

They stayed out in the starlight for some time, John giving information about the grove, details of expenses etc., telling the price of land in that section when they purchased several years ago. Then he went in and had a little talk with his father. Later he wandered over to the plane and sought out Richie Wainwright again.

"Father says he'd be glad to sell," said John Saxon. "He says Mother needs to get away, and he knows she's been longing to go north again. He'd be willing to sell at almost any figure that would cover what he's actually put out."

"All right. I'll see what I can do in the morning," said Cousin Richie, trying to appear most casual.

"Well, it would be great, of course," said John Saxon, "but I'm not entertaining any very high hopes. Florida has slumped, you know, and people are not running around paying anything for isolated orange groves in the wilderness."

"You're sure your mother won't mind? You don't have to ask her first?" said Cousin Richie.

"No, we'll tell her the good news if it ever happens," grinned John Saxon. "That will be better for her than hoping for something that never could be."

"Well, we'll try it out in the morning," said Cousin Richie dryly. "Now you run home and get some sleep, and don't fret about things."

John Saxon said good night and went to his bed. He was not taking the matter of a possible sale very seriously. He thought this rich man did not understand the present state of the market for Florida property, and he had even more serious problems to face than the possible loss of the grove. He couldn't rightly exult in the love of the girl he had chosen because the way ahead looked dark and blank. He couldn't possibly marry Mary Elizabeth in his present penniless state, and he had a struggle with himself to lay the whole matter before the Lord and go quietly to sleep, but he finally did, and the new day dawned with a joy over the whole little group that could not be daunted by poverty or pain or anxiety of any kind. John Saxon's mother was getting well and what more could be desired?

In the morning Cousin Richie borrowed John Saxon's old flivver and drove in to the village. In about an hour he returned and said that his friend in New York had offered a sum twice as large as the highest hopes of the Saxon family had ever dared go. Old Mr. Saxon sat with an incredulous look upon his face and laughed when they told him. It took a lot of talking to make him understand that the offer was genuine. When he was at last convinced he sat and beamed.

"How about this furniture?" asked Cousin Richie. "Old family heirlooms? Have to keep it or want to sell?"

"It's all very cheap furniture, bought down here, no heirlooms," said John, looking about him at the things that had made up his background of home for the last fifteen years. "It's not worth much, and not worth taking north. But you wouldn't get anything for it."

"Well, I told him I didn't know if you wanted to sell the furniture of course. I told him it was plain and comfortable, nothing fancy, but it would be worth a thousand more if it was left furnished. He said all right, that would be good. Then I could select a care-taker who could live here and get right to work on the grove. Know any such person?"

"Oh, yes," said John Saxon. "Eric Tanner over in the next county is an expert with orange trees, and he'd be glad to get the job. He lost a lot of money in the slump. But really, Mr. Wainwright, this furniture isn't worth a thousand dollars. It isn't worth half that, not even when it was new."

"That's all right. It's worth that much to the new owner, just to get the grove taken over right away. We'll fix up the papers this afternoon and take them with us to sign in New York. Now, how soon do you think you could get away? Are there any things Mrs. Saxon would want to keep? Better find that out right away, and after lunch I'll take a flivver or the plane and go hunt Eric Tanner."

"Gee!" said Sam, standing in the doorway listening.

"You certainly are a fast worker!" said John Saxon, looking dazed. "It seems as if this was too good to be true."

"It certainly does," said John Saxon's father. "I'm afraid the man will think he's been cheated when he gets down here and sees everything."

"Oh, he won't get down here," said Cousin Richie easily. "He's just buying this on speculation. He'll put money into it and make it a success. He'll sell it for a lot more by and by when things come up from the slump again. Don't you worry about him. He deals in large interests and buys widely. He's taken my word for it that this is worth buying, and I feel sure it is, if one has the money to develop it. There's land enough all around to buy up, too, and enlarge, if he wants to. He's glad to know about it!"

"Well, it's just a miracle," said the old man sweetly, "just another miracle our Heavenly Father has let you be the instrument of bringing to us. We can never be thankful enough to you for your part in it."

Cousin Richie hurried away from praise as from a plague, and he came out into the orange grove rubbing his eyes and clearing his throat. He had never met people quite like these before.

Sam watched him away and then he slipped out into the kitchen where Mary Elizabeth was doing some work.

"Say, Mary Beth, did Cousin Richie buy this grove himself?"

"Why, he *says* that a man named Westgate bought it," said Mary Elizabeth turning a radiant smile on Sam.

"Oh *yeah?*" said Sam speculatively.

25

IT was decided that Mother Saxon was well enough to be told one or two of the things that were about to happen. Father Saxon was to do the telling while he sat with her for a few minutes. He was warned that it must be done so that it couldn't possibly excite her.

"Well, Mother," said Mr. Saxon, settling down in his chair, "do you feel strong enough to hear some good news?"

"Good news?" said Mother Saxon slowly. "Why surely. Good news never hurts anybody, does it? I really think, dear, that I'll be well enough to sit up in a few days, don't you think so? What better news could there be for me than that?"

"Well, we'll have to ask the doctor about when you can sit up," said Father smiling, "we're not going to have any relapses, you know. But listen, Mother, the unexpected has happened. We've had an offer for the grove. How about it, shall we sell?"

"I suppose they haven't offered enough to pay half what you've put in," said the wife. "Are you sure it's a genuine offer? Or just another one of those fakes, people trying to get property for nothing?"

"No, it's genuine enough. A man in New York. Mr. Wainwright knows him. I'm pretty well convinced we should sell. I'd like to take you back north, at least for the summer."

"But Father, not at a great loss! I can't bear to have you lose everything you've put in. And all your hard work!"

But when he told her the price that was offered she gasped delightedly.

"Why, Father, it's just like the fairy tales I used to dream out when I was a child going to sleep! You're not 'kidding me' are you, as John says?"

"No, I'm not kidding you. It's a genuine offer. He wants to take it over right away. He wants to buy the furniture too. He'll pay a thousand more for everything just as it stands. Of course you're to take out anything you very much prize. Or, of course, if you want to keep the furniture you can."

"No, there's nothing but the old clock and grandmother's bureau and chair that is worth keeping," said the pleased old lady, "but I can't make it seem real. Why _uld he want furniture he'd never seen?"

"_'_ _oing to put a man in right away to work the grove. He _._ _' it would save time and trouble to have a place all ready for him to live."

"How soon does he want us to get out? We'd have to pack our personal things of course."

"Yes, but that wouldn't take long, I guess. The man would like to take over the place this week."

"But, dear, does the doctor think I'd be able to get up by then? And where could we go, with you not able to walk yet without a crutch?"

"Not to say exactly up," said the smiling old man.

"Yes, up, up in the air perhaps," he smiled again. "But he says you'll be able to be moved. And we're invited to a house party! Mary Elizabeth Wainwright has invited us to a house party at the seashore and the doctor says you can go!"

The old lady looked dazed.

"But I couldn't possibly go to a house party," she said, "I've nothing fit to wear. It's very lovely of her of course, but I couldn't possibly do it. Everything I have is quite worn and old. It was well enough for down here, but it wouldn't do for a seashore place nor a house party. And besides, I haven't even anything fit to wear traveling!"

"Well, you talk with Mary Elizabeth about it, Mother. She'll explain it all out to you. And John, he thinks it's all right!"

"He would!" said the woman who had come back to earth again from the borderland of heaven, and realized that her fig leaves were entirely out of date. "John is a dear lamb but he doesn't know about clothes!"

"Oh, but I do!" cried Mary Elizabeth entering at just the right minute from her station outside the door. "I'll tell you all about it. You see it isn't a fashionable summer resort where you are going. It's a dear old house where I used to go when I was a child, and I love it. There are no fashionable people around, and anyway our house party is just going to be us, and clothes don't matter."

"But I've really nothing to travel in, dear," said the old lady who had begun to love the lovely girl who seemed to be a sort of assistant to the nurse, and was yet a cousin of Jeffrey Wainwright of whom she was so fond.

"Oh, but don't you know, you're just going to travel in your nightie, so that needn't bother you at all," laughed Mary Elizabeth.

"In my *what?*" exclaimed Mother Saxon in horror.

Then appeared John Saxon on the scene.

"Mother, you see it's this way. You've got to go very quietly. You've been too sick for us to risk any excitement. So we're just going to carry you over across the road and put you in a nice bed, in an airplane. You know you've always wished you could ride in one, and now you've got your wish!"

"An airplane! Oh, John! And how much will that cost? Just because you are selling the orange grove for more than we expected, don't go and get extravagant. I can perfectly well go in the train. I couldn't think of letting you pay a lot for an airplane."

"But it isn't costing anything, Mother!" assured John with a lot of joy in his eyes and a more rested look than Mary Elizabeth had seen on his face since they came down. "Mary Elizabeth's cousin Richie is taking us all back in his plane that he brought the doctor and nurse and Sam and Mary Elizabeth down in. Isn't that nice? Now, will you tell us, please, just what you want to keep of the furniture in the house? Sam and I are going to pack whatever you want to keep this afternoon. We'll go away and leave you a while and let you think about it, but you mustn't get excited."

"Excited!" said Mother Saxon. "I guess I have a right to be excited over all that! But can't you wait till I'm up before you pack?"

"No, we can't! We've got to get out of the house! Is there much you want beside the pictures, and the chests and trunks in the attic? I'll send everybody else out and sit down beside you now with a pencil and write down all you think of, and then you must go to sleep. Those are the doctor's orders."

"There isn't much, dear. Our personal things. The curtains perhaps?"

"Leave the curtains," advised John. "You can get new

ones when you have a new home. It will make the house look more homelike to leave them."

"Why, of course!" said Mother, relaxing with a smile. "It's a little bit like going to live in heaven, isn't it? You won't need the things you leave behind because you'll have better ones."

John Saxon stooped and kissed his mother, with a breath of thanksgiving in his heart that she was not leaving them for heaven yet, and then went back to his list.

In ten minutes he came out and Mary Elizabeth went in, and wafted a big palm leaf fan till the sweet old invalid dropped off to sleep.

John Saxon went through the house picking out the things that had to be kept. He realized that now he had hopes of getting his family into the safety of a cooler world, nothing else seemed to matter. The actual packing was not arduous. John produced two big boxes from the little shanty that was dignified by the name of garage and he and Sam stowed away books and pictures, and the few little precious trifles that are found in every home.

Cousin Richie borrowed John's flivver and went to make arrangements with Eric Tanner, saying as he left that he would arrange to leave the Saxon belongings stored in the attic until fall till they would know where to have them sent. Things were assuming quickly the attitude of departure.

The doctor came and went with a light of satisfaction in his face. He had saved another life, and that was better to him than anything else in the world. He watched his patient carefully without seeming to do so. He stepped in several times during the afternoon, watched her breathing, listened to her heart, touched her pulse lightly, and slipped out again with almost a grin on his rugged face.

The nurse was washing out garments and hanging them to dry in the back yard. The doctor came out to her.

"I believe it's done her good to be told. Her pulse is as strong and steady as I've seen it." There was a ring of triumph in his voice.

"Perhaps!" said the nurse doubtfully.

"Perhaps, nothing of the kind," muttered the doctor. "The sooner she's out of this heat the better."

So the work went steadily, quietly on. In the sick room, Mary Elizabeth, cautiously opening drawers and folding garments, sorting them in neat piles, was selecting the things that would be needed by Mrs. Saxon on the way.

Night came on and found things well on the way to readiness for the journey.

Mary Elizabeth went over to the plane for the night and looked up at the velvet star-studded sky thinking how things had worked out even in the very small details so that there seemed to be nothing to worry about anywhere. She wondered if God would always do that with troublesome details, if she would trust them absolutely to Him?

But out on the highway, Boothby Farwell was speeding along in the blackness of night, turning over in his mind his well laid plans to ship that impertinent kid, Sam Wainwright, home to his mother on the first train, and kidnap Mary Elizabeth! He had hoped to make his destination by that afternoon, but in some unaccountable way he had got off the highway, and had to go miles to get back again. He must stop at the next possible resting place and wait till morning. He was almost out of gas, dog-weary and terribly thirsty. But in the morning he would start early and arrive in time to get the kid off on the night train. Then Mary Elizabeth would find out whether it was worth while to trifle with him or not!

But unfortunately for his plans someone had left a lot of broken glass in the way, and Farwell was not driving carefully through the night. The result was that he was laid up for several hours waiting for his car to be put in running order again, and thus it was the morning of the second day before he reached the village for which he was aiming. Still he felt reasonably sure that his prey would not escape. How could they get by him? This was the only highway, wasn't it?

26

A GREAT deal was accomplished the next morning at the bungalow before the invalid awoke, and during the day Mary Elizabeth and Nurse Noble did their best to keep her quietly interested in getting together such of her own garments as she wanted to take with her. Then when Mary Elizabeth felt she was getting a little weary she would tell her about the sea, and the whispering pines, and gently sing her to sleep.

It was planned that they should leave the next morning as early as possible, and Cousin Richie had spent time on his plane, getting it in perfect order for the start. John Saxon had errands here and there preparatory to leaving. Then toward night Eric Tanner arrived and had to be introduced to the needs of the grove. There really hadn't been any too much time anywhere since the decision had been made to start, and Mary Elizabeth had been busy too, for there were telegrams to send to Father, and Uncle, and the Bateman caretakers, to be sure that there were supplies in the house and a meal ready to serve almost any time.

It was with great eagerness that she got up the next

morning and dressed in her last clean white dress, ready to leave. They didn't even have to wash the breakfast dishes, Mr. Tanner had said, for he would do them. Though they did wash them. Nurse Noble wouldn't hear to anything else.

And indeed there was time enough, for at the last minute a man came to buy John Saxon's old flivver, and Eric Tanner offered to give a little more than the other man, and John Saxon had to do some dickering between them.

Then, just before they were to take Mrs. Saxon out to the plane the doctor discovered that his bottle of rubbing alcohol was empty, having been upset by somebody's carelessness when the cork was out. Also one or two other things needed replacing from the drug store. Sam eagerly offered to go for them on John's old bicycle, the flivver obviously being otherwise occupied at that moment, and so there was a short breathing space in which everybody went around being sure that nobody had left anything.

Sam was glad to have an outlet for his excitement. He bent low over the handle bars of the bicycle and rattled along over the resonant board walk, the little gay scared lizards whisking along before him and darting beneath the boards whenever they got too near. The sun beamed down hotly and the perspiration streamed down Sam's face, but he wore a broad grin of satisfaction, and he could scarcely restrain himself. Sometimes he whistled and sometimes he sang:

> *"Everything's all right in my Father's house . . .*
> *There'll be joy, joy, joy all the while!"*

But when he approached the sleepy little hamlet and drew near to the store he sobered down, and put on a grown-up air. He leaned his wheel against the building and sauntered in casually, in the regular boy way. No one would have dreamed he was in a terrible hurry, or that anything exciting was going on that morning.

He handed over the doctor's prescription and the bottles that were to be filled, and sauntered back to the end of the counter examining the dusty articles there on display.

The sound of an automobile horn drew his attention, and a great car flashed up, brilliant with chromium, a car with a familiar look about it. Sam turned and squinted at it carefully. He even came forward a step or two to make sure.

"Good night!" he said softly to himself. "If that poor fish hasn't butted in again!"

He stood there in consternation and watched the man get out of his car and come toward the drug store. Yes, it was Farwell, no mistake about it!

Sam stuffed his hands in his pockets and ducked casually behind the counter out of sight, keeping both eyes and ears open to developments.

"Is there a man named Saxon living around this neighborhood?" asked Farwell in his condescending tone.

"Yep!" snapped the clerk clipping off the string that tied Sam's alcohol bottle. "Lives about five and a half miles west of here, up the first road to the right, turn at the cross roads. You can't miss it!"

"Thanks! That sounds easy! Have you got anything to drink?"

The clerk named the various drinks as he sauntered back to Sam with his bundles.

Farwell gave his order curtly and then said:

"By the way, are there any people visiting these Saxons? A young woman and a red-haired kid?"

The clerk gave a quick startled look at Sam, met a deadly wink that only Sam's eye knew how to give, and sauntered back slowly, answering:

"Couldn't say. There might be and there might not be. You'd havta go and see." Slowly he went at the work of preparing the drink, and looked back where Sam had been standing. But Sam had made good his escape, informally, out of the back door.

"Good night!" thought Sam again. "I can't get out there ahead of him on this bike. I gotta do something! If he gets there before we get started he'll gum the works entirely! *Good night!*"

Sam gave a quick look at the big blue car with its silver trim, took in its direction from the window by the soda counter and ventured forth furtively.

Darting out into the road opposite the car, he stooped down, his bicycle leaning against his back as if he were doing something to its pedals, and reaching out a quick hand back of him he turned a tiny cap on the rear tire of the big blue car. A soft whistling sound ensued. Sam slid a length to the front wheel and did the same thing to that. Then with a furtive glance toward the drug store window, noting that the enemy was still standing with his back to the window, sipping his drink in a leisurely way, Sam slid his wheel around behind the car and doctored the other two tires, in spite of having to struggle with one cap that resisted.

He caught up his own wheel then and whirled out of sight, taking a short cut through the woods, which, though bad for bicycling, would at least hide him from immediate view.

Sometimes he had to jump down and run beside his wheel to make any time at all, until he came into the road again and could take to the rickety board walk. Then he raced along madly. How long would it take for that dumb fish to find a garage and get his tires pumped up again? Could he make it to the house and get the folks to start at once?

The alcohol bottle in its thin paper wrapping bumped around in the wire basket that was fastened to the front of the wheel. He must look out. If he broke that bottle there would be more delay.

The last half mile he was puffing like a porpoise, and he looked like anything but a neat boy prepared to go a journey.

Sam arrived just as they were carrying Mrs. Saxon across from the house on a mattress. John Saxon was carrying the head, Cousin Richie the foot, the nurse and Mary Elizabeth on either side.

Sam held his breath till they had lifted her up and carried her into the plane. Then he slid the old bicycle into its place in the garage and came on the run, just in time to help Mr. Saxon, who was trying to get along by himself to save trouble.

As he upheld Father Saxon he cast a furtive glance down the road looking for a flashy blue car with silver edges, but all was quiet and empty on the highroad so far.

"Is there anything else in the house to go?" he asked Cousin Richie when he had seated his passenger comfortably. "There's some poor fish down at the village on his way to find Mary Beth and I happen ta know she don't want him. Can't ya get started before he gets here?"

Cousin Richie cast a speculative eye at Sam, a keen glance at Mary Elizabeth, who was smiling down and giving some direction to John Saxon, and then said:

"Sure thing, son. Run after John and help him bring the rest of the things. There aren't many, and I'll get the engine ready."

Sam scuttled off, his eye down the road again.

Three minutes more and they were back with the last load, and nobody in sight yet. John Saxon was lingering to say a few last words to Eric Tanner. Would he never be done?

At last they were off. Sam felt the smooth vibration of the engine, the slow movement that seemed to be scarcely motion at all, for the ride was to be a quiet one not to excite the invalid. And now at last they were rising, a little, and a little, and now the ground was really quite far below them. Sam drew a deep breath.

Then, looking down the road from the height that gave him a better view he saw a great blue car flash into view, its shining trim casting sharp brightness in the sun. Sam looked down and grinned.

He cast one more look at the ground, measured the possibilities of turning around and going back again for callers and decided they were nil, then he slid over to Mary Elizabeth's side pointing down.

"There goes that poor fish of a Farwell, coming to call. Do you wantta go back and entertain him?" he said into her ear.

Mary Elizabeth gave a quick glance back and saw the bright car slowing down before the bungalow, saw Eric Tanner coming out to meet it, and a look of amazement grew upon her face. It couldn't be that Boothby had found out where she was and had dared to follow so far! It must be another car, like his, of course.

"What makes you think that is Mr. Farwell, Sam?" she asked.

"Because I saw him down at the village when I went after the alcohol. He was getting a drink, and asking the way out here! He wanted to know if the Saxons had company, a girl and a red-haired boy!"

Sam's face and voice expressed the scorn and disgust he did not put into words.

"But I don't understand," said Mary Elizabeth, "Why didn't he get here before you did? It's a long way into the village and you had only a bicycle?"

"Sure, I fixed him so he couldn't. I let the air out of his tires!"

"Sam! You didn't! Not *really?*"

"Sure I did! I wasn't going to have that poor dumb fish coming here gumming things all up just as we were getting off."

Suddenly Mary Elizabeth put her head down and laughed and laughed. Then she said:

"Sam, there are a great many things I have to thank you for, and this is not the least of them. Oh, Sam, Sam, for a person who knows as much about the Bible as you do, you certainly are the limit!"

Then Mary Elizabeth's eyes turned away and rested with great tenderness on John Saxon who was bending over his mother, smiling and holding her hand, helping her through the first startling idea of riding in the air.

The great bird lifted and soared aloft, smoothly, evenly, and suddenly the young man who had come out seeking a wild free thing, to bind and bend it to his will, found that his bird had flown away, and wildly he lifted a futile shout, and raised his hand in a gesture of command. Then he ran with all his might forward toward where the plane had been, dashing into the deep untrodden sand without looking where he stepped, and wallowed along screaming and shaking his fist up toward the vanishing plane. Suddenly his head and shoulders were going faster than his feet could get there, and the inevitable happened. Boothby Farwell went down ignominiously in the sand and literally bit the dust, sand in his eyes and sand in his ears and sand in his mouth, a sorry figure, stunned, and blinded, and so angry he was stupefied for the instant.

And the girl he was chasing did not even see him. She had eyes for only one man and he was up in the air with her.

Only Sam saw the downfall of his enemy and stood grinning with all his might and finally laughing aloud in a great boy roar, but the engine drowned the sound and nobody was the wiser.

THE great plane came to earth on the smooth, broad beach almost exactly in front of the Wainwright summer estate, taxi-ing over the hard, white sand as lightly as over a marble floor, and the invalid who had been greatly intrigued and unexpectedly invigorated by her flight, scarcely knew she had lit upon earth yet.

Almost at once, there appeared around the plane Mary Elizabeth's father, Sam's father, Frank Bateman wheeling an invalid chair-cot, and Susan Bateman, her hands wrapped in a neat white apron, standing respectfully in the background. It had the air of an occasion, almost of a celebration, and Mary Elizabeth's eyes shone with satisfaction as she looked upon the group. Not one of them was missing! Dad had been equal to the occasion as she knew he would be, as he always had been since she could remember, and Uncle Robert Wainwright was right behind him. They were great brothers, those two, of the House of Wainwright, and Mary Elizabeth was proud of them.

Then her glance went to John Saxon, who had suddenly straightened up from assuring his mother they had landed, and was taking in the situation. John Saxon's face was tense with a dawning comprehension of what all this might mean, suffused suddenly with a deep embarrassment, and then a quick misty realization of the kindness that had prompted it all.

Oh, he had met them both, those Brothers Wainwright, at the wedding; big, successful, kindly, blustering, but polished men of the world. Under the guise of a best man he had shaken their hands and let their hearty greetings at introduction roll off from his consciousness as something that didn't mean a thing to him personally, being only a part of the wedding ceremonies.

But now, suddenly brought face to face with them in a personal way, with the weight of a great debt of gratitude to them hung about his neck John Saxon was overwhelmed.

Mary Elizabeth saw and understood. It was like Mary Elizabeth to understand, even if he hadn't been John Saxon, and dearly beloved. Mary Elizabeth had an understanding mind. And quickly she moved over to stand beside John Saxon, and share the meeting, share the experience of whatever her man was passing through, and take the sting with him, protect his pride with her own hands and her own smiles, so that its gay plumage should not be permanently damaged.

"It's Dad and Uncle Bob!" she exclaimed, sliding her hand into John Saxon's! "Oh, aren't they the old darlings, John! They would leave their business and rush down to have fun with us when we arrive! They're just like kids! They couldn't wait to see you, and to help all they could!"

Somehow her words, and her shining eyes that she lifted to John Saxon's face, took the sting from the mortification, and suddenly put John Saxon and his honored father on a level with the whole Wainwright tribe. It made him forget that he was poor and struggling, and utterly presuming to dare to have aspired to the hand of Mary Elizabeth Wainwright, heir to millions, and choice of the whole universe of women.

Suddenly his hand folded the hand of Mary Elizabeth close in his own, and looking down into her shining happy eyes he felt for the first time utterly that he and she were one, and that it didn't matter if those two relatives out there on the sand had been a whole battalion of royal soldiers come out to battle with him for a princess, she would never leave him, nor would he have to let her go, for they belonged together, now and through eternity.

It was Sam who alighted first and did the honors of the ship as if he had been commander.

"Well, here we all are!" he announced importantly. "Howareya, Dad? Hello, Uncle Sam! All ready for us, aren't ya? Well, we're all okay!"

His father enveloped him quickly with a strong possessive arm and said with a relieved voice:

"Sure! I knew you would be! Great son you are, Kid! I'm proud of you. How's the invalid?"

"Oh, she's fine. The doctor says it did her good! She's a good sport, she is!" swaggered Sam as if she were a protégée of his.

Then all was quiet orderliness. Mary Elizabeth's father came forward and grasped John Saxon's hand as he alighted from the ship.

"Glad to see you! So good you could bring your mother right here. Nothing like sea air. Now, here's the outfit. Think this will be comfortable for her? Get her right up to the house in a jiffy and into her bed. How do you want this wheel-chair arrangement set? Head this way? Frank can wheel it and we'll steady it, or we could carry it if necessary. This the doctor? Glad to meet you,

Doctor. Great work you've been doing, I hear. Now, we're here to serve, just tell us how to move to cause the least excitement. And we've brought a wheeled chair for Mr. Saxon—"

Quiet, pleasant, business-like voices, steady, composed air as if they were all one family bent on doing the very best for the invalids. He was perfect, thought his daughter, listening with overflowing heart of joy. Dear Dad!

With the least noise and fuss possible the little procession formed, bearing the invalid gently, steadily up the beach, into the great grilled gateway, under the whispering pines, and into the hospitable old-fashioned mansion.

"I'm Mary Elizabeth's father," said Samuel Wainwright to the invalid just before they started, "and we're very glad to welcome you. Now we aren't going to bother you with any more introductions to-day till you're rested from your journey!"

Mother Saxon lifted her sweet eyes and smiled, and the brothers dropped behind to escort Father Saxon in his wheeled chair as if he were a king among his subjects.

So they came down from the sky, and went up from the sea, and the old Wainwright summer home came to life after many years of quietness.

Before she could possibly realize what was happening Mother Saxon was tenderly lifted and laid in the softest bed on which she had ever been and was swallowing a glass of orange juice in a fragrant darkened room, with flowers dimly lifting fairy faces in quiet corners. There was the dull gleam of old mahogany, the smooth feel of linen sheets and pillow cases, the soft murmur of whispering pines above, the deep undertone of the ocean not far away, all mingling softly into a delicious sleepy atmosphere, with the memory of Mary Elizabeth's soft lips, brushing her forehead, and her boy John's tender pat on her hand. Could mortal happy woman keep awake under those circumstances?

The doctor tiptoed in, touched her wrist, her brow, winked in satisfaction at the nurse, and nodded his approval, tiptoed out again and she never knew it.

Out around the side of the house Mother Saxon's old lover sat in a deep comfortable chair with his hurt foot on a cushion and enjoyed a real old-time talk with men of his own age and education, discovering mutual friends, similar experiences, and links of their younger days that made them friends at once. Till Mary Elizabeth and his son John suddenly descended upon him and swept him off to the little room adjoining the invalid's room, and made him take a nap.

Cousin Richie had taken the doctor up the beach fifty miles or so in his plane to visit a convalescent patient about whom he was a bit anxious, Mary Elizabeth and John Saxon had gone off down the beach hand in hand, and it was then that young Sam had his innings, sitting on the side steps with his father and his Uncle Sam who were lying back in two big old beach chairs listening to him proudly.

By the time the rest came back there was not an incident of the trip down and back that had not been recounted, and the two old men had laughed till they wept over the story of the deflated tires and Boothby Farwell wallowing in the sand, shaking his fist at the departing plane.

"Well, Samuel," said Robert Wainwright at last, wiping the tears from his pleased old face. "All I've got to say is, that girl of yours is smart as they make 'em. She knows her onions! And she certainly has picked a rare one! I like that John Saxon! Even if my Jeff hadn't picked him first as the best man he knew, I'd still have liked him!"

"Yes," said Mary Elizabeth's father with a faraway look in his eyes, "I consider that I've had a very narrow escape, to say nothing of Mary Elizabeth! Of course, we may be a little previous. They haven't said anything about it, but it sorta looks that way," and he nodded down toward the beach where a man and a maid could be seen walking very slowly along the bright sand.

"It certainly does!" agreed the uncle, "no mistake about that. Haven't I just been through one wedding? Can't I tell the look in the eye of a young lover? You certainly had a narrow escape if you ever considered that young ape of a Farwell in the light of a son-in-law."

"Well, I didn't know what to think, one time there. I didn't know but I was going to have to take Mary Elizabeth around the world again, or up to the moon or something. I guess I've got young Sam to thank for showing him up several times! Good work, Kid! Good work! I shan't forget it! Mary Elizabeth was telling me something about some empty bottles in a case of liquor. Sam ever tell you that tale, and the mystery of how they got empty? Get him to tell you that, Bob. It's a good one!"

And then they were off again listening to young Sam and laughing.

The days went by and the invalid improved in leaps and bounds. Dr. MacKelvie lingered a few days to be sure that all was well and then hurried away to his neglected vacation and patients, returning occasionally when Cousin Richie brought him down for a day or two to watch Mother Saxon.

The summer was slipping away fast now, and the invalid was able to walk on the piazza a few steps every day leaning on the arm of her strong son. Sometimes Mary Elizabeth walked on her other side encouraging her.

There came a day when John Saxon felt he might be spared to run up to New York for another interview with the great man who was to be his instructor during the winter.

While he was gone Mary Elizabeth and Sam took the honors of looking after the invalid upon themselves. Of course the nurse was there yet, but Mary Elizabeth knew that Mrs. Saxon felt a little formal with her in spite of the long weeks of her ministrations. So when the invalid was taken out on the piazza, either to walk or just to sit and enjoy the air and listen to the beating of the waves, or to watch a white sail flit, it was Mary Elizabeth who came out and occupied a chair near by with a nice book, often reading aloud to her; and it was Sam with his knife and a stick who sat on the top step not far away, whittling, sometimes softly whistling, ready to run for a glass of milk or orange juice, or a cup of broth or the medicine.

Sam was very happy in these days. It seemed to him that this last few weeks had been a special dispensation of Providence to show him exactly what like Heaven was going to be like some day.

He had been almost entirely free from being told what to do, or what not to do. In fact he didn't seem to want to do anything except what the people around him most desired. He had had long hours of close companionship with his beloved hero–doctor, walking on the beach, fishing, crabbing, swimming, and often getting a Bible lesson when he least expected it.

Mary Elizabeth, too, had often been with them, and that made it all the better. Sam believed that there were no two better in all the world than Mary Elizabeth and John Saxon. And he often marveled that they were willing to have him around when they were together. He had noticed that the way of the world with a man and a maid was that they had no time for small boys. So he adored them all the more, and was most humble and grateful, and as unobtrusive as possible.

In some of the long walks with John Saxon he had learned of a boys' school not far from home, where there were Christian teachers, and where many of the boys were Christians also. Listening to his friend's stories of the head master of that school Sam had acquired a deep desire to attend it.

He broached the matter to his father one weekend when he came down to the shore to see if his son were in the way and ought to be removed. His father had been interested, had read the catalogues carefully which Sam diligently acquired, and had written to the head master, finally giving his consent that Sam should go. Sam felt that a new world was opening before him. Of course there might be trouble when his mother arrived on the scene. This calamity was due to happen almost any day now, Sam realized, for it was getting toward the time for migrations back to the city, but his father had given him his word of honor that he would tell his mother that he felt it was time that Sam had a change of environment and that his father should choose the next school, because Sam was growing up. Jeff had written also his hearty approval of the plan, added his own knowledge of the head master to the argument, and promised to speak to his mother. There was due to be a battle, of course, but Sam had reasonable hopes of coming out victorious, and so he was very happy.

Mary Elizabeth had a quiet starry look in her eyes as she went about humming snatches of little tunes. Sam was sure she was happy.

One day her father talking to her over the telephone,

happened to mention a matter which the summer had entirely erased from his memory until then.

"Say, Mary Elizabeth, do you know, I promised Jeff that I would get you to run out sometime this summer and see if Camilla's mother is getting on all right, and it entirely slipped my mind. It won't be long now before Camilla and Jeff will be coming back from their trip, and I'd hate to say I hadn't even told you. I had it in mind that you might ask her and her companion down for a week-end sometime this summer but I guess that's out of the question now, isn't it, while the folks are there? Might be too many for the invalid. But can't you get away to run up to the city for a day and go out and call there?"

"Why, of course," promised Mary Elizabeth. "I've meant to do that all summer only there didn't seem to be any time. But I'm coming up to the city to-morrow, Dad, and I'll make it a point to call. I've got to get another nurse. The one we've had all along thinks she's got to get back to New York to look after her affairs, so I said I'd try and get another. Sam's driving up with me, wants to see his father about his new school, and why can't you come on back with us for over Sunday?"

"Well, perhaps," said her father. "I'm glad you can see Jeff's mother-in-law, that's weighed on my mind."

So Mary Elizabeth called on Camilla's mother. To her delight she discovered that the companion who was staying with her during Camilla's absence was a trained nurse, and before the call was concluded Mary Elizabeth arranged that the two should come down to the shore for the next week, Nurse York taking the place that Nurse Noble would leave vacant in a few days. It seemed an altogether happy arrangement. And so it proved to be.

John Saxon's mother was delighted to have the

mother of her son's dearest friend to visit with, and the two dear elderly ladies spent pleasant hours on the piazza together, drinking in health, and conversing like two girls of their life's experiences.

John Saxon came back from New York with a new light of hope in his eyes. He had not only made satisfactory arrangements about his winter's work with the great specialist, but he had spent an evening with Dr. MacKelvie in his city office, and had been offered an out and out partnership with that great man!

It would mean of course that his future was practically secured. A professional connection with Dr. MacKelvie was beyond compare. There was none better in the land.

"I'm getting old. I need help," said the doctor. "My son who had a bent toward medicine is dead. I've never seen a man before that I cared to work with till I knew you. Will you come and join forces?" He had sat back in his chair and studied the face of the younger man with a kind of wistful yearning.

"But I'm not through my studies yet," said John when he had recovered from his astonishment enough to speak. "I won't be worth anything to you for some time."

"That's all right," said the doctor wearily. "I want you to finish your course. But I believe you told me you were planning to work part time? Well, why not work for me in what leisure you have, and gradually work into things? No, this isn't a philanthropic proposition at all,—" he waved his hand impatiently as he saw that John was going to offer objections,—"I *want* you! I *need* you! There'll be times when I can leave matters with you that I wouldn't trust with an ordinary assistant. See? Because I know you as a man, and I know you've got something that will be dead sure to lean on. I need to lean on you sometimes when I'm hard pressed. Do you think you can stand it to hitch up for a time to an old crotchety man who is getting near the end of his career? I'll see that you don't lose anything by it."

The whole thing seemed too spectacular to be true, and on the way back to the shore John Saxon began strongly to suspect that Mary Elizabeth was somehow at the bottom of such a wonderful proposition. But when he told her about it he saw by her quick surprise and delight that it was as much a surprise to her as to him.

"It means," said John Saxon with a wonderful light in his face, "that now I can go to your father and put myself on something like a working basis with him. It's time he understood how things are between you and me, Mary Elizabeth."

"Yes?" said Mary Elizabeth, lifting her sparkling face with a twinkle in her eyes. "But you know, I sort of think he knows already."

"You haven't been telling him, Mary Elizabeth?" said John Saxon suddenly appalled. "You know I asked you not to till I could have some definite financial future in view."

"Oh, no!" grinned Mary Elizabeth. "I didn't need to tell him. My father has average intelligence. He doesn't need to be told what I like and what I don't like."

Mary Elizabeth's father came down to the shore that night for the week-end, just to look his family over and see how things were getting on. After dinner while it was yet sunset, and the waves were tossing rubies and diamonds and sapphires and amethysts and topazes and pearls about on their crest, John Saxon and Mary Elizabeth's father took a walk out along the many-colored sands together, while the younger man told of his love for Mary Elizabeth.

"Good news, Son!" said the old man in a hearty voice. "You couldn't tell me anything that I'd like better! I never saw a man before that I was willing to have marry Mary Elizabeth, and there's been a-plenty of 'em, I'm telling you! But I feel that you'll be a real son and I can welcome you heartily into the family. I'm going to feel comfortable about Mary Elizabeth with you for a husband. You see I was beginning to be afraid I'd been mistaken about you two after all, and maybe the way would still be open for that nincompoop Farwell yet. You never can tell what a woman will do you know, and that Farwell has ways past finding out. I didn't know but I might have to go out and shoot him or something to get rid of him, and I couldn't die happy leaving my girl open to such as he."

"I wanted to tell you at once, sir," said John eagerly, "but you see I hadn't so much as a shadow of prospect for the future until to-day."

"Stuff and nonsense!" said the father with happy eyes. "As if it wasn't prospect enough just for you and Mary Elizabeth to be together. My girl will have enough for both of you, and you're not to worry about prospects and money, do you understand, young man? You've got something worth far more than money. If we'd wanted more money that cur Farwell has gobs of it. But we didn't, Mary Beth and I, we wanted a real man, and I'm satisfied we've found him. You have my best wishes."

Wainwright put out a strong hand in a hearty grasp, and John Saxon had a sudden rush of warm liking for his girl's father come into his heart.

"There's another thing, too, John," said the older man, "better get married right away. You'll need your wife this winter in New York, and Mary Elizabeth needs you. It isn't as if you didn't know your own minds, and I don't see hanging around and being lonesome when a question like that is really settled."

John Saxon gave his future father-in-law a quick searching look, and then in a wistful voice:

"I wish that were possible, Mr. Wainwright, but I won't begin to have an adequate income for a little while yet, you know. I can give Dr. MacKelvie part time, and can't in honesty accept much for that. Of course, if I were to give up the idea of taking that special work with the other doctor—. But I should lose out in the end, for that special work is going to make me worth more money in the end."

"I understand all that of course," said the old man with a gesture as if he would brush the idea of such folly from the scene. "You must have all the advantages that are to be had. And as for income, that's all poppycock! There's no question of whose income it is between a husband and wife if they're both the right kind. Of course if you were some other style of man I might take your point of view, too,—a man who was out to get his hands on his wife's fortune,—but you're not. And Mary Elizabeth needs your care. I'm an old man. I can't look after her right. And besides, I may not last long. I wish you'd get married soon! I really do. It will be better for you both."

John Saxon's voice was husky with feeling.

"I certainly appreciate your confidence, sir," he said. "I'll never forget what you've said. But you don't real-ize, perhaps— You see, I couldn't possibly keep your daughter in the way she should be kept, not yet. I hope it won't be long before I can,—but—"

"Nonsense," said the old man testily. "Put your pride in your pocket and forget that idea. Mary Elizabeth has knocked around a lot and she would rather knock around with you than waste away in a mansion waiting for you. She's not so hard to please! And anyhow you wouldn't starve, I'd see to that. Oh, I know, your precious pride! But look here now, be reasonable! I want a chance to watch you two be happy a little while before I die, and if I get more pleasure out of using some of my money that way instead of hoarding it up for you to inherit when I'm gone, haven't I a right? Now, listen to me. I've got an apartment in New York, looking out on Gramercy Park. I've owned it for years, and the family used to live in it winters the years we summered down here, when Mary Elizabeth's mother was living. It's old-fashioned, and the neighborhood is not stylish any more, but I like to keep it because of old times. It's big and roomy and comfortable. There'd be plenty of room for your father and mother to be with you winters, at least till they want to go back to Florida, though privately I don't believe they should. I think they need to be with you and be looked after, especially not till your mother is thoroughly strong again. I know Mary Elizabeth thinks so too for she told me so. And there'll be room for me to drop in over night whenever I have business in New York, so I can keep in touch with you all now and then. Come, will you be reasonable and think it over? Here comes Mary Elizabeth now. Here, Mary Beth, come take your future husband and talk turkey to him. I've been offering him the New York apartment for you all to live in this winter. It's all repaired and done over, and if you want any more changes it's all right with me. Now you two run along down the beach and have it out. I'm going back to talk with Mr. and Mrs. Saxon a while. It's getting chilly out here for my rheumatic shoulders."

Mary Elizabeth came running up catching John's hand, the last glow of the sunset in her face, and together they walked slowly into the dying glow of the evening.

And so it came about quite quietly, that there was a

wedding in the old house at last, although there were almost no preparations.

Mary Elizabeth hunted out her mother's fine old wedding veil from a carved chest where it had lain wrapped in satin paper, for many years. And there was a sweet little white dress, very simple and plain and lovely, among her Parisian clothes, a dress which she had been keeping for some special time. There wasn't a thing that Mary Elizabeth needed to buy but a clean pair of white slippers, and those she could telephone for, and they would arrive the next day. In fact a half hour's telephoning completed all Mary Elizabeth's arrangements.

She called up her uncles and she called up her aunts, and a few favorite cousins, and invited them to come down for a house party. She called up Cousin Richie and asked him to meet Jeffrey and Camilla when their boat docked at New York, and fly them down also. He was to tell them that it was a celebration of their home coming and they *must* come! Then she called up the doctor, and the family caterer, giving a brief simple order, and Mary Elizabeth was ready. She didn't bother with any of the long lines of social acquaintances and friends. This was a family affair.

John Saxon's problems were not so easily solved. He had to get a suitable ring wherewith to wed a Wainwright, and he couldn't begin to afford the right kind.

He stayed awake half the night and came down to breakfast all perplexed, announcing that he must go up to town right away.

However, his mother called him to a conference and placed in his hand a little velvet box that he had often seen as a child, but had forgotten long ago.

"These were your Grandmother's, John. I was wondering if you wouldn't like to use them—at least for a little while till you could afford to get something more modern? They are tiny, but Mary Elizabeth has a very small hand. I think she could wear them. Do you think she would like them?"

John Saxon took the worn little velvet box reverently and pressed the tiny pearl button that sprang the lid open, and there were the dear old rings, the wonder of his childhood, in a setting of so long ago that it was almost modern. A plain gold band, and another with a great ruby like a drop of blood, and a pearl of rare luster.

"Oh, Mother!" breathed the son. "But they belonged to your mother! I couldn't let you give them up!"

"It's what I've been keeping them for, Son," said the mother with a pleased light in her eyes. "But you're not to make Mary Elizabeth wear them unless she really likes them."

"Mary Elizabeth will like them, I'm sure!" said John Saxon, stooping to place a reverent kiss on his mother's forehead. "Dear Mother!"

Mary Elizabeth did. They called her and she did. She said she would wear them always. She didn't want them changed for diamonds, ever! She loved them as they were, and when they went up to town John would put her name and his under the quaint old inscription that was still clearly to be read in the ring, announcing the former wearer and its giver.

Then John Saxon had only to telephone to a florist's shop in the city and get a bouquet.

It was Mary Elizabeth's father who supplied the minister. Mary Elizabeth was just back from a drive with John to get the license when he telephoned. She hadn't so much as remembered that a minister would be needed. She gave a little gasp when her father asked her who was going to perform the ceremony. The summer guests who might have a minister among them, had mostly gone back to the city now. Mary Elizabeth didn't number many ministers among her friends, and John Saxon had gone up the beach with Sam so she couldn't ask him what to do.

Mary Elizabeth hesitated so long that her father grew impatient. He waited another second or two and then said:

"Well, if you haven't anybody in mind, how would you like me to bring somebody down?"

"Who is he?" asked the bride-to-be in a perplexed tone.

"He's the young man who married your mother and me, only of course he isn't a *young* man any more. But he was young then and your mother and I thought there wasn't any minister like him, I remember. I just happened to run across him in the city to-day and it occurred to me you might like the idea. I could bring him down and park him at the hotel until the time for the ceremony so there wouldn't be any wondering about him, and then send the chauffeur after him when we're ready."

"Oh, Dad, that would be great!" said Mary Elizabeth delightedly. "I simply hadn't thought about a minister, and there isn't anybody I can think of I'd like. It would be lovely to have the same one you and Mother had!"

"All right!" said the father, "then I'll bring him down. I suppose there's still some place open where we can park him? Some hotel or boarding house open, either there or up the beach a way?"

"Oh, yes," said Mary Elizabeth. "I'll see to that. I'll send Sam up to engage a room somewhere as soon as he comes back. You'll be down early, won't you Dad?"

"Sure thing!" said the father happily. "I might come the night before. All right! Then that's settled."

The servants from the city house were to come down for the house party, but Susan Bateman had everything in such apple-pie order that they found little left to do until the guests arrived, so they made a regular holiday out of it.

Mary Elizabeth and John Saxon wandered off down the beach in the moonlight with no cares at all the night before the wedding.

Mary Elizabeth wore a simple little blue organdy the day of the house party. Of course it happened to be made in Paris and had very lovely lines, but for all that it had a simplicity about it that fitted seashore life, and its color matched her eyes. John Saxon told her so a dozen times an hour.

The guests came fairly early for they wanted to be on hand when Jeffrey and Camilla arrived. They thought it was merely a surprise party for them.

Uncle Warren Wainwright was there with Aunt Fannie, sleek and placid and beaming on everybody, enjoying the view and the pines and reminiscing delightfully about the house and grounds.

Father Wainwright came the night before as he had threatened, having parked his minister safely a mile up the shore, and went about doing the honors, introducing the elder Saxons delightedly as if they belonged to royalty, as in reality they did.

Sam's father and mother arrived a little late as usual, that is later than the rest, and it was plain to be seen that it hadn't been Uncle Robert who had been the cause of the delay.

"I really hadn't a rag left fit to wear," Aunt Clarice declared in apology, glancing down at the elaborate flowered chiffon she had finally elected to wear. "You know I'm only just back from the mountains, and everything is simply unspeakable after the entire summer away from home."

"Oh, but it's a very lovely dress," said Mary Elizabeth

cannily, pouring a few drops of her own sweet personality on the aunt who most frequently troubled the family waters.

"Well, it had to do," sighed the poor woman, dismissing the subject and lifting her lorgnette for a glimpse around at the place.

"Why dear me! The old house really looks quite livable again, doesn't it? I suppose you had to do a lot of replacing and repairing, and it was hardly worth it, was it? So utterly out of date, but it's nice to see it again, a quaint old setting of an age that is gone!" and Aunt Clarice heaved a sentimental sigh.

"And where is my infant son?" she next demanded, bringing down her lorgnette from a survey of fluted columns and giving a quick alert look about for Sam.

Now although Sam was fond of his mother, he had rather dreaded her coming, for she was apt to belittle him, and it embarrassed him exceedingly to be called her infant son, but he had prepared for the meeting by an elaborate toilet, the like of which he had not attempted since he last saw her, which explained the present immaculateness of his garments. They had lain in a bureau drawer all summer.

He came forward now dutifully with a gravity and grace that was astonishing considering his years, and gave his mother the kiss she expected. It quite took her off her balance, it was so unusual. Heretofore he had always had to be admonished about it before he reluctantly welcomed her.

She stood back and surveyed him through her lorgnette, as she had the fluted columns. Sam bore it very well. He had scrubbed unmercifully behind his ears, he had polished his shoes, cleaned his fingernails to a nicety, and put on a necktie he hated but knew she liked. What more could he do? Besides, he was going to a real school now and one had to concede something.

"Why Sam!" she exclaimed in pleased surprise, "you're quite grown up, aren't you? You did that very well. Betty dear, I believe you must have been good for him in spite of everything, though I do think you went a little beyond the limit when you took him up in an airplane."

"Oh, I didn't take him, he took me," laughed Mary Elizabeth.

"And what's this ridiculous idea I hear of, that you've been putting notions in his head about a new school?" said Aunt Clarice putting aside the matter of the airplane for a future time when she could hope to do justice to it. "I really can't think of countenancing his going away from home again when he's been away all summer—"

But just then to the distraction of everybody the buzz of an airplane was heard, and all heads were turned to the heavens. Presently Cousin Richie's big plane came sailing down neatly on the beach and taxied right up to the big iron gateway.

Aunt Clarice watched the performance with a shudder, and several gasps.

"I don't see how he dares!" she said in a terrified voice. "And to think he presumed to take my angel child and his bride up into the sky! I think it was criminal!"

But nobody heard her. They were all rushing down to greet Jeff and Camilla and Cousin Richie. All but John Saxon's mother who lay in her invalid chair, relaxed and happy, and amused at it all. For did she not know a secret that none of the other guests knew?

The dining room was ready in festive array with flowers that had been ordered from the city, a long family table, made up of several sections, a reminder of other days. There was no hint of the big bridal cake that had been hidden away. Not even Mary Elizabeth knew about it. For Mr. Wainwright had given the family servants carte blanche to order what was needed and nothing had been forgotten. But in it all there was nothing to suggest to a casual guest passing through that it was to be a wedding luncheon, and not just a plain house party. It was all quite simple and informal, and the various guests looked about upon each other smiling and relaxed, and thinking how nice it was for them all to be together once more like a big family.

They settled down to talk like a bunch of magpies, and Sam stood about grinning to himself at what was to come. It was going to be swell. Nothing to interfere with the fun, everybody here, nobody missing, no frumpy old cousins that were not wanted, just the ones who belonged. He smoothed a wrinkle out of his white linen coat, adjusted the unaccustomed, throttling tie, and smiled to himself. There were few duties ahead now, and those nice ones. Sam did a great deal of grinning to himself that morning, and in between he ran little pleasant errands, brought Mrs. Saxon's shawl, brought her a better footstool, adjusted the pillows for her, got Mr. Saxon's cane, hovered in the wake of his idol John Saxon, and admired his returned brother and the new unknown sister-in-law from afar.

No one saw the Wainwright car drive in from the back gate and the elderly stranger in a frock coat who got out and followed Sam up the back stairs to a room appointed for his use. No one even noticed that Mary Elizabeth had disappeared for a few minutes. It was getting near to lunch time and they were growing hungry. She had likely gone to give orders to the servants.

When Sam and Miss York helped Mrs. Saxon into the living room they merely thought she was chilly out on the piazza, and several of the guests drifted inside also. Then Sam appeared at the door and called the rest, supposedly to lunch.

"Will you all come in now?" he said pleasantly in quite a grown-up tone, and they responded to the call eagerly.

But inside they stood about uncertainly in the big living room, thinking how lovely it all looked with the airy muslin curtains blowing in the fresh sea breeze, and gorgeous fall roses in great bowls and vases everywhere, wondering why Mary Elizabeth didn't give the signal to come to the dining room.

They could see the long table through the archway now, and it looked so festive and inviting.

Then suddenly Mary Elizabeth appeared at the top of the stairs, with her father just behind her. She had changed her dress! She was wearing white! How strange! She must have soiled that pretty blue one! What a pity, it was so becoming! And what was that she was wearing over her hair? A veil? They gasped softly in amazement, those who stood in the hallway and saw her.

At that instant soft strains from the piano began to sound. They turned about and saw Camilla sitting at the old grand piano playing. Just soft chords, at first, blending in delightful harmony.

Then at the far end of the room, the place that strangely had no chairs in it, Jeff and John Saxon appeared, and a stranger with them, an elderly man! A stranger! In a frock coat! The family stiffened, and prepared to resent the stranger.

Then the music widened and grew stately and became unmistakably the wedding march!

Why, what was this? A wedding? Why, where was Mary Elizabeth, and had that really been a veil over her head?

But Mary Elizabeth was walking into their midst now, on her father's arm, smiling with happy eyes, looking toward John Saxon, and stepping to the well-known measures of the wedding march. That rare old lace that draped her head and flowed down over her lovely new white frock must be her mother's wedding veil. Aunt Clarice was studying it through her lorgnette as it passed her, and recognizing it as if she had memorized every flower on it long years ago.

A low, soft exclamation in chorus broke from all their throats and then they looked up to differentiate the group at the lower end of the room and single out the bridegroom.

John Saxon! Jeffrey Wainwright's best man!

And Mrs. Saxon was sitting in a deep comfortable chair just at the side where she could watch the faces of the two beloved children! She had come north to John's wedding even as she had dreamed! Ah! Was this what had been going on all this quiet summer? And Mary Elizabeth had done this, put this over on them!

"When she might have had that lovely rich Boothby Farwell," sighed Aunt Clarice into a costly handkerchief.

Then the quiet voice of the elderly stranger broke the silence of wonder:

"Dearly beloved, we are met together to join this man and this woman in the bonds of holy Matrimony—"

Sam standing in the doorway his hands gripped together behind his white linen back held his breath listening to every word, storing it away for the time when some great experience should perhaps come into his life, getting a sudden vision of what it might mean to join two souls in such a bond, remembering how John Saxon had taught him that marriage was meant to be a picture of Christ's relation to His true church. Sam's eyes grew misty with tenderness, big and faraway and serious, and his expression startled his mother as she suddenly turned and saw him standing there! Sam was growing up! She must get at him and teach him how to behave in society, she thought with a fleeting sense of her social duties, and then she turned back to take in the lovely scene again, to watch Camilla, playing so exquisitely! That was a revelation, too. She never knew that her new daughter-in-law was a musician. Perhaps she wasn't going to be so bad after all. And Camilla's mother over there in the corner really looked very smart in that lovely gray chiffon. She must ask her how she managed to keep so slim at her age.

Then it was over with a tender prayer. John Saxon had kissed his bride, and Mary Elizabeth was kissing her father, and everybody was stirring happily and milling around, trying to say how surprised they were, and rushing to congratulate the bride and groom.

There was so much gay laughter and talk going on that nobody heard the big showy car drive around the house and stop before the door. That is, nobody but Sam.

Sam caught a glimpse of the enemy approaching up the steps and grinned to himself.

"Good night!" he murmured under his breath. "Just too late, as usual! But let him come! He can't do any damage now."

And Boothby Farwell, frowning at the sight of the family gathering, walked into the hall without ceremony, and was in the midst of the living room staring grimly about him before he realized what was going on.

It was Mary Elizabeth who saved the situation.

"Why, Mr. Farwell!" she called cheerfully, "you've arrived just in time to congratulate me! How nice! Come over and meet my husband!"

Boothby Farwell with a baleful glare at the bridegroom, walked over and did the proper thing, but severely, disapprovingly, and then with an offended glance about him he turned and stalked out of the room.

Only Sam bothered to watch him as he strode down the steps, sprang into his car, and drove furiously away. Sam had to slip out on the porch after that, behind one of the fluted columns, and whistle. Then he heaved a sigh of utter satisfaction and whistled again. All was as it should be to his way of thinking, for the maid of honor had become the bride of John Saxon! What more was there to be desired?

About the Author

Grace Livingston Hill is well known as one of the most prolific writers of romantic fiction. Her personal life was fraught with joys and sorrows not unlike those experienced by many of her fictional heroines.

Born in Wellsville, New York, Grace nearly died during the first hours of life. But her loving parents and friends turned to God in prayer. She survived miraculously, thus her thankful father named her Grace.

Grace was always close to her father, a Presbyterian minister, and her mother, a published writer. It was from them that she learned the art of storytelling. When Grace was twelve, a close aunt surprised her with a hardbound, illustrated copy of one of Grace's stories. This was the beginning of Grace's journey into being a published author.

In 1892 Grace married Fred Hill, a young minister, and they soon had two lovely young daughters. Then came 1901, a difficult year for Grace—the year when, within months of each other, both her father and husband died. Suddenly Grace had to find a new place to live (her home was owned by the church where her husband had been pastor). It was a struggle for Grace to raise her young daughters alone, but through everything she kept writing. In 1902 she produced *The Angel of His Presence, The Story of a Whim,* and *An Unwilling Guest.* In 1903 her two books *According to the Pattern* and *Because of Stephen* were published.

It wasn't long before Grace was a well-known author, but she wanted to go beyond just entertaining her readers. She soon included the message of God's salvation through Jesus Christ in each of her books. For Grace, the most important thing she did was not write books but share the message of salvation, a message she felt God wanted her to share through the abilities he had given her.

In all, Grace Livingston Hill wrote more than one hundred books, all of which have sold thousands of copies and have touched the lives of readers around the world with their message of "enduring love" and the true way to lasting happiness: a relationship with God through his Son, Jesus Christ.

In an interview shortly before her death, Grace's devotion to her Lord still shone clear. She commented that whatever she had accomplished had been God's doing. She was only his servant, one who had tried to follow his teaching in all her thoughts and writing.

Don't miss these Grace Livingston Hill romance novels!

You can find Tyndale books at fine bookstores everywhere. If you are unable to find these titles at your local bookstore, you may write for ordering information to:

Tyndale House Publishers
Tyndale Family Products Dept.
Box 448
Wheaton, IL 60189